Lethal Storm

ALSO BY PAULINE ROWSON

THE ART MARVIK MYSTERIES
Book 1: Deadly Waves
Book 2: Dangerous Cargo
Book 3: Lost Voyage
Book 4: Fatal Depths
Book 5: Lethal Storm

THE SOLENT MURDER MYSTERIES
Book 1: The Portsmouth Murders
Book 2: The Langstone Harbour Murders
Book 3: The Horsea Marina Murders
Book 4: The Royal Hotel Murders
Book 5: The Isle of Wight Murders
Book 6: The Portchester Castle Murders
Book 7: The Chale Bay Murders
Book 8: The Farlington Marsh Murders
Book 9: The Oyster Quays Murders
Book 10: The Cowes Week Murders
Book 11: The Boathouse Murders
Book 12: The Thorney Island Murders
Book 13: The Guernsey Ferry Murders
Book 14: The Rat Island Murders
Book 15: The Luccombe Bay Murders
Book 16: The South Binness Murders
Book 17: The Hayling Island Murders
Book 18: The Chidham Creek Murders
Book 19: The Tipner Lake Murders

INSPECTOR RYGA HISTORICAL MYSTERIES
Book 1: Death in the Cove
Book 2: Death in the Harbour
Book 3: Death in the Nets
Book 4: Death in the Dunes
Book 5: Death on Board

THE ART MARVIK MYSTERIES

Lethal Storm

PAULINE ROWSON

JOFFE BOOKS

Joffe Books, London
www.joffebooks.com

First published in Great Britain in 2025

Cover art by Dee Dee Book Covers

ISBN: 978-1-80573-340-9

CHAPTER ONE

Marvik's head throbbed, the scar on his face itched like blazes and he was hungry. The night was drawing in. All he wanted to do was eat and then crash out in his cottage on the Isle of Wight, but his last brief conversation with Strathen on Saturday morning gnawed away at him like a sore. Strathen had asked him if the operation had been completed — he'd been engaged with the UK's National Intelligence Marine Squad on the continent. Marvik had told him they were closing in on the people smugglers and arrests were organized for early Monday morning. Everything had gone to plan. His part in tracking the gang members by boat around Europe was done and he'd handed it over to the various European organizations who he'd been working with undercover, alongside the UK squad he was occasionally seconded to. Marvik hadn't had a great deal of time to consider Strathen's words, but now they returned with clarity and concern.

'I'm sailing to Ballycotton in Ireland,' Strathen had said. 'I might not come back.'

'It's that dangerous?' Marvik had asked, shocked.

'Yes. And it's not one of Crowder's assignments.'

Strathen ran a private intelligence agency as well as assisting their boss on the squad that they both occasionally worked for as freelancers. That was all Marvik had got before the line had gone dead. Either he'd switched off the mission mobile they used for intelligence-based conversations, which couldn't be tracked or bugged, or the signal had given out. Strathen had also turned off his boat's Automatic Identification System, as Marvik would expect if he hadn't wanted to be tracked. And clearly that was his purpose. So what was he working on and for whom?

He ran a hand over his face, fighting off the fatigue, and corrected his course as the rain swept across the English Channel. Soon he would see the island on the radar. He had tried Strathen early that morning before leaving France. There had been no signal. He wondered if he had left a message in his apartment at Hamble. Perhaps he should head there instead. How could he sleep if Strathen was in trouble?

His personal mobile rang, startling him. He hoped it was Strathen, but the number was one he didn't recognize. Even though he had no intuition that this would be bad news, Strathen's words haunted him. He steeled himself to answer.

'Is this Art Marvik?'

'Speaking.'

'This is Garda Denyse Berry of the Irish police.'

Marvik took a silent breath.

'Do you know a Shaun Strathen?'

'Yes.' His heart began pounding.

'We're sorry to have to tell you this, sir, and over the phone . . .'

His stomach clenched. It was as he had feared. He cursed himself for being on that operation and for not being able to head straight to Ballycotton. 'You've found his body?' He put the boat into neutral.

'No, sir, not yet. It's believed he went overboard.'

'Then he's missing?'

'Yes.'

And missing was not dead. Marvik's relief was so overwhelming that he felt physically sick.

'His boat was found off Ballyandreen Bay. There was a note at the helm, which gave us your name and mobile number.'

'What does it say?' he asked, eagerly.

'I can send a copy to your mobile.'

'Thanks. Can you also read it out to me?'

She cleared her throat. '"Art, sorry it's come to this. I've tried to come to terms with my injuries but I can't. I'm holding everyone back. The pain of pity others bestow on me is far worse than any physical pain. Look after things for me and take care of my boat. Per Mare, Per Terram."'

Strathen had had it tough losing his left leg from just above the knee in combat in Afghanistan, but he'd adapted well. He would never have taken his own life. 'Is the note handwritten?'

'No, typewritten.'

That cheered Marvik further.

'And where is his boat now?'

'The lifeboat crew have taken it into Ballycotton Harbour.'

'Is there a mobile phone or laptop on board?' He didn't ask if there was a typewriter. He was certain there wouldn't be one, not on the boat, but in his apartment, yes.

'Not that we could find, sir. He must have ditched them in the sea. Do you know who his next of kin is?'

'He hasn't one. I'm his sole executor. Can you keep the boat there until I arrive? I'll get the first available flight and let you know when I get into Cork. I'll ask Mr Strathen's solicitor to confirm my identity and authority. You'll notify me if you find his body?'

'Yes, sir. You have our condolences.'

'Thank you.'

He rang off, letting out a heavy sigh of relief, which was short-lived. Strathen could still be dead, not by his own hand but by that of whoever he had been after. The typewritten note, though, gave him some hope. It meant he had prepared it before leaving and that no one had forced him to write it in order to make it look like suicide. Not unless whoever he had been after had found the pre-prepared note and utilized it for that purpose to cover up murder. He didn't even wish to consider that.

His head swam with theories but they wouldn't get him anywhere. He throttled up and changed course for Hamble Marina, where Strathen usually kept his boat. As he did, his phone pinged. He read the letter Strathen had typed. Marvik's initial reaction of shock returned. Rapidly, he tried to still his swirling emotions, and urged himself to think rationally. No, even if he believed that Strathen would take his own life, he would hardly have gone all the way to the coast of Ireland to do so when he could so easily have jumped overboard in the Solent or the English Channel. And he would not have left a self-pitying note like this. Nor would he have signed it off with the Marines' motto: *By Sea, By Land*.

He put the boat on autopilot and made himself a coffee to help keep him alert. Then he radioed up Hamble Marina to say he was arriving and would put in on Strathen's berth. He knew all too well that commandos could, and did, suffer from post-traumatic stress, which broke down their mindset of courage, determination, unselfishness and cheerfulness. He needed now to apply the ethos that had been drilled into him over his years in the Marines: first understand, then adapt and respond, and finally overcome — in this case, find Strathen.

Eventually, as he drew closer, the marina lights blinked in the fine rain. The pontoon was deserted. It was gone nine. After mooring up he stuffed his rucksack with some overnight things, his two mobile phones and two powerful torches, locked his boat and made his way to the car park.

Strathen's Volvo estate was parked under one of the lights. It yielded nothing but a rug, some tools and a large golfing umbrella. Not that Strathen played golf, but its purpose was obviously to keep the elements at bay. There was

4

no one about, and, as far as he could see, no one taking any interest in the car. He didn't think there would be, not unless someone had seen Strathen arrive, tracked him to Ireland through having planted a device on his boat, killed him and then returned to see who showed up at the marina. Strathen, though, would have found any such device on his boat by using his surveillance-detecting equipment. Maybe he had and had left it intact because he had wanted to draw someone out. Who, though, for goodness' sake, and why? Marvik didn't even know why he had gone to Ireland. Perhaps something in the apartment would give him an indication.

As he headed for the large Georgian manor house that backed onto Southampton Water, he wondered how thoroughly the Garda had examined Strathen's boat. Other questions ran through his head. How long had it been in Ballyandreen Bay? Had the boat been anchored? Who had reported it? And why had someone gone on board anyway and discovered the note and the boat owner missing? These were all questions he had subdued while talking to Garda Denyse Berry, but they were ones he would ask when he met her — and more. For example, had Strathen's tender still been on board?

He stopped in front of a pair of large wrought-iron gates and pressed the fob against the panel. The gates slid silently open. Marvik slipped into the grounds. Security lights flashed on as he marched briskly up the driveway and through the porticoed entrance. He stepped into the well-decorated, spotlessly clean silence of the grand hallway, turned immediately to the left of the sweeping pale-blue-carpeted staircase and let himself into Strathen's apartment. It certainly hadn't been forcibly entered, but if Strathen had been held prisoner, or killed, his keys could have been taken from him.

Quickly moving through the rooms though, Marvik noted that everything was in its rightful place. Strathen was meticulously tidy and, unless the intruder was an expert searcher, he didn't think anyone had been here. In Strathen's operations room, he met with the same result. It seemed strange not to see him working at one or more of his four computers and odd to be met by silence and blank plasma screens on the walls. There was nothing on the two whiteboards, or in the fax machine or typewriter, all of which served the purpose that they didn't leave an electronic footprint.

He ran his finger over the typewriter ink roll. It came back smudged, as he had expected. He took a piece of paper and placed it around the roll, then withdrew it. There was a faint imprint on it, not enough to see clearly what had been typed and nothing to say when, or that it was the suicide note. He folded it and stuffed it into his jacket pocket. The wastepaper bins were empty. The whiteboards had been thoroughly cleaned.

Next, he tackled the computers. The screws on one of them were loose and it didn't take him long to discover that the hard drives had been removed from each. Was that Strathen's doing, to safeguard information getting into the wrong hands, or was it the work of another party? The external disk drives that took the old three-and-a-half-inch floppies and another that took the even older five-and-three-quarter-inch ones that Strathen occasionally came across in the course of his work were still there. There were no disks. Marvik hadn't really expected to see any — they would be in the safe, secreted behind a false wall. Marvik didn't have the combination; that was at Strathen's London bank in a safe deposit box. There was no sign of Strathen's laptop, as he had also anticipated. And the Garda officer said it hadn't been on board the boat. That could indicate he was alive and had taken it with him, or alternatively that someone had seized it, because Marvik didn't believe Strathen would have tossed it overboard, as Denyse Berry had suggested, before taking his own life.

He slipped out of the house, walked round to Strathen's garage and pressed the key fob. The door opened silently and smoothly. Nothing of any value would have been kept here and this was quickly confirmed. There were some tools, all-weather clothes, two wetsuits and a drysuit.

Back in the house, he pushed open the door to the base-ment, which Strathen had turned into a gymnasium. He said he was the only person to use it, the majority of the residents being elderly. Not that it precluded them from being fit, but perhaps they got their exercise elsewhere.

The house had at various times been a sports and social club, an apprentice training school and owned by a corpora-tion, before being converted to luxury flats. Long before that, in the Second World War, it had been occupied by the US Marines, who had made an escape route in case of bombing or invasion. Strathen had located it and they had used it when someone had been hot on their heels. The hatch was locked. Marvik unlocked it, recalling that Strathen had fitted it with an electronic sensor linked to his phone and com-puter. As he climbed from it into the grounds, he wondered if Strathen had picked up that signal, or perhaps his captors had, *if* he had been taken prisoner. That would have alerted them to the fact that someone was sniffing around. Perhaps they'd dismiss it as being one of the residents.

Swiftly, Marvik made his way past the tennis courts to a dense patch of shrubs and some trees. Beyond the trees was a solid-looking fence. He removed the panel, as Strathen had previously shown him, and squeezed through. Only he and Strathen knew of it, and it didn't look to have been used for a long while. It gave direct and quick access to the shore through a dense copse on a rough path.

Marvik stepped out into a small clearing, in front of which was a dinghy park, farther along than the one that adjoined the manor house. Beyond it was the ripple of Southampton Water. Strathen's kayak was there, as he had suspected, but he needed to make certain in case he had taken it on board with him.

Back in the flat, he made himself a drink and something to eat and then called up the internet. He badly needed sleep, and unless he got some soon he'd start to make mistakes. But first he needed to book his flight to Cork. It would have been easier if he could have flown from Southampton airport, but there were no direct flights. The earliest he could get, though, was better than he had expected. Gatwick at 11.15 a.m. He booked himself on it. It would be an early start from Hamble to Southampton and then on to Gatwick via a change at Havant, but he could reach the airport just after nine thirty. He was running out of clean clothes but he and Strathen were of similar build and height, so he put some clean ones of Strathen's in his rucksack.

Next, he called up the location the Garda officer had given him. It was twenty-four miles by road from Cork, a dramatic and picturesque rocky coastline nestling under the clifftop. Ballyandreen Beach was a small, pebbly bit of sand. Could Strathen have swum ashore? Possibly. He'd have had his water-proof prosthesis on board. Or had he piloted his tender or an inflatable? But what would he have done with it? He couldn't have hidden it unless there was a cave in those cliffs, and Marvik couldn't see him hauling it up to the clifftop. Someone in the houses dotted at the top would have seen him. Marvik was itching to get over there and view the boat and the terrain.

Alternatively, Strathen could have gone ashore else-where along the coast. Marvik widened out the pictures. The only other places that looked likely were closer to Cork — Ballycroneen Beach and a stretch of sand called Ballybranagan Beach. The latter looked to be possible. It had a longer line of access, and wasn't as rocky. But it also looked to be popular in terms of visitors. There weren't as many houses as close to it as at Ballyandreen. Strathen could have taken one of the tracks across country. But, again, if he had gone ashore in a tender, where was it? Had one been reported as being found on the beach?

The alternative was that he had gone with someone on their launch, either voluntarily or under coercion. But the fact of the typewritten note still remained.

He retrieved from his jacket pocket the paper he'd run through the typewriter and lightly rubbed a pencil over it, trying to pick up the impressions of the letters and their order. With a magnifying glass from a drawer in the operations room, he examined it. Yes, he was certain this was the suicide note, though he could make out only a few letters.

After taking two Panadols to ease his pounding head, he showered and retired to Strathen's spare bedroom. He knew the kind of sleep he was likely to get was the half-waking type with many questions regarding Strathen's disappearance playing merry-go-round in his mind. Tomorrow he would need to call Strathen's solicitor and ask him to email verification of his identity and his authority to Garda Denyse Berry. He could do that on the train or plane. He might also need to notify Howard Goodley, who managed Strathen's considerable country estate, which he rarely visited. Strathen's father had been in the diplomatic service and had died in China when his son was just five. More than that Marvik didn't know, except that he had been raised by his aunt and both his aunt and his late father had left him considerable fortunes, which Strathen had eschewed, apart from buying his boat and this apartment. But perhaps he wouldn't have to worry Goodley, because tomorrow he very much hoped to locate Strathen — alive.

CHAPTER TWO

Tuesday

'On holiday, sir?' the taxi driver asked as they headed towards Ballycotton, a forty-five-minute drive from Cork. 'Ballycotton gets its fair share of tourists, as does Cork. Not everyone goes to Dublin as the papers and internet would have you believe, unless it's a stag night or hen do.' He tossed Marvik a grin that showed he hadn't visited a dentist in years, and didn't wait for an answer. 'Those wanting to walk and have some peace and quiet come to this coast. Is it the walking you're after?' he fished, once more taking his eyes off a practically deserted road to gaze at Marvik's scar with a quizzical stare. 'Recovering from an accident, maybe?'

'No, I'm hoping to take my friend's boat back to England,' Marvik answered, generating raised bushy eyebrows.

'A boat now, is it? Dangerous waters around here. You have experience?'

'Some.' Marvik wasn't going to tell him he'd been a commando in the Royal Marines' Special Boat Services division. He wasn't sure how well being a former member of the British armed forces would go down here. While most in the Republic of Ireland and across the border in Northern

10

Ireland, over two hundred miles to the north-east, were content to live peacefully, there were still some who resorted to violence to achieve their aims and saw service personnel as the enemy. The violent conflict and terrorist activity in Great Britain and Northern Ireland had spanned the decades from the 1960s to the late 1990s, with the Irish nationalists and republicans — who were mainly Catholic — wanting Northern Ireland to leave the UK, and the unionists and loyalists — who were mostly Protestant — to remain. An agreement to end the 'Troubles' had been made in 1998. But violence still continued, albeit not on its previous scale. Had Strathen been following up something in connection with a terrorist cell intent on stirring up violence? If that were the case, even though he knew Strathen was highly trained and capable of taking care of himself, Marvik didn't hold out much hope for his chances. His body could eventually be washed up somewhere with a bullet in his head or back.

'Where's your friend, then?' The taxi driver broke into his thoughts. He had his occupation's natural nosiness combined with the famed curiosity of his countrymen. 'Not ill, I hope, or maybe he's run off with a woman,' he joked.

'He's meant to have committed suicide.'

'You don't say!' His eyes widened and he seemed to spend a whole minute gazing at Marvik instead of the winding country road. Not that there was any traffic, but they could end up in a ditch. Marvik was about to urge him to concentrate on the job in hand when the driver focused his gaze back on the road. 'You said, "meant". You don't believe it?'

'I don't want to. His boat was found in Ballyandreen Bay.'

'Then why are you going to Ballycotton? Ah, I know — they took his boat into the harbour there. Was there a note?'

'Yes.'

Marvik could see the taxi driver was itching to ask what it said but a semblance of sensitivity prevailed.

'Do you take many fares out this way?' Marvik asked.

'No. Mostly it's from the airport into the city. Though I have taken some to the marina at Cork, them as is staying on board with friends, or picking up a boat that's for sale and taking it back to wherever. Was your friend staying there before he . . . you know what?'

'I won't know until I see his logbook.'

The taxi driver sniffed. He didn't seem to know which way to go with the conversation. From his sidelong glances and lip-licking, he looked as though he ached to ask Marvik how he'd got his scars. He'd have lied anyway. It was easier to say he'd had a car accident than been wounded in conflict in Afghanistan.

'From London, is it?'

'No, the Isle of Wight.'

'An island like this then?' he cried, delighted.

'But smaller and busier when it comes to traffic. We get a lot of tourists.'

'Ballycotton gets a fair few, although most don't come by taxi. They come by air or ferry and hire a car. Some come by boat. It's a pretty place and quite famous in its own right. Do you know about the heroism of the lifeboat men back in 1936?'

Marvik did but there was no point in saying so because the taxi driver would still have told him. He launched in on the tale of how, having spent forty-nine hours in mountainous seas, the crew had rescued those on the Daunt Rock lightship, which had broken away from her moorings. The lifeboat crew were justly awarded medals for gallantry.

As the taxi driver merrily chatted on about the area, the state of Ireland and the world, Marvik — giving the occasional monosyllabic response — let his mind wander. That morning he'd informed Strathen's solicitor of what had occurred, and had promised to keep him updated. He'd requested that he send the necessary authorization over to the Garda for him to take possession of *Sea Fever*. He'd then called Garda Denyse Berry and they had arranged to meet on the quayside at three thirty, which gave him time to take a look around the village. He'd looked it up during his flight, which had gone surprisingly smoothly. Ballycotton nestled between the sea and countryside overlooking the bay. It had a few pubs, cafés and restaurants as well as a couple of hotels if he needed one, but he hoped to stay on board *Sea Fever*. He didn't know how long for. That depended on what he found.

Soon the Celtic Sea lay out before him in grey, relative calm. Whitewashed bungalows and some brick-built houses appeared on his right, with palm-like plants swaying in the strengthening wind at the head of long driveways. They passed a children's playground. There was no one in it. All at school, Marvik assumed. Then came a church and the road narrowed, with the dwellings more plentiful. The driver pointed out the small police station, a single-storey white-washed building with an equally small car park behind it. They passed a post office, a couple of tearooms and a hotel, the driver giving a running commentary as they went, but Marvik's concentration was on the tiny harbour he could see below them through the gaps in the houses, with its twin piers and sheltered waters, its small red-and-white trawlers and angling boats, but before he could pinpoint Strathen's boat the view had gone as the road twisted down towards the harbour.

Within minutes, the driver pulled up. 'This is as far as I can go without me feet and engine getting wet.' The pier narrowed and, beyond it, Marvik could see the lighthouse, high on its rock. He paid the driver, who wished him luck.

Marvik rapidly took in his surroundings. The lifeboat building was at the landward mouth of the harbour, and to his right a sign showed a path that led up to the clifftop. There was no one about. It was low tide. There didn't seem to be any visiting yachts, which didn't surprise him because this little harbour wasn't really equipped for leisure craft. There were moorings outside the harbour but he couldn't see any boats on them either. Strathen's substantial motor cruiser, though, was at the end of the main quay, and even from where he was standing Marvik could see the tender was on board. He wasn't sure if that was a good or bad sign. It could mean a number of things: Strathen had thrown himself

13

overboard — unlikely in his opinion — he had an inflatable on board, he swam ashore for some reason, he was taken against his will, or he went willingly.

Marvik was keen to go on board, but he didn't have the keys. He consoled himself with the fact that there would be time enough for that later, after he'd spoken to the Garda officer.

He made his way to the nearest pub, a short stroll up the road. He was hungry. There were seats outside but no one occupying them. Perhaps it was too chilly and dank for al fresco dining. It was also quiet inside, with only a couple in their early sixties dressed in walking clothes and another couple in their early thirties, their heads bent over their phones. At the bar he ordered a sandwich lunch and a Guinness — 'What else in Ireland?' he said with a smile at the attractive dark-haired woman behind the counter.

'On holiday, sir?' she asked politely, making a valiant effort not to gaze at his scarred face, her light-brown eyes not quite sure where to rest.

'Sadly no.' He repeated what he had told the taxi driver.

'It's such a terrible shame. And he was such a nice man.'

Marvik did a double-take. 'You met him!' This was a stroke of luck, or was it? Strathen had told him he was going to Ballycotton. Marvik just hadn't expected him to be walking around the village and eating in one of its pubs. But why not? He'd have got hungry too and this was the first hostelry you came to on leaving the harbour. Maybe Strathen had been fishing for information.

'That I did. He came in late Sunday morning.' She put the Guinness in front of him. 'I'm sure it must have been your friend.'

'He's about my height and build, powerful upper body, muscular, keen grey eyes, and he has a prosthetic left leg. Not something you forget about a person.'

Despite her best efforts, her eyes went to his scar.

'He lost his leg in a motorbike accident,' he lied. If Strathen had chatted to her about his amputation he wouldn't have told her the truth. That was the story they

14

had both agreed to use, if needed, a while ago. 'These are from a car accident.' He indicated his scars.

'Dangerous places, the roads.'

'Did he put into the harbour?'

'He did, sir. I'll just put the order through for your sandwich.'

Marvik drank some Guinness, mulling this over. He was now even keener to read Strathen's logbook, although he wondered if it would say much. He wouldn't have risked documenting his real reason for being here and his views on this place.

The woman returned with a burly, auburn-haired man in his mid-forties. 'This is my husband, Tom Gilley. I'm Laura. Tom was on the lifeboat that went out to your friend's boat when the fishermen reported it in Ballyandreen Bay.'

'I'm sorry you've had such sad news,' said the woman's husband. 'Terrible thing. Poor man must have been at his wits' end, though Laura says he didn't seem it when she spoke to him. I was busy in the kitchen when he came in.'

Laura said, 'He was very cheerful and friendly. But you never know, do you?'

Marvik looked suitably sorrowful. 'You don't, no.' He addressed Tom. 'Did you go aboard *Sea Fever*?'

'I did. I brought her into the harbour. The keys were at the helm along with that terrible sad note.'

'I'm Art. He mentioned me in it.'

'Ah, that he did.'

Laura said, 'I was surprised that he took his own life because he said he'd come here to see a friend who'd recently moved over from England. Maybe he had some unfinished business with this friend that upset him so much he couldn't see any way out. Or this friend gave him some terrible news that sent him over the edge. Who knows?' She leaned forward and lowered her voice as though there were crowds of people listening, when in fact there was no one even close to them. 'He might have come here to say his farewells.'

Marvik knew Strathen hadn't come here for that. Admittedly he didn't know all of his friends, but his gut

15

told him there had been a reason why he had called into this pub, aside from food. And a reason why he had spun the landlady this yarn. Thinking quickly, Marvik said, 'Do you mean Giles Milton?' He plucked a fictional name out of thin air, and sipped his Guinness, keen to see the publicans' response.

Laura answered, while her husband looked guarded. 'No, that wasn't it. Now, what was the name? Daniel Larmer or Larton. No, I think it was Larroc, something like that, but I told him there was no one of that name. It's a small village and Tom and I know most people, but we've never heard of him.' Her husband nodded in agreement. 'There was someone who we were told was English, who bought the old stone cottage up above the village — over the clifftop, along Ballytrasna way — but that was years ago and it's not been lived in for ages. Your friend said he'd take a walk up the cliff path anyway and that the view would be worth it. I thought it might be too much for him, what with his leg 'n' all. Not that I said so. You have to be careful what you say to people with disabilities — no offence meant, sir.'

'None taken, and Shaun wouldn't have been offended either if you had said as much.' Strathen could outwalk and outrun most people who had two legs. If he had gone to this cottage then he'd returned to Ballycotton because he'd taken his boat over to Ballyandreen Bay. He addressed Tom. 'What time did the lifeboat get called to *Sea Fever*?'

'It was just after eight yesterday morning. John Walsh and his crew on the *Ellie May* were returning from a night's fishing on the high tide and thought it strange that it was still in the bay.'

'Still?'

'They saw it there when they went out.'

'And what time was that?'

'On the high tide the previous night, just after eight.'

'Why did they think it strange for it to still be there?' asked Marvik over the top of his glass. 'It was only just over twelve hours.'

Tom's eyes narrowed slightly. 'They had to go quite close to it and it looked to be deserted.'

'Shaun could have been below deck.'

'He could, but John wondered if the man was ill. He might have overtaxed himself because of his leg, or got injured walking, and although he'd managed to make it back to his boat his injury could have got worse during the night.'

'John Walsh knew then that Shaun was an amputee?'

'Well, yes.' Tom blinked. 'He saw him around the harbour in the daytime. John hailed the boat and, getting no answer, called me. I said we'd best come out and take a look.'

Marvik was growing ever more dubious about this story but didn't show it.

'I hailed the boat. Still nothing. I thought it best we boarded her. That's when I found the note. I brought the boat into the harbour and called the Garda.'

'Was the boat drifting?'

'No, it was anchored.'

So why anchor when you're intending to do yourself in? It would hardly matter to a suicidal person if the boat drifted onto the rocks, or ran aground or into another vessel. OK, so Strathen had a conscience — injury might have been done to others if there was a collision — but in Marvik's experience people intending to take their own lives weren't thinking logically. But then Strathen hadn't.

'Did you see the logbook? He might have written his feelings or intentions in it.' Marvik knew he wouldn't have.

Tom scratched his head. 'It was on the shelf by the navigation table. I read the last entry in case it could help but it was only a short, factual note: "Made it into Ballycotton Harbour. Looks a quaint place. Going for something to eat."'

'Nothing written on his return?'

'No.'

'Did he talk to anyone else in the village or here in the bar?'

Laura answered, 'I don't know about the rest of the village, but he didn't speak to anyone here. Not that I noticed. Although, it being Sunday, it was busy.'

'Were there any strangers in here, tourists, or people off their boats?' Tom was looking ever more guarded. Perhaps, Marvik thought, he was pressing too hard too soon. 'I just wondered if there was anyone else I might be able to speak to who Shaun exchanged some words with. I guess I'm hoping to find a reason why he took his own life,' he added sorrowfully.

It seemed to do the trick; Tom's expression relaxed. 'No one from a boat, was there, Laura?'

'No. Aside from some regulars, there was a couple from Wales and a man from Liverpool. Ah, here's your sandwich,' Laura added brightly, as a young woman put a plate on the bar. 'I'll leave you to enjoy your lunch.' She gave him a dazzling smile. Tom nodded and slipped back into the kitchen.

Marvik took his refreshments to a seat by the window and tucked in while he contemplated Tom's unlikely story and along with it Strathen's mention of this man called Daniel. Why had Strathen come here to see him, if he had? Perhaps he'd plucked the name out of the air, just as he had done with 'Giles Milton'. If so, why? As an excuse to talk to Tom and Laura? Or perhaps there had been others in the bar, aside from the people the publicans had mentioned, who Strathen had wanted to throw off course. And why had the fishermen reported the boat? In Marvik's experience, craft could stay anchored in a bay for a long time before anyone thought anything of it. And fishermen were usually more intent on getting their catch back to the shore. This smelled wrong and it increased his concerns about Strathen's safety.

After swallowing the last of his sandwich, he took the empty plate and glass back to Laura at the bar. 'I'd like to talk to John Walsh. Do you know where I can find him?'

'Could be anywhere at sea. I've got his mobile, but he doesn't always answer when out. In fact, he rarely does and there's not always a signal.'

Marvik said he'd take it anyway. He thanked her for the appetizing sandwich and made his way to the quay, where he examined the fishing boats. The *Ellie May* wasn't one of them. On returning, he found Garda Denyse Berry waiting patiently for him in the drizzling rain not far from Strathen's boat. He apologized for being late, even though he wasn't, introduced himself with a show of his passport and also showed her the email on his phone from the solicitor, which she confirmed had been sent to her.

'Nothing's been touched or removed, except the suicide note,' she said, as they made for the blue-hulled motor cruiser. She was about Marvik's age, mid-thirties, with an open face, tanned complexion and warm brown eyes. She hardly blinked at his scarred face — either she was a very good police officer to mask her reaction so successfully, or she'd been forewarned. His gut reaction told him it was the latter. He had an inkling that Tom might have called her while he was eating his lunch. He wondered why. Perhaps just a case of small-village gossip.

They climbed on board. Marvik let her enter the cockpit and the helm ahead of him. A swift glance confirmed this was how Strathen would have left it — pristine. There was a table and seating for several people to his left. The table was bare. Behind it, facing for'ard, was another seat and, across the aisle, the skipper's seat. She gestured to the chart plotter behind the helm. 'The note was propped up on the screen. Tom Gilley moved it to pilot the boat. He didn't want it to fall on the deck, so he put it in his pocket.'

And had anyone else's prints, save Strathen's, been on it before then? wondered Marvik. Not that he would say, and there was no point asking for it to be examined in that respect because he would need to explain too much. Besides, he didn't think there would be any other prints to lift now except Gilley's and the Garda officer's. 'Can I see it?'

'Of course.' She delved into her pocket and handed it over.

It wasn't even in an evidence bag, but then why should it have been when to all and sundry this was suicide? There was no foul play, not even the hint of it, as far as the Garda and others here were concerned. She remained silent while he read it.

'Have you searched the boat?' he finally asked.

'Only cursorily. I looked for other evidence that could tell us about the poor man's state of mind but didn't find anything.'

'Did you find a typewriter?'

'No.' She looked puzzled.

Marvik knew she wouldn't have done, but he'd wanted to see her reaction. 'This has been typed. Don't you find it strange that he should type it and there's nothing on board to type it with?'

'He must have brought the note with him, having typed it elsewhere, with the intention of taking his life. Can you think of why he should do so here? He's not from Ireland. Does he have relatives or close friends nearby?' Her expression gave no indication she knew about Strathen's conversation in the pub. And how did she know he wasn't Irish — had she found his passport? Or perhaps she'd run a check on him.

'I wasn't aware he did, but I've just learned from Laura Gilley that he might have a friend living somewhere in these parts, a man called Daniel Larmer, Larton or Larroc. Do you know him?'

She shook her head. 'No.'

It looked to be the truth. He didn't see any need to repeat what the Gilleys had told him. She could find out for herself if she wished, or maybe she already knew. Marvik stepped down into the saloon. Again there was nothing on the table, and only cushions on the seats and some charts on the shelf between lockers. Strathen was always neat.

'Will you attempt to locate this Daniel?' he asked.

She looked taken aback. 'Only if we need to. But I can't see how he could help when it's clear what happened.'

Not to me. It would be a simple enough task for her to run the names Larmer, Larton or Larroc through the police computer to establish if he had a criminal record. And she could also easily check if he was an Irish national and living locally or if he had come through border control, but she obviously wasn't going to do so. Maybe she would when she returned to the station. He didn't press it. He was certain Strathen had made that name up. But he had come here for a reason. If only their conversation hadn't been cut off before he could tell him more. There was no indication of foul play or any kind of struggle on the boat. Not unless there was evidence of it in the aft master cabin and for'ard cabin, and he didn't think there would be. He was glad she had accepted the suicide theory. That left him to continue undisturbed.

He said, 'I'll be taking this boat back to England. I assume that's OK with you and the coroner?'

'It is. I have photographic evidence of the boat, the location where it was found, the note and pictures of the helm. You know how to handle the craft?'

'I've been on board many times and I have a similar boat. If I could have the keys and keep the note.'

'I'll need the note for the inquest, but you can have the keys.' She handed them over in exchange for the note. Marvik had suspected as much but had thought it worth a try.

'When will the inquest be held?' he asked.

'I couldn't say for sure, sir. About a month, maybe two. I can let you know. I don't think you'll be called but I have your details and will pass them on to the coroner. I'm sorry there's not anything more I can tell you.' She made to turn, then hesitated. 'You don't believe your friend took his own life, do you?'

Should he say no? Would she spread the word, which would prompt whoever Strathen had been after into the open? This Daniel, possibly. Or would it delay his investigation because she might decide to make further enquiries and get in his way?

'I'm not sure what to believe,' he said. 'It's been such a shock. Maybe I just don't wish to believe it.'

'I can understand that. I'm sorry.'

He watched her walk down the quay. She stopped to talk to a couple of fishermen. They didn't seem interested in him, or the boat, and yet every fibre of his being, every sense and all his training, told him he was being observed. He didn't know by whom and where they were, but he was convinced the news of his arrival had spread fast among the fishing community, just as Strathen's had. And that Tom and Laura Gilley and the fisherman, John Walsh, were involved more deeply than it appeared. Perhaps Garda Denyse Berry was too.

CHAPTER THREE

He dumped his rucksack on the unmade bed in the for'ard cabin. A swift search of the lockers yielded nothing. Crossing to the master cabin, he saw that Strathen's bed was neatly made. His clothes hadn't been disturbed and there were no hidden hard drives or notes. In the heads were Strathen's shaving tackle, soap, aftershave, towels. In the galley he found enough provisions to keep him supplied for a short time; along with some tinned food and packets of pasta and rice, there was also bread, milk, eggs, Irish butter and cheese. Not the kind of food supplies a man contemplating suicide would stock up on. They were all fairly fresh, which indicated Strathen had bought them either in Cork or here at Ballycotton.

He returned to the helm. Before reading the logbook, he inserted the key. Both fuel tanks were almost full. Strathen must have refuelled at Cork, which was confirmed in his logbook. He'd also topped up two large containers. They must be in the lockers on deck or in the engine room. That in itself was interesting. Again, it was hardly the act of a man about to end his life.

Eagerly he read on. Strathen had reached Cork Marina at 14.00 on Saturday having made a good and speedy crossing from Hamble, which he had left the previous day at just after 15.00. It was a journey of almost four hundred nautical miles. The weather had been fair. He had got up on the plane and had managed to do twenty-four knots in the daytime and seventeen knots at night. Like him, Strathen was well versed in sailing at night and in all weathers. He had needed to reach here quickly. There was no explanation for the journey, no thoughts or reflections. It was factual only. Why hadn't Strathen flown to Ireland? But then he had reached here swiftly without having to hang around at airports, rely on taxis and show his passport. He didn't have to book into hotels either. The boat gave him privacy, speed and independence.

On arrival he had bought some food in the marina shop, then stayed there for the rest of the day and overnight, probably catching up on his sleep as he'd made the journey nonstop. He'd made for Ballycotton on Sunday morning, and had moored up in the harbour on high water at 7.24. His entry said the weather was wet but calm and he'd spend some time taking a look around Ballycotton. The following entry mentioned him eating in the pub. After that, nothing.

Marvik sat back, his mind swimming with unanswered questions. The critical one being why hadn't he written up his journey to Ballyandreen Bay? What time had he left here and arrived there? Tom Gilley had said Walsh had seen *Sea Fever* in the bay when they had gone out to sea on high water Sunday night at just after eight. That was right on sunset. Strathen could have taken his boat out of Ballycotton Harbour, say, any time from 17.00 or thereabouts, a couple of hours before high water but not after it, if Walsh and Gilley were to be believed. Why hadn't Denyse Berry and Gilley been curious as to why Strathen hadn't written up his log on returning to his boat and taking it out? Had they assumed his state of mind was so unbalanced he hadn't wished to record it? What had he done after eating in the pub? The obvious answer to that was he'd gone for that cliff walk to the stone cottage. And the simple explanation for the absence of a log entry was that Strathen had never returned from there. Someone else had taken out the boat. There was no entry in the log because it was handwritten and they couldn't fake Strathen's handwriting.

And that was where Marvik was heading, that stone cottage. He would wait until it was dark; he didn't wish to be observed. That left him with a few hours to kill.

He searched the boat thoroughly in case Strathen had left him a message, but he didn't find one. He explored Ballycotton, greeting a few people as he went but not stopping to hold a conversation with any of them. He appeared to be just another tourist. He hesitated over asking any fishermen around the quay if they had seen *Sea Fever* go out on Sunday night, and decided not to. He was certain that would get back to the Gilleys and Walsh, and he didn't want to seem too curious and as though he disagreed with the suicide verdict. As far as anyone here was concerned, he had accepted it.

On his return to the boat, he could tell no one had boarded it in his absence. After eating he called up a map of the area on his phone and studied it, recalling what Laura Gilley had told him. The countryside above Ballycotton heading towards Cork was peppered with a handful of properties. Most looked to be farmhouses, but there were two isolated dwellings and one in particular with high hedges and trees around it. That would be his first port of call. It could, of course, be a trap. She had told him about it to lure him there. So be it, he'd go anyway.

He studied the terrain and the direction. Then, after packing his rucksack with water, some of Strathen's biscuits and a chocolate bar, he checked the batteries in his powerful torch and the thin pencil one. Taking these and his small binoculars, he locked up the boat.

He stood for a few moments in the dark and rain. He was alone and, as far as he could tell, no one was on board their boats. The *Ellie May* still hadn't returned. He turned to the cliff path without using his torch. His night vision was good, and only when he was away from the last of the houses did he switch on the torch.

The rain had stopped but he knew there was more to come. He could feel it heavy in the air and in the stiffening wind. From the map, he judged the stone cottage with the hedges to be about three miles to the south-east. To him that was a short distance, but it was across rain-soaked fields and ditches and a couple of times he had to crawl through gaps in the hedges where there was no gate to climb. Soon, though, the stone double-storeyed building loomed. Marvik switched off his torch. The house was in complete darkness and Marvik's senses were on full alert. There was the possibility the occupant had seen him coming and extinguished all lights. Alternatively, he could have left. The house might not even be that of this Daniel.

He approached through a rickety gate that was hanging off its hinges, and even in the dark Marvik could see the garden hadn't been touched for years. The bushes were overgrown and merged together in a tangle of brambles. The grass against his wet walking boots was long and weed-strewn, and what path there must once have been leading to the door had long since vanished. The undergrowth didn't look to be trampled, but he wasn't going to risk using his torch to confirm it.

His heartbeat picked up as he stealthily made his way to the front of the house, rapidly checking for a surveillance device as the rain began to sweep in from the sea. But even if one were there, he wouldn't be able to see it in the dark. The door appeared to be firmly shut, and he was about to go round to the rear when he saw that it was slightly ajar.

Pulse racing, and body poised to counter any attack, he quietly and gently pushed it open. It gave a low creak. He froze. No one came. Silence greeted him. He stepped onto a dirty stone-flagged floor and again paused, listening for the slightest sound of movement or breathing. There was a scurrying, scratching sound, which he judged to be mice or rats, but above them the hum of something else that was more revolting. The damp, musty smell was cloying but it wasn't that which turned his stomach. It was the nauseating smell of rotting flesh. All he had to do was follow the sound of the buzzing and, despite not wishing to, he knew he had no choice.

His heart was hammering against his chest, his body taut with fear, not for himself at the thought of being attacked — his senses told him he was alone — but for what he might find. Not just a body, but that of Strathen.

As he inched forward, steeling himself, his mind ran on. This was why Strathen hadn't returned to his boat. This was why someone else had taken it out. This was why the suicide note had been used, because someone had lain in wait here for Strathen. This Daniel had been forewarned that Strathen would be heading for him and had killed him. What the hell had he been working on?

The door to the kitchen was open, and in the far corner by the rear door lay a bundle. The stench was overpowering, the flies disgusting. Bile rose in Marvik's throat. He grabbed a handkerchief from his jacket pocket and put it across his mouth. Best to get this over with. His body was like steel. The shape of the bundle had Strathen's build. As he moved forward, his torch flashed over the corpse and an enormous sense of relief washed over him so powerfully that he swayed slightly before quickly recovering. This man had both his legs. It wasn't Strathen.

His relief was so overwhelming that he felt sick. He had to take some steady deep breaths even though the awful smell of the decaying corpse nearly made him gag. His torch played on the battered face with the flies and maggots eating it. Suddenly he was experiencing a flashback to the ravages of war. He found his hand shaking and sweat pricking his brow. Urgently, and with an effort, he summoned his commando training. Remain professional and observant. It wasn't Strathen and nor was Strathen the killer because clearly this man had been dead longer than three days. But would he find Strathen's body elsewhere in the house or in the garden?

Although he didn't want to, he went through the dead man's pockets. Nothing. Perhaps the killer had taken the items, or Strathen had, if there had been any, and *if* he had reached here. A perusal with his torch showed this man had been bludgeoned violently several times on the back of the head. And, although he couldn't be certain, he thought the man might be in his thirties.

Marvik stood and listened. He caught a faint sound outside but reasoned it was just the wind and rain. He suspected that any evidence in the house as to the identity of this corpse would be long gone but he searched anyway, and not just for that but in the hope he wouldn't find another body — Strathen's. It was with considerable relief he didn't, although there were still the grounds and a small outbuilding to search.

There was nothing in this house to tell him who the dead man was and why he had been here. It was sparsely equipped with some basic items of furniture, all of which had seen much better days. There were some threadbare rugs and a sleeping bag on some cushions taken from the sofa and placed in the one bedroom upstairs. There was an old range in the kitchen that hadn't been operative for a long while. There were also some food wrappers, empty tins and plastic bottled water. No bathroom or toilet, the latter of which he found outside.

As Marvik went over the grounds and poked about in the stone outbuilding, he wondered if anyone was watching the boat in Ballycotton and, finding it deserted, would know he had come up here. Would they tell the police? Even if they did, the police would soon realize the deceased had been killed long before he or Strathen had arrived in Ireland. But explaining things to the Garda would take time and he didn't have that on his hands. Nor did he know what to tell them, as he knew nothing about the murder or the situation here.

He found some grimy blankets in the outhouse and some tins of food. The latter didn't look to have been there a long time. Perhaps the killer had hidden out here waiting for his victim to arrive. Maybe then he had also waited for Strathen, but if so where was his body?

He made his way back to his boat, his mind turning over the latest discovery and what it meant. He put himself in Strathen's shoes. What would he have done after finding the corpse? Why hadn't he returned to his boat in the harbour? The answer to the last question was because he knew, or suspected, the same treatment would be meted out to him. Someone would be waiting at the bottom of the cliff or on the quayside to dispense with him.

He could have hidden at the house for a day or two, before heading on foot to Cork. Could those blankets and the food have been his? Or had he trekked to Cork immediately on finding the body? Perhaps he had gone to Shanagarry, farther to the east and about twenty miles from Cork, the next modest-sized conurbation to Ballycotton. Marvik recalled it from his earlier perusal of the map of the area. It was about five miles on foot and across country. And from there he might have been able to get a bus or taxi to Cork airport. But would he have willingly left his boat? The words Strathen had typed in that suicide note flashed before Marvik's eyes: *Look after things for me and take care of my boat.* And of their snatched conversation: *I might not come back.* Perhaps Strathen had never gone to that house at all but had been overcome before he reached it.

Marvik hurried down to the harbour as fast as he could, given the driving wind and rain and the black night. He was still cautious about switching on his torch. He half wondered if he would find *Sea Fever* gone, but there she was, in darkness. There wasn't a soul about, but as he climbed on board he stiffened. He sensed movement from below. The door to the saloon was open. It was too late to turn back now. The killer was here waiting to strike him on the back of the head as he entered. Silently and stealthily he descended, steeling himself for the attack he knew would come.

CHAPTER FOUR

'I thought you'd never get here.' The voice that came from the dark was one Marvik knew well and his relief was overwhelming. The man who faced him was no assassin. Marvik wasn't naturally demonstrative but this called for more than a handshake. Pulling away, Strathen grinned. 'Nice to have been missed.'

'What's going on, Shaun?'

'I'll explain everything later. We'd better get underway before any nosy parkers come sniffing around. And we've just got time to make it out of the harbour before the tide is too low. I'll keep out of sight. I'm meant to be dead. We've got plenty of fuel, unless the fishermen have swiped it.'

'They haven't.'

'Good, then we'll make for Plymouth in one hit. We should reach there by midday, weather permitting.'

'Plymouth? OK, I'll save the questions for later. The forecast is fair.' Marvik started the engine. 'This rain will soon be behind us as we get farther out into the Celtic Sea, and the wind is set to drop.' He alighted and cast off, trying to quell the thousand and one questions running around his head, glancing about to see if anyone was watching him and wondering why he was leaving at night and so abruptly. But

30

the quay was deserted. Back on board, he throttled up and swung the boat out of the small harbour into the choppy sea.

'I need to get this damn prosthetic off. Having kept it on nonstop since Sunday, and mountain climbing in it, it's a bit past its sell-by date,' Strathen joked.

Marvik knew his limb stub would be very sore.

'And I need a shower, a shave and a change of clothes.' Strathen ran a hand across the stubble on his chin. 'It's a wonder you didn't smell me when you came on board.' His clothes were grubby and soaked through, and his chiselled face etched with fatigue. It reminded Marvik so much of when they had been on ops together.

'You could also do with some sleep,' Marvik said.

'Later.'

It wasn't a pleasant voyage to start with but Marvik had been in much worse seas. And this boat, like his own, was well equipped and built to withstand many sailing conditions. As they headed farther south, the rain eased and the wind dropped. After showering and changing, Strathen, without his prosthetic but still managing to balance, reached up a coffee to Marvik. 'I'm cooking a kind of risotto with what we have on board. It might be an acquired taste.'

Before long, he brought up their food, and more coffee to help keep them awake. Not that Marvik needed that — he wasn't tired — but he could see Strathen did. He put the boat on autopilot and they sat at the table at the helm.

Strathen tucked in. 'This is cordon bleu compared to biscuits, cold baked beans and tinned spaghetti for three days courtesy of our dead man. I wasn't going to cook, sleep or wash in that cottage. Not that I was squeamish about it, you and I have been in tighter jams, but I wasn't sure that his killer wouldn't return. I was in the outhouse.'

'I saw some blankets there. I assume you saw me on the quayside or on the boat with the Garda officer.'

'I did, and I saw you arrive in the taxi and walk up to the pub.'

Marvik raised his eyebrows.

Strathen grinned. 'But if I'd stayed any longer with my sore eyes fixed to those damn binoculars most of the day, they'd have left ruddy great indents under the already deep bags there. It was after seeing you leave the boat that I moved from my luxurious quarters and slipped down here. Thankfully it was raining and no one was about.'

'You could have stayed in the house and been a welcoming committee.'

'I could but it's nice to be home.' He gazed with affection and relief around the boat.

Marvik ate. 'This is good.'

'Thanks. I knew you'd come. We've been on too many missions, including those for Crowder, not to know each other's moves and thoughts. I made a calculated guess that you would follow in my footsteps.'

'I got the message from the note: *take care of my boat*.'

'Yes, and I knew that the lovely Laura or Tom would tell you that the man with one leg had come asking. It was obvious you'd call there, it being the closest pub to the harbour.'

'Is the dead man this Daniel you asked about?'

'Larroc. I suspect so. There was no ID on him, only this crucifix.' He reached into his trouser pocket and handed it across to Marvik. It was gold, on a tiny chain, with a small stone that looked like a diamond in the centre.

'The killer missed that,' Strathen continued between mouthfuls. 'Too busy rifling through the dead man's pockets. That's assuming he had ID on him and a mobile phone. And I also assume he had a rucksack, or holdall, which was missing. From what I could see of the discarded tin cans, empty packets and bottles of water, Larroc had been hiding up in that cottage for several days.'

'It couldn't have been pleasant for him holing up there.'

'No. And it suggests he was desperate to stay hidden.'

'Was he on the run from someone who finally caught up with him?'

'That's the obvious explanation, but why I don't know. What I do know is, it's connected with Jarinder Vaidya's death.'

Marvik took a millisecond to register the name. Shocked, he repeated, 'Jarinder's dead?' Instinctively, his hand went to his scar. He recalled the brilliant plastic reconstructive surgeon he and Strathen had first met on tour in Afghanistan and then in the Royal Centre for Defence Medicine at Queen Elizabeth Hospital, Birmingham, where Jarinder had also overseen Strathen's amputation. Since then he had moved to the hospital in Plymouth and also worked at the navy recovery centre, which supported all service personnel. It was based in HMS *Drake*, part of His Majesty's Naval Base Devonport, a huge site of over six hundred and fifty acres, making it the biggest naval base in Western Europe.

'Sadly, yes.' Strathen's expression hardened. 'He came off the road on a sharp bend and ended up in the river. No way out for him. No doubt it will be put down as accidental death. But it was no accident, Art. He was forced off that road. And he was killed because he was on his way to see me.'

'This was Thursday night?'

'Yes. Jarinder phoned me late Thursday afternoon. He was very disturbed, which as you know is not like him. Surgeon Commander Vaidya was not a man to be scared. God, he had the Green Beret and worked in as many conflict zones as you and me, with clinical tours during the Iraq War and Afghanistan. And he never turned a hair — we've witnessed it. He was calm, fearless, professional and caring. But his voice when he spoke to me reflected acute anxiety. He said he needed to discuss something of the utmost urgency. I was surprised and worried.'

This was indeed troubling, and it was horrific that he had been killed. Marvik's mind scrambled to make some sense of why anyone would murder him.

Strathen continued, 'I pressed him but he wouldn't say what was distressing him. I said I'd leave for Plymouth immediately but he insisted on coming to me.'

'He knew where you lived?'

'He had my address from my NHS record, which gives the Hamble apartment, not that of my estate. And he had my mobile number — we've kept in touch over the months since my discharge from the Marines. He said he'd be with me in the early hours of Friday morning. Well, Friday morning came and there was no sign of him. I rang his mobile. No reply. At first I thought he must be in a black spot, or concentrating on driving having set off later than he'd anticipated. I tried again half an hour later and then after another half an hour. By this time it was ten thirty. I called the hospital and was eventually put through to Heather Carter, his secretary, who was in tears, and told me that Jarinder had been killed in a car accident. No other car had been involved, or so she had been informed by his son, Nishan.' Strathen paused to eat. Marvik also thought it was to compose himself. 'I thought fatigue and worry had distracted him so that he'd lost control. I searched the internet on the route Jarinder would have taken to reach me, to see what I could pick up on the accident. There wasn't much, it being too recent, and no name released. There was mention of a fatality, which I assumed must be Jarinder, and the police were appealing for witnesses, but it had been very late on Thursday night so I thought it unlikely that anyone would have been about. I was debating what action to take when I got his letter. It arrived in the post just after eleven.'

Marvik quickly caught on. 'He'd posted it before he'd spoken to you.'

'Yes, to catch the first-class mail, hoping it would reach me either when he was with me on that Friday, or by Saturday morning, Monday at the latest, and by then he hoped to have told me what was wrong. He'd also posted it in case he never made it.'

'And by using the postal service he knew that it couldn't be intercepted or destroyed.'

'Yes. As you know, Art, I make sure that my mobile phone and computers aren't traceable, but Jarinder's call to me could have been tracked via his mobile, and my number obtained. It's possible someone could have got my details from that, or from the address on the letter, if they saw it being posted, or before it was posted.'

'Which was why you took out your hard drives in case someone broke into your apartment. They're in your safe.'

'Yes, and no one can get into that, not even the most experienced safe cracker — if they managed to find it. I'm hoping everything is still intact because I haven't been able to get a signal to verify that.'

'Everything is fine. No sign of any entry, so, unless someone is exceptionally talented, I'd say no one's been there. What did the letter say?' Marvik asked eagerly.

'The envelope was typewritten and the note was written in Hindi with a fountain pen, possibly in a hurry because it is smudged at the end. I scanned and uploaded it for a translation. This is essentially what I got from my memory, which isn't as good as yours, but good enough, especially as I've gone over it again and again. I have the original in my safe. It translates: "*I am in danger. I have been warned to keep silent or they will kill me and hurt my family. I cannot let it go. It is my duty to tell but I cannot do it alone. One man was on my side. He is in Ballycotton, Ireland. If I do not make it to see you, Shaun, go to Ballycotton. See Daniel Larroc . . .*'

'So we can assume the dead man is Larroc.'

'Jarinder says he "was" on his side, then he "is" in Ballycotton — either the computer-generated translator has the tense mixed up, or Jarinder wrote it incorrectly, or he wrote it deliberately. Meaning he knew that Larroc was dead.'

'Or suspected it because he couldn't speak to him. If the signal is that bad, Jarinder might have been trying him and couldn't get through. It looked to me as though Larroc had been dead about ten days to two weeks when I saw him, judging by what I saw of the maggots and flies.'

'I agree. I'd say he was about our age, mid- to late thirties, light-brown hair, slim, a sedentary worker, not manual, judging by the hands. Chain-store clothes. No visible tattoos or obvious birthmarks, but I wasn't going to undress him. He must have brought that discarded food I saw with him, and the supplies I helped myself to, or it was previously put there, possibly by Jarinder, but I think the former more likely so as not to alert anyone as to his whereabouts.'

35

'And how long was he there before he was found and killed?' mused Marvik. 'How did the killer find him?'

'He might have been tracked through a device sewn into, or planted on, his missing rucksack or holdall. He could have confided to someone where he was going. Obviously Jarinder knew. And if Jarinder's mobile was bugged, then the killer would have listened in to their conversations and read any messages sent between them.'

'I wonder if the police found Jarinder's mobile phone on his body.'

'I'll see if I can hack into his call log.'

Marvik rose and checked the radar. There were no hazards or shipping ahead and the sea state was relatively calm. He still needed to know more, and about the suicide note, but Strathen looked all in.

'Let's call a halt,' he said. 'You need sleep. We can pick this up in the morning.'

'No. I'll bring you fully up to date first.' He pushed away his empty plate and swallowed some coffee before continuing. 'What is clear is that Larroc was hiding out there. And he'd done so in a hurry. I couldn't research him on the internet because, as I said, there was no signal, and I had to keep my wits about me in case I had the same visitor. I'll get onto it as soon as we get to Plymouth, where hopefully the marina will have a good connection.'

'And we're going to Plymouth because Jarinder worked and lived there, so we hope to pick up the trail of why he and Larroc were killed. But couldn't we have dug a bit deeper in Ballycotton?' Marvik added, as he tried to pull together the threads of this deadly mystery. 'Why did you stay in that cottage? Why not return to your boat? And why the suicide note?'

Wearily, Strathen said, 'I'll take the last question first as it leads into the others. It was in case I needed to go into hiding. Let's say that Jarinder's phone was bugged, or that he used the satnav in his car to reach me and he was tracked through that. I asked myself, why hadn't they followed him to my apartment and then taken us both out? The answer was because that would have been too difficult, and would need too much explaining. The police would be suspicious at finding two bodies, and there was the chance that I would fight back and the assassin would fail.'

'A very strong chance.'

'They couldn't take him out on his return journey because they couldn't risk him telling me what the hell was going on.' He again swallowed some coffee. 'When I knew he was dead, and then received the letter, I anticipated it would only be a matter of time before an accident befell me, if they suspected Jarinder had told me something. But if they didn't know about the letter, but knew Jarinder had been on his way to confide in me, they'd wait and see what I did. Would I accept the accident theory? Would I begin to ask questions? And if I did, where would I start? How much did I know? The starting point for me had to be Ballycotton. I prepared the suicide note in case I had to disappear for a while and in the hope that you would have finished your mission with Crowder and come to find me. I showed up there three days after Jarinder's death, on Sunday, asking about a man called Daniel Larroc, which set off alarm bells. And I'll tell you how I know that—'

But Marvik interjected. 'Tom and Laura Gilley had been primed that you might arrive. If I had stayed in Ballycotton, I might have got the ID of the killer from them.'

'I doubt it. This guy is too smart to betray himself in that way. Even if he was careless enough to do so, we wouldn't get the why, Art, because I doubt they've been told. They could have been spun some yarn about me and Larroc. Don't ask me what, because I don't know.' He rubbed his eyes. 'They might have been paid to pass on their message or intimidated into doing so because they have a secret to protect.'

'Smuggling?'

'Possibly. Or they were told I was a bad boy and they would be assisting the police or the intelligence services, or something like that. Whatever, it was obvious to me that they'd been forewarned, even though they tried to disguise it. I duly went where they said, not then knowing if I was walking into a trap. Larroc mightn't be where they'd hinted at. Someone else could have been waiting to take me out. And I didn't know Larroc would be dead, although I suspected it because of Jarinder's note. The Gilleys might have told me about that stone cottage in order to get me off the boat and away from the village, knowing nothing about Larroc being dead inside. I thought I might not come back, so I left the note I'd prepared for just such an eventuality, knowing you would pick up on the clue and come after the boat. If the purpose was to get rid of me, then having a nice get-out clause — the suicide note — would suit their purposes. They wouldn't destroy or attempt to disguise the boat and abandon it somewhere.'

'You left it propped up on the chart plotter?'

'No. On top of the nearby navigation table.'

'Why would Tom Gilley tell the Garda officer otherwise?'

'Maybe the fisherman moved it. After I found Larroc, I turned the night glasses on the harbour. If anything was going to happen to my boat, I anticipated it being around the high water, and they would need to take it outside the harbour. They wouldn't want to risk doing anything in the harbour. I was right. I couldn't see who came on board. He had a sou'wester hat rammed low over his forehead, and was wearing a ruddy great oilskin and boots. It was wet and windy. But a fishing vessel left shortly after my boat — in fact, it practically followed it out. Someone had to take the skipper off my boat and back to Ballycotton.'

'Or out fishing.'

'Yes.'

'He could have used the tender, adding more weight to the fact you'd gone off in it and then taken your own life. I wondered why it was still on board.'

'Maybe they weren't creative enough to think of that.'

'I take it they unlocked the helm with a skeleton key.'

'Must have done. I didn't leave mine, that would have been *too* easy.'

'It took some skill to do that.'

'Perhaps one of our fisherman, or the friendly publican, was a locksmith in a previous life, or a crook. I just hoped they wouldn't scupper the boat.' Strathen gave a wry grin. 'But they would want it to look as though I had killed myself.'

'Wouldn't they have thought you'd come back and ask where it was?'

'They'd been told to take it out, make it look as though I'd had an accident and fallen overboard, until Gilley found my prepared letter and had a better idea. If I showed up after the boat had vanished, maybe Gilley was told to offer me bed and breakfast and the fishermen no doubt would have volunteered to take me out the next morning to look for my boat, which had been stolen.'

Strathen had been shrewd and prepared. Marvik said, 'I wonder what they thought of that suicide note.'

'Maybe they didn't stop to think.'

'The killer might though.'

'And if he's clever he'll wonder if I'm really dead. I expected him to arrive but no one came. Why?'

Marvik had been running scenarios quickly through his mind. 'Perhaps he underestimated you — he thought you'd be an easy target and couldn't get far with one leg. He didn't take into account the fact that you're an ex-Marine commando, clear of mind, trained for endurance and ready to fight. Larroc was perhaps easy prey. Jarinder wasn't quite so easy, so they ran him off the road. This killer thought he'd soon catch up with you if you went on the run after finding the body. And that could be why your boat was moved, to force you to run. He didn't care if you saw it being taken out. In fact, he hoped you did because he knew Jarinder had been in contact with you, and told you something about what was going on. He never expected you to return to the village and innocently report a murder, not if you believed it was linked to Jarinder.' Marvik took a breath, his mind racing. 'Or perhaps the killer was unavoidably delayed. Or we could be looking at two killers — one in Ireland, hired for the purpose, another in England. Although there is a time lag between the murders, so they could have been carried out by the same man. He contacted Gilley and told him what to do. He and the others must have been well paid. And now that I've been there and disappeared in the night on your boat, they'll report back to the killer and he'll need to find out how much I know.'

'Yes. And if you believe I'm dead.'

'And whether you confessed more to me about Jarinder's concerns before taking your own life.'

'Correct.'

'So I ask questions and stir up some action. I lure this killer out into the open.' Much as he did on assignments for Crowder at the National Intelligence Marine Squad. 'So where do I start? With his family, friends, colleagues?'

'Jarinder's children — Nishan, Rohan and Tarina — work and live in London but they'll be in the Plymouth house for the mourning period. I don't know who Jarinder's close friends were, but one of them might be able to tell you that. As to his colleagues, I can't see him confiding in them, but they might have picked up something of his concerns and they might also know Daniel Larroc. I would say Amanda Nightingale would be your best bet.'

Marvik agreed. Amanda was a highly skilled plastic surgeon, forthright, intelligent, and had worked with Jarinder when he'd moved to the Plymouth hospital three years ago.

'I don't have her contact details but Heather should be able to give those to you or pass on a message to Amanda. There's also Jarinder's connections with the recovery centre, not only as a physician — he has a personal interest in it.'

'Elaine.' Marvik snapped his fingers. He recalled the friendly, happy sixty-year-old who worked in the café there and knew everyone and everything.

Strathen gave a weary smile. 'Yes, the font of all knowledge and very fond of Jarinder.'

'And vice versa. His death will have come as a blow to her.'

'And to many others. We're going to find the bastard who did it and why. I'll get busy on my research into Larroc and that cottage. It means using the marina's Wi-Fi but I'll encrypt my internet searches so that each time I connect to a web server it'll be routed through a random array of nodes before heading to the final destination. Even then an internet service provider can still be detected and I could be traced.' He rubbed his chin, stifling a yawn. 'There are other tools I can use, though, which I won't bore you with, to make my searches look like unencrypted traffic so that it doesn't draw undue attention. I'll do what I can.'

'Surely the chances of them picking up your trail from it are small.'

'Not if they're monitoring any searches or links to Jarinder, the *Ellie May*, Ballycotton or even Cork.'

'You think they're that canny?'

'I hope not. But I'm afraid they might be.'

Marvik rose and took the boat off autopilot. 'Get some sleep, Shaun. Let's get started on this tomorrow. We'll prompt them into taking action.'

Strathen hauled himself up. 'Hopefully not before we get to the truth.'

Marvik hoped so too.

CHAPTER FIVE

Wednesday

Elaine Cornish's smiling countenance behind the counter lifted Marvik's gloom, which had descended on him as he'd entered the recovery centre, conjuring up memories of when he and Strathen had spent time here recovering from their injuries. It had been here that the psychologist had told him that one day he would have to face up to the deaths of his parents. He'd been seventeen when they'd been killed in an underwater explosion while on a diving exploration of the Straits of Malacca. He'd only recently learned that their deaths had been no accident. Their expertise in marine archaeology and oceanographic turbulence had been exploited by people they had trusted, those same people who had been instrumental in their murders. They in turn were now dead, not by his hand, although it had been a close call. That didn't give him satisfaction but it did give him closure of a kind. The anger and deep resentment had gone, but there was still a hollow inside him that might have more to do with the uncertainty of his future than the past.

He pushed away such thoughts as Elaine moved around the counter and threw her arms around him. The warmth of

42

her greeting threatened to overwhelm him for a moment; it fleetingly made him think that perhaps what was missing in his life was a meaningful relationship.

Stepping back, she looked him over with a gleam in her eye. 'Still as handsome as ever.'

'Even with this?' He pointed good-naturedly at his scar.

'Especially with that. It makes you look exciting. I told you that before. If I was thirty years younger, no one would stand a chance with you.'

'And if I was thirty years older I'd be sweeping you off your feet.'

'You can do that now, I've no objections.'

He made to do so and she laughed and gently pushed him away. 'I'll get the sack.'

'I doubt it, you're too valuable for that.'

'I'm only a catering assistant.'

'There's nothing "only" about that or you. Can I buy you a coffee? I want a bit of a chat.'

'I thought there would be an ulterior motive. So it's not me and my wonderful personality you've come to see.'

'It is, because I know you'll help and as usual be the font of all knowledge. Go and sit down. I'll get you a coffee and a sticky bun.'

'I'll be told off for idling.' She looked back at the counter, where another woman in her fifties was working. It was mid-afternoon and the café was quiet. They had made good time on the boat and had moored up at King William Yard Marina just after one thirty. Strathen had grabbed five hours' sleep on the journey and looked much the better for it. He'd then relieved Marvik at the helm for five hours. When Plymouth had come in sight, Strathen had ducked out of view and Marvik had moored up alone. He'd paid for the visitors' berth, telling the marina office he wasn't sure how long he would be staying, and, after eating, had left Strathen to his research below decks while he'd set out by taxi for the naval base and recovery centre some four miles away. His veteran's card had gained him entry to both.

43

'I'll square it with the boss,' he told Elaine, then did so, saying he wouldn't take up too much of her time. He bought the promised refreshments — forgoing the sticky bun for himself — and joined her in a seat by the windows overlooking the gardens, where trees and shrubs were swaying in the brisk breeze.

'How's Shaun?' she asked, spooning three sugars into her cup.

'Missing. It's why I'm here.'

Her lined face fell. 'When? What's happened?'

'It's believed he took his own life.'

Her eyes almost popped out of her head. 'He'd never do that. Even in his darkest moments he'd not contemplate that.'

Elaine thought of all the personnel who came through these doors as her children. She felt for each one of them but never showed pity, and that was her gift — she treated each and every one as though there was nothing different about any of them, always with a smile on her round, lined face and a joke on her lips.

Marvik felt a heel for deceiving her. He wondered if this was the right strategy, especially with Elaine. He drank some coffee before continuing. 'His boat was found off the coast of Ireland. There was no one on board and a note at the helm saying he'd come to the end.'

Elaine was shaking her head vigorously. 'I still don't believe it.'

He studied her carefully. 'Nor do I. I've been to Ireland and brought his boat back here. He told me before he went that Jarinder had been killed in a car crash. He was upset and angry about it. So am I.'

Elaine was looking downcast, an expression Marvik had never witnessed on her pleasant face before. 'I can't believe that Jarinder is dead,' she declared. 'It makes me sick to my stomach and that furious. All that talent, and a good man, gone to waste. And now you're telling me Shaun could be dead. He couldn't have killed himself because of Jarinder's death. I know they were close but Shaun would have tried to make sense of it, as are we all, but there is no sense to accidents is there?' she added sorrowfully. 'It's about being in the wrong place at the wrong time, or making a foolish mistake — not that Jarinder would have done that, but he could have been distracted, or tired. You know how hard he works . . . worked. Why is it the good people get taken and the evil bastards live for ever?'

'I can't answer that.' He wished he could. 'What do you know about Jarinder's accident?'

'Only what I've read in the local paper and heard around the place. I'd like to pay my respects but they do things different in the Hindu religion. They don't have a cremation in the same way as we do — by that I mean it's not ordinary mourners who go, only family, and then only the men. I don't rightly know what to do.'

'When the body comes home, you can visit the house, but that's up to you. The coffin will be open.'

'I've seen dead bodies before. Maybe I will.'

He drank some coffee while she bit into her sticky bun. 'Elaine, when was the last time you saw Jarinder?'

'A week ago. It was last Wednesday morning, but I didn't speak to him. He was in the garden talking to a man. And he didn't look very happy. I've never seen Jarinder lose his temper, but he looked close to it with this man. I'd have said they were having an argument, but I can't see Jarinder arguing with anyone.'

Marvik's ears pricked up at this piece of information. Not that it might mean anything, but on the other hand it could be significant.

'Did you recognize this other man?'

'No, he was wearing a black motorcycle helmet.'

'And he didn't take it off or lift up the visor when he was speaking to Jarinder?'

'Not when I saw them.'

That was irregular, in Marvik's experience, and if this man had been an employee, a visitor to one of the patients or a supplier, then surely he would have done so. And he would have needed to show ID to get through the naval base security. He'd also have needed to sign in. How had Jarinder recognized him? Had he introduced himself? His voice would have been muffled because of the helmet.

'They were over by those trees,' Elaine continued. 'I was wiping down this table and happened to look out. Jarinder turned away and this other man grabbed his arm. Jarinder went ramrod stiff and drew himself up. He had a lovely bearing, handsome too.' She sighed. 'He looked steadily at this man and said something, but I couldn't hear from here or lip-read. Then I got called to the counter.'

'What time was this?'

'About eleven thirty.'

'I know you couldn't see his face but can you tell me what he was like, his build and anything else about him?'

'About your height and build, although he could have been bulked out by the clothes he was wearing — motorcycle leathers with a red stripe down the side and big boots.'

'Did you notice any badges or logos on the clothes?'

'No, sorry. Is it important?' She looked concerned as she licked her fingers.

'Probably not but I'd like to trace this motorcycle man and talk to him.'

'He could have been a courier. He had a jiffy bag in his hand, a small, square flat one, not bulky. It might have been some medical supplies and Jarinder was furious because the man had brought the wrong thing, or was late delivering it.'

'Did Jarinder take it?'

'Not that I saw, but he might have done after I got called away.'

'Have you mentioned this to anyone?'

'No. Should I?'

Marvik gave a smile. 'No. Like you said, it could have been a small dispute over some medical supplies.' He didn't for a moment think that. This sounded as though it could have some bearing on what had followed, but how and what

46

he didn't know. 'If you see this man again, would you phone me?'

'Of course.'

'Give me your number and I'll send you a message so that you'll have my number on your phone.'

This she did, and he messaged her back while she finished her bun.

Despite what he had told Elaine, he was certain this encounter meant something. But what? And what had happened to this package? Had it been found in Jarinder's office? Or perhaps it was in his house and his children would find it. Or had it been in the car when Jarinder crashed on his way to see Strathen? It could have got lost in the carnage. Had someone taken it? Was it even relevant?

'Did you ever hear Jarinder, or anyone, speak of a man called Daniel Larroc?'

She shook her head. 'No.'

'Did he, or anyone, mention Ballycotton? It's a small harbour village in Ireland.'

'No, why?'

'It's close to where Shaun's boat was found.' He quickly changed the subject by asking her about her family, her grandchildren and where she had gone for her holidays. After a while she said she'd better get back to work.

Marvik made his way to the reception desk, where he asked if he could see the signing-in log for 13 September. It was the same receptionist who had been here when he'd been recovering, and he told her that he was trying to contact a man who had known Jarinder to inform him of what had happened. She produced the file and Marvik scanned the list of names, which included the name of the patient they were visiting. There were only two who had signed in at 11.10 and 11.20 a.m. The first was a woman.

'This is the man I'm looking for, Gary Reide. He was visiting Alan Jennings. Do you have contact details for either of them?'

'We do for Alan but I can't give those to you, Art.'

As he had expected. 'Army, navy or Marines?'

'The first.'

'Was his visitor Reide wearing motorbike clothes?'

'Not that I remember.'

'Has anyone signed in wearing them, with a red stripe down the side?'

'No.'

That ruled out Reide then. He asked though when Alan Jennings was next at the centre and was told he was due there Friday morning at ten. Marvik thought he'd come back then and see if he could get Reide's contact details. Reide might have seen the man on the motorbike and might be able to tell him more about him and the bike. He asked if Jarinder had visited the centre the morning of 13 September. The fact that Elaine had seen him obviously indicated that he had, but Marvik wondered if Jarinder had been drawn here specifically to meet with this motorcycle man, rather than to see a patient.

'I can't remember or say for certain,' was the receptionist's reply. 'And I no longer have access to his records. They've been stopped now that he's deceased,' she added sadly. 'I think I remember seeing him here that day but I couldn't swear to it. The days merge into one, they go so quickly.'

'Do couriers and delivery drivers have to sign in?'

'At the main gate but not here. Our medicines management nurse, Roy Searle, usually checks that the couriers have delivered what has been ordered and that they've come from the correct and legitimate source and are not fakes. Do you want to speak to him?'

'If he's available.'

She located Searle, who appeared a few minutes later, a bulky, short man in his forties, with large dark-rimmed spectacles and a cheerful countenance. Marvik apologized for taking him from his duties. 'I want to know if a man delivered any medical supplies to you on the morning of the thirteenth of September.'

'I'll check the records.' He moved round to a computer and keyed something in. Marvik looked over his shoulder at the list with dates beside it. Most had been noted as received, checked and signed in by Searle. A couple had an annotation beside them of being out of stock. 'No. Nothing on that date.'

'Do you recall seeing a man about my height and build wearing motorcycle clothes with a red stripe on them?'

'Sorry, no.'

This gave further confirmation to Marvik that it was not Gary Reide. But this motorcycle man had been here and someone other than Elaine must have seen him. Still, he could hardly go round asking the prosthetic and orthotic nurses, consultants and doctors if they recalled him. He might need to if he drew a blank elsewhere, but he'd come to that later. Before leaving, he asked Searle if he recognized the name Daniel Larroc. He didn't. Nor did the receptionist, who also looked it up on the database, with a negative result.

Making his way back to the main gate, he considered what Elaine had told him. Was it a stroke of luck that he'd picked up something of the trail that could ultimately lead to the truth behind Jarinder's death? Or was it, as Elaine had said, a private courier delivering something Jarinder had ordered and he'd got it wrong?

He called Heather Carter, Jarinder and Amanda's secretary. Getting her voicemail, he left a message saying he had learned of the tragic death of Jarinder and would like to speak to Amanda Nightingale if Heather would pass on his mobile number and message. He didn't expect Heather to return the call immediately, or for Amanda to be available and contact him.

He asked the security officer if he recalled seeing the man on the motorcycle on the morning of 13 September, but the officer was non-cooperative and monosyllabic. He vehemently denied Marvik access to the security log. Irritating but correct. Marvik had no right to demand to see it. For all the security officer knew he could be a terrorist, or perhaps someone testing the fastness of security.

Outside the main gate, he rang Strathen on the mission mobile. Marvik relayed what Elaine had told him.

'Sounds interesting but could be nothing,' was Strathen's view. 'There's no news from Ireland on the body being found, which could mean one of several things. One, no one cares why you and I were asking about the man who took occupancy in that house; two, his body's been moved; or three, they're all keeping schtum out of fear, obstinacy or for money, the latter of which gets my vote.'

'Hang on, my other phone's ringing. I've got to go.' Marvik abruptly rang off and answered his mobile because the caller, to his amazement, was Amanda.

'You want to talk about Jarinder?' she said peremptorily.

'Yes. I—'

'You're here in Plymouth. Where?'

'Outside the naval base.'

'I'll pick you up in ten minutes.'

She rang off, leaving him staring at his phone. Amanda was always blunt, which made her bedside manner an acquired taste, but she was an excellent surgeon, and both he and Strathen preferred a direct and honest diagnosis and prognosis to waffle and sympathy. So did the majority of their injured ex-comrades. With a thrill of anticipation, he hoped this meant Jarinder had confided something to her that could help them get to the truth.

CHAPTER SIX

'It's good to hear from you, Art, although not concerning the subject matter,' Amanda said, as he climbed into the new white Range Rover.

He stared at her perfectly made-up oval face framed by shoulder-length fair hair. She was early forties, trim and dressed in a tight-fitting blue dress that complemented her blue eyes and creamy skin, which despite her age had not a single line on it. She wasn't everyone's picture of a surgeon consultant. She looked more like a City banker.

'Does the scar bother you much?' she asked, unable to prevent her profession from creeping in and stalling his questions. She indicated into the traffic.

'It itches like blazes from time to time. Otherwise I forget it's there until I look in the mirror or I see people step back from me or stare at it.'

'Does that worry you? Because if it does, something might be able to be done about it.'

'And let you loose on it with your scalpel? Not likely,' he joked.

'How are the headaches?'

'They come and go. But—'

'You're not here for a medical consultation. I know. And I haven't got much time. I'm late already for my private clinic. I'm afraid you'll have to make your own way back from there. Jarinder's death is tragic but the biggest shock and the most devastating is what's happened since.' Her blue eyes bored into his as they stopped at a set of traffic lights. 'Before I say more though, tell me why you're asking — the real reason, don't fob me off about wanting to come here to pay your respects, although I know you do want to.'

'Before his death, Jarinder was in touch with Shaun Strathen. He said he was worried about something that he'd like to discuss with Shaun. He never made it and I don't know what it was.'

'And Shaun is curious. So why isn't he here to ask me, or is he?'

'Shaun's boat was found anchored up in Ballyandreen Bay, Ireland. There was no one on board. There was a note from Shaun saying he was taking his own life.'

She snorted. 'Impossible. Not Shaun.' She pulled away. 'You don't believe it either.'

'No.'

'Why not, aside from the fact that he wouldn't do anything like that? Shaun is not a quitter and we both know that, you more than me. There's another reason. I can see it in your face.'

'There are several. For a start the boat was anchored, not left to drift. Why bother to do that? His laptop and mobile had gone. Yes, I know he could have jumped overboard with them—'

'But unlikely.'

'And there was a full tank of fuel and another in reserve, enough for me to bring his boat back here to Plymouth. A suicidal man would hardly fill up his tank for a return journey. And why go all the way to Ireland to throw himself overboard when he could have done so anywhere in the Solent on his doorstep?'

'Does Ireland hold any special memories for him?'

'Not that I know of.'

She pulled up in some traffic. 'Then why write a note telling a lie that would worry you?'

'Because I believe it's somehow connected with Jarinder's death, and when I find out what was troubling Jarinder then maybe I'll discover where Shaun is. I'm convinced he must still be alive and in hiding somewhere.' That much was true.

'Perhaps because you want to believe it. He could have had an accident and fallen overboard. He could have had a sudden seizure. Although that doesn't explain the note.'

'Or the fact that he went to Ireland.'

'Shouldn't you have stayed there to look for him? What are the Garda doing?' she fired at him, driving off.

'Nothing as far as I'm aware, and I don't think the answers lie in Ireland but here with Jarinder's death.'

It was a moment before she spoke. 'Jarinder was having an affair with a former patient.'

It was Marvik's turn to scoff at the bombshell. He stared at her disbelievingly. 'Never.'

'That's what I said. Anyone less likely is hard to imagine. It goes against everything he believed — his religion, his ethics, his professionalism — and he was still in love with his wife even though she's been dead for many years. And he would never do that to his family. Perhaps that's what Jarinder told Shaun and it so disillusioned him that he . . . No, I still can't believe Shaun would do that, and I can't believe Jarinder would have an affair, but it's there in black and white, in his emails, so they tell me.'

'Who are "they"?'

'Our wonderful IT department. Explicit emails between Jarinder and this woman.'

'He wouldn't have been so stupid to correspond with a lover, especially a former patient, at work,' Marvik declared, still reeling from the shock and trying to fathom what it meant.

'It's there, nonetheless. After his death, his computer files were lifted by the IT department, as is usual. Obviously his patient list has to be reallocated — some have come to

53

me, others to Rufus Jarrow. Jarinder's emails also needed to be scrutinized, passed on and answered. They found evidence of correspondence of a sensitive and explicit nature between him and a woman called Debbie McCleary. I don't recognize the name. I've never heard Jarinder speak of her, nor has his secretary.'

'But Heather must know her. She'd have had access to Jarinder's emails. I take it they found this correspondence on his hospital email address.'

'They did, but Heather would only have seen the ones he copied her into, not these. The rest of the team are being questioned about this Debbie creature. From what I've been told, which is precious little, the affair had been going on for some years. We've all been sworn to secrecy. As if any of us would blab about it! Everyone loved Jarinder.' She pulled into the private hospital's car park and into a space reserved for consultants. After silencing the engine, she swivelled round and gave him a hard stare. 'No one wants to see his reputation tarnished.'

It seemed someone did. It wasn't enough for them to kill him, he thought with fury. They had to disgrace him, even after death.

She said, 'It would be dreadful if the media got hold of it. I shouldn't even be telling you.'

'Have the police been informed?'

'Not that I know of but I don't know everything. And I can't see that they'd be bothered anyway. It's a matter for the General Medical Council, but even they can't do anything because Jarinder is dead. And he's no longer in the Marines, so he can't have his rank stripped from him. It'll be hushed up, unless this Debbie McCleary wants to blab about it. I'm assuming someone in the IT department is trying to trace her. The chief executive might have engaged a private security company to investigate.'

'Have the family been informed?'

'I doubt it and I sincerely hope not. But when, and if, Debbie is found and told about Jarinder's death, she might very well turn up to pay her respects.' She opened the car door and climbed out. Marvik followed suit.

'What was Jarinder treating Debbie McCleary for?' he asked. 'There must be a patient record.'

'I couldn't find it, and yes I did look, but then I suspect it was removed from the system as soon as they found the link between her and Jarinder. Or it might have been archived some time ago. I don't have access to all the archived records. It could have been a skin cancer treatment or cosmetic plastic surgery.'

'Has anything been found on his private patient list?'

'No. I went through it with Rufus. He's a talented surgeon with the same interests as Jarinder, managing complex wounds, major limb trauma and limb salvage as well as reconstructive surgery both on the NHS and privately. Jarinder rated him highly and vice versa.'

They halted at the door to the hospital. Marvik sidestepped an elderly couple leaving. 'Was the affair still active when Jarinder died?' He wondered when the last correspondence between them would have taken place.

'I've no idea. I'll see if I can get any more information. I'll let you know what I find. Which marina are you in?'

Marvik was reluctant to tell her. She might take it upon herself to visit him and find Strathen on board. If he refused to say, though, or fudged where he was moored, Amanda might be suspicious. She was bright enough to speculate about why. He told her, adding that he wasn't sure how long he'd be there. 'It depends what I get from Jarinder's family.'

'When will you see them?'

'Tomorrow morning. Is there anyone else in the meantime you think might help me?'

'Only this Debbie McCleary, and goodness knows where she is. Don't let on I've told you about her. I'll ferret around tomorrow as soon as I can. I'm in theatre most of the day, so it won't be until late or perhaps even the day after, Friday. Will you call me if you get anything?'

'Yes.'

He watched her waltz inside before making his way out of the grounds and walking briskly back to the marina. He was certain the emails were phoney. Someone had hacked into the system and put them on it, but how and who? And why? They were questions he put to Strathen some forty-five minutes later after bringing him up to speed. Strathen didn't believe the affair either.

'Someone was out to ruin Jarinder, but is it the same person who we believe drove him off the road and killed Larroc?' Strathen pondered.

'It has to be. Does it mean it's someone within the health authority? Motorbike man? That would explain how he got into the naval base and the recovery centre. He had a medical pass.'

'Maybe. On the other hand it could be an outsider, a black-hat hacker as they're called, paid by whoever silenced Jarinder to get into the system and plant the emails.'

'That can't have been easy.'

'It's not. It takes expertise in coding and programming. Jarinder's letter said, "*I have been warned to keep silent or they will kill me.*" The warning could be those emails, and when he saw them and told whoever was behind them to go to the devil — possibly this motorbike man — he was killed.'

'And they were left on the system to discredit him after his death in case anything came out about what he was doing. But what's the motive behind this?' Marvik said, exasperated.

Strathen looked thoughtful. 'OK, some options. Blackmail for money. Although Jarinder wasn't rich, and certainly not super rich, the hacker could think he'd pay up several thousands of pounds, or even hundreds of thousands if he sold his house, to stop the emails from being exposed. This same trick could have been practised on other senior consultants who had a lot to lose if their reputation was smeared.'

'Amanda didn't tell me, or even hint, that any other consultants seemed to be troubled.'

'She might not know because they're in a different field of medicine. And it might not just be the Devon health authority. This hacker could have his grubby fingers in other pies around the country.'

'A blackmailer wouldn't kill the goose who laid the golden egg.'

'He would if he thought his dirty secret was going to be exposed. But I agree with you. Someone clever enough to get into the NHS system would be clever enough to cover his back and make doubly sure Jarinder's reputation, and that of his family, would be so tarnished that many would believe it. Especially if this blackmailer had fabricated other evidence to back it all up. So, second option: espionage, which I think we can also rule out.'

'But can we?' Marvik eagerly interjected. 'Jarinder is ex-navy. He could have information that a terrorist group would be very keen to get their hands on. Alternatively, one of Jarinder's patients might be, or might have been, an agent of the intelligence services of another country and Jarinder became privy to some sensitive material. The threat of revealing the skilfully planted information about Debbie McCleary was to get him to tell what this agent had revealed. Jarinder refused.'

'He could have communicated that to a British agent.' Strathen looked disturbed.

'The dead man at Ballycotton.'

Strathen nodded. 'Our expert hacker, or whoever is behind this, got into Jarinder's phone and emails and he tracked Larroc to that location. A hitman was sent to eliminate Larroc and then Jarinder, as we've previously discussed.'

'Would Crowder tell us if Jarinder or Larroc were in the pay of British Intelligence? Maybe I should find out. What other options do we have on motive?'

'Vengeance against Jarinder for some injustice, or perceived injustice. This email hacker wants to see Jarinder and his family suffer by destroying him completely. He could have harboured a grudge for some time. It could be a family member of someone Jarinder didn't save, or someone this person believes Jarinder deliberately let die.'

'In combat?'

'Or on the operating table. Then again it could be motivated by jealousy,' Strathen added reflectively. 'Perhaps this killer, who might also be the hacker, never made it to the top of his profession, a medical one. He saw Jarinder do so. He took to cybercrime to get even.'

'The two don't seem compatible to me. Medical man and IT expert,' Marvik posed.

'Why not? A brilliant analytical, diagnostic brain and a high intellect is required for medicine, the same for a cyber expert. Not all medical people are good at the patient relationship. In fact some are appalling, and others prefer dead bodies — i.e. pathologists — or medical research, which fits more with the profile of our cyber expert. Maybe Jarinder isn't the target though.'

Marvik quickly caught on. 'All this is being done, including his murder, to hurt or threaten a family member. His sons or daughter? But I can't see how the body at Ballycotton fits with that.'

'We might if we could find out who he was. I can't find any Daniel Larroc on the databases I can access. Nor can I discover who owns that cottage. It's not listed with the Irish Land Registry.'

'Anything on this Gary Reide? Even though I don't believe he's our man, I still think it might be worth talking to him, just for the fact that he was visiting Jennings at about that time motorbike man was and he might be able to tell me more about him.'

'I agree. I've found three Gary Reides: one who lives in Scotland and is in his eighties, another in Southend in his late sixties, both of whom I think we might rule out. The third is more interesting — he's in the army reserves at 165 Port and Maritime Regiment, based here in Plymouth. Given that Jennings is army, it sounds likely his visitor was genuine.' Strathen shifted.

Marvik could see he was restless. 'What is it, Shaun?'

'It's being holed up here. I'm severely hampered by the slow Wi-Fi and only being able to work on one computer at a time. I haven't got the same range and power as at the flat. I need to return, Art. No one's gone near the place in the last couple of days since I've been able to get a signal, so our killer might believe I've topped myself. I can live like a hermit there, no one will see or hear me, and my security is good.'

'I think you're right. Amanda asked me where I was moored, and, while I don't expect her to pay me a visit, it's possible she could and therefore risky. Better if you're not here. It would be natural for me to take your boat back to Hamble — after all, that is what I should be doing. But I've got to speak to the family and Jennings first. And I need to stick around in case you can find Debbie McCleary or Amanda comes up with something.'

'I agree. I can take the train. I'll stay here until after you've spoken to Jarinder's children tomorrow, then slip away. I'm not sure when the cremation will be but I doubt if it's tomorrow. It's probably too early, although the body might be at home by now.'

'Did you find anything on the post-mortem?'

'No. I've found the statement put out by the health authority regretting Jarinder's death, saying what a skilled surgeon he was and offering condolences to his family, the usual bland thing. This might have been before the discovery of Debbie. There's also a statement from the British Association of Plastic Reconstructive and Aesthetic Surgeons, and the charity Jarinder was associated with, along with the General Medical Council and the British Medical Association.' Strathen eased his prosthetic leg. 'The BBC also picked it up, through the local newspaper, which features a sizeable article on Jarinder. No doubt the one Elaine read. It's dropped down the BBC menu now as other news stories take priority. There's a fair amount on social media from naval personnel, his patients and former patients — service-men like us, as well as NHS and private patients. Jarinder didn't have a social media profile but his sons Nishan and Rohan do, on the professional networks only. Nishan is a well-respected barrister, and Rohan an investment manager with FXL Wealth Management. I haven't been completely idle.'

Marvik smiled. 'Never thought that for a moment.'

'There's nothing for Tarina, but she might post under a pseudonym, if at all.'

'I won't mention the emails to them, not unless one of them raises it.'

'Meanwhile, I'll carry on searching.'

Marvik could offer to help but, as Strathen had said, they were hindered by not having ultra-fast access to the internet and by the lack of computers. While Strathen halt-ingly tried his best, cursing every now and then, Marvik felt he was wasting time sitting on the boat when he should be out there discovering who and what had driven Jarinder and Larroc to be killed.

For the umpteenth time, he questioned whether he should have stayed in Ireland and put pressure on the Gilleys. He could also have questioned the fishermen and perhaps got a lead on the killer. He toyed with the idea of calling Crowder, who would be able to mobilize a whole team of researchers to look into Larroc, McCleary and anyone else whose name came up in connection with the investigation. But this wasn't a National Intelligence Marine Squad mis-sion. Crowder didn't even know that Strathen had suppos-edly taken his own life. Perhaps he should tell him what was going on. But neither of them were employees, just seconded to the team as and when needed.

Strathen urged him to sleep on it and see what the next day brought. Marvik somewhat reluctantly agreed. The adrenaline of the completion of his mission in France and of finding and bringing Strathen back had worn off, leaving him dejected and drained. There was nothing for it but to sleep and hope that his interview with the Vaidyas might yield something that he could take action on.

CHAPTER SEVEN

Thursday

Jarinder's house was an impressive whitewashed, semi-detached Victorian villa in a tree-lined conservation area a mile from the city centre. Set back from the road with an expansive driveway leading up to stout stone pillars either side of the front door, the property was arranged over three storeys and would certainly fetch a considerable sum of money if sold. But Marvik didn't think the motive for this was blackmail, not for money anyway. Nor did he believe it was espionage, as they had discussed yesterday. It had to be revenge — for what, though? So far Strathen had had no luck on his searches for Debbie McCleary, and, although he would continue throughout the day, he didn't think he would get very far. He would also continue to monitor anything that came up from Ballycotton.

Marvik pressed the brass doorbell and heard it echo throughout the house. There were four cars parked in the driveway and a top-of-the-range Porsche in front of the double garage slightly distanced to the side of the house to his left. A woman in her early sixties in traditional Indian dress answered the door. She looked startled and confused. Marvik hastily apologized for the intrusion and asked if he could speak to Nishan or Rohan in private, outside. He didn't wish to intrude on their grief but said he was a former patient, colleague and good friend of Jarinder's.

The woman pushed the door to and Marvik waited. A few seconds later, a fit man in his early thirties wearing expensive casual clothes stepped out.

'I'm Rohan Vaidya, what do you want?' he demanded sur- lily. His restless dark-brown eyes roamed over Marvik's face, registering the scar with suspicion. His fingers fiddled with his phone. Marvik noted the diamond-studded ring and gold bracelet. His unshaven face was etched with grief but it was hos- tility that gained the upper hand. He seemed unable to contain his energy or impatience, his eyes constantly on the move as though seeking an escape. As if to confirm this, they frequently flicked to the Porsche. His, Marvik suspected. Maybe he was finding it hard to be confined to the house among so many relatives, and perhaps Jarinder's body had been brought home and he was uncomfortable and distraught over that.

Marvik hastily said, 'I served alongside your father in the Marines. He was a good man. Please accept my sincere condolences. I'm sorry to trouble you at a time like this but I believe there was something disturbing your father and I'm keen to find out what it was.'

'What good will that do? He's dead.'

Marvik hid his shock at the blunt reply, knowing grief could make people behave in all kinds of different ways. He gently pressed on. 'Did he speak to you about any concerns, or hint at what was troubling him?'

'No.'

'Did he mention a man called Larroc?'

'No.'

'Or a woman called Debbie McCleary?' Marvik watched him carefully for a reaction.

The eyes narrowed and his mouth tightened. 'No.'

That was a blessing at least, if it was the truth. 'I—' but Marvik didn't get any further because Rohan's eyes looked

62

beyond him at the sound of a car approaching. A black Mercedes slid into the drive and swung round to park in front of the garage next to the Porsche.

'My brother, Nishan,' Rohan said curtly. 'Ask him your questions. I've got—' His phone rang and he put it to his ear eagerly. He strode round to the side of the house without acknowledging his brother, who looked after him with a scowl before approaching Marvik. Rohan disappeared from view, obviously into the back garden.

Marvik hastily introduced himself to the slender man in immaculate pale slacks, highly polished brogues and a beige designer polo shirt. He looked as though he could have stepped out of a fashion magazine. He was slimmer than his brother and his features more aquiline. His eyes were deeper-set but just as dark and not so restless or suspicious, though they held curiosity.

'I'm Nishan Vaidya. You must excuse my appearance.' He ran a hand over his stubble. 'But we do not shave until the end of mourning. How can I help you?'

His voice was calm, well educated, his manner polite; there was nothing about him of the restless anger that his brother exhibited. Marvik recalled that Strathen had said Nishan was a barrister. Marvik thought he might be an exceedingly good one.

'I'm here to pay my respects but also to ask you about your father's state of mind before he died.'

Nishan's shrewd eyes studied him. He remained silent, forcing Marvik to continue.

'He spoke to a friend of mine shortly before his death and my friend has gone missing. I'm trying to discover if anything Jarinder said to him could help me find him. He, like me, was one of Jarinder's patients, an amputee, Shaun Strathen. We served in the Royal Marines and met your father when he was operating under combat conditions. Did your father confide anything to you that was troubling him?'

Nishan showed no reaction to the name. But then Jarinder might never have mentioned Strathen, or any of his patients, to his son.

'No. He didn't confide in any of us. It wasn't his way.'

'When did you last speak to him?'

'The Monday before his death.'

Marvik didn't know why but he felt there was something wrong here. Perhaps father and son had quarrelled.

'And he never mentioned anything troubling him?'

'No.'

'Did he mention a place called Ballycotton?'

'That's in Ireland.'

'Yes. You know it?'

'I conducted a trial in Cork about six years ago. I'm a barrister. And we used to sail there, and along that coast, when we were children, when Father wasn't away on service or working, which wasn't often.'

Did Marvik detect a note of bitterness? He'd forgotten that Jarinder had enjoyed sailing, but then they'd only spoken of it briefly and some years ago. 'Did he still own a yacht?'

Nishan looked a little surprised at the question, but answered lightly enough. 'Yes. None of us sail, so it will be sold. It's in Mayflower Marina. I haven't been on board for some time and I don't think my brother or sister have.'

'Did your father speak of a man called Daniel Larroc?'

'Not that I can recall.'

'Or a woman called Debbie McCleary?'

'No.'

'So your sister wouldn't know if anything was disturbing her father?'

'No. I expect you asked my brother. He won't be able to help you. Rohan is more concerned about a sizeable investment deal and is desperate to get back to London. He's an investment manager in the healthcare sector.'

There was just the hint of a sneer in the voice, as though Rohan had chosen an unworthy occupation. Marvik had witnessed the friction between the brothers with Rohan's abrupt withdrawal. Had it always been there or had the death of their father prompted the dissent? Bereavement didn't always bring families together. It could often tear them apart.

'Who are these people you mention?' Nishan asked.

'Just names I'd heard at the recovery centre,' Marvik lied. Nishan too, from his reaction, hadn't been told about the emails, thankfully.

'Well, I'm sorry I can't help you.' He looked at his designer wristwatch, clearly indicating his time was limited. 'The undertakers brought my father's body home on Monday. There are more family members coming to mourn him, and as the eldest son I have certain duties to perform.'

'I understand.' But Marvik hadn't finished yet. 'Did the post-mortem find anything?' Nishan would know that the results would be made public at the inquest.

'There was no evidence he had a seizure and my father didn't drink or take drugs. It was just one of those things. He might have been sleepy and lost concentration for a moment, or a deer ran out in front of him. The police are still appealing for witnesses but no one has come forward.'

'Was anything found in his possession — his mobile phone, laptop, or a note or letter?'

Nishan's tired eyes narrowed, but only perceptibly. He answered politely and neutrally. 'His mobile phone was smashed to pieces. His laptop was here in the house and there was no note or letter on my father's body. Why do you ask?'

'I believe Jarinder was on his way to see Shaun when the accident happened, and I wondered if he'd written anything that might help me find out why my friend's gone missing.'

Nishan's expression softened. 'I'm sorry then that I can't help you. Perhaps there is no connection between the two incidents. I can't think how my father's death could have caused your friend's disappearance. I wish I could give you some answers, but grief can do terrible things to people. Perhaps hearing the news of my father's death tipped your friend over the edge.'

'You could be right. His boat was found off Ballyandreen Beach in Ireland. It's close to Ballycotton Harbour.'

'Which was why you asked about the place.'

'Yes. There was a note on board to say he was taking his life. I just don't want to believe it.'

'I'm sorry.' Nishan's eyes flicked beyond Marvik as though he was waiting for someone to arrive. Family members, possibly. He put his eyes back on Marvik. 'The cremation is tomorrow at eleven thirty. It's a private ceremony. It's not like Christian funerals — only close family can attend, and in our instance only males, although I draw the line at watching my father's coffin enter the furnace and pressing the button as some Hindus do. The funeral was held yesterday afternoon, and, as is the Hindu custom, it was in our house over my father's body. You are welcome to come in and pay your respects if you wish.'

'Thank you, I'd like that. But I haven't brought a gift of fruit.'

Nishan looked momentarily stunned that he knew the custom. 'That's not necessary,' he said dismissively.

Marvik removed his shoes. Nishan led him through the hall into a large airy room that overlooked a terrace and the immaculate rear garden. The coffin lay on trestles, and around it were baskets of fruit and food, and inside the coffin flowers. Sitting around it were four women and two men. Two of the women were in their early thirties, both wearing traditional dress; one of them had a cut on her face and a deep bruise. Her eyes were red and her expression harrowed.

Marvik stared down at Jarinder, feeling a knot of pain in his stomach. Accidents were one thing but murder quite another, and the bastards who had done this still hadn't finished with him. He didn't know who had laid him out, the undertakers or family, but whoever it had been had done a good job at concealing the worst of the ravages of a motor crash on the face of the man who had worked steadily and professionally under fire. As Elaine had said, this was such a waste. Quietly, he said, 'He was a brave, kind man.' He turned to Nishan. 'I apologize for intruding on your grief and thank you for allowing me to pay my respects.'

Stepping out of the room, he almost collided with Rohan, who looked stunned for a moment before pushing the kitchen door to behind him, the moody look returning to his face.

'Rohan and I will return to work once the official period of mourning ends, which for our caste, Brahmin, is ten days. We're taking the time of mourning from that of our father's sudden death. We end the period of impurity following death on the ninth day after death, which is Sunday. Some disagree and say it should be the sixteenth day, but that's just not practical. I have a major trial starting at the Old Bailey. And Tarina has to get back to St Thomas' Hospital, where she's a doctor. She was here when Father was killed. You might have noticed the woman with a cut and bruised face. Tarina was mugged in London on her way home from the hospital. She lives with Rohan at Clink Wharf.'

Marvik's heart skipped a beat. The letter to Strathen: *I have been warned to keep silent or they will kill me and hurt my family* . . .

'I'm sorry to hear that. That must have been terrifying. When did it happen?'

'Tuesday before last.'

Two days before Jarinder had telephoned Strathen and asked to meet him. 'Did the mugger get anything?' He wondered if Tarina's mobile phone held messages from her father that could explain what had worried him and could possibly implicate the killer.

'No. Fortunately a resident in the same apartment block as Rohan, George Ferrer, scared him off. The police say they're investigating, but what's one more mugging among others?'

A car pulled into the driveway and came to a halt. More relatives arriving, it seemed.

'Will there be a memorial service for your father? I know a great many people will wish to pay their respects.'

'If someone wishes to organize it,' he answered distractedly.

Marvik again thanked him for his time, and walked away. He recalled the memorial service for his parents, held at the National Oceanographic Centre, Southampton. He, as a young man of seventeen, had sat there while people had paid their tributes. He'd hated every moment of it. He'd been too angry at their deaths to take it in, and too confused and hurt. The same might be said for Jarinder's children if they attended such a service, and, even though they were older than he had been at the time, the anger might still be there. He'd seen it in Rohan. But would such a service be held? Was Jarinder's killer going to tarnish his reputation so much that it would be felt to be in bad taste?

At the entrance to the driveway, Marvik looked back. Nishan was on the steps leading to the house. Marvik knew he had lied. Jarinder had said something to his eldest son, but what? And why not confide it to him? But then why should he? Nishan didn't know him. And maybe he didn't trust him. There was no reason why he should. Being a barrister he would be naturally cautious, and Marvik hadn't produced any evidence to say he was a former Marine, or that he really knew Jarinder. He could have been anybody. Even if Nishan had believed him, he was a man who would weigh his words carefully. Perhaps there was nothing to give away.

And what of Rohan? His hostility had been all too evident. But although the brothers might know their father was disturbed, and might even know the reason why, or part of it, they weren't involved in killing him or Larroc, and they wouldn't have wished to smear their father's name by a false email campaign.

Marvik made his way into the town, mentally going over the conversation. What information had he gleaned? Tarina had been attacked the day before Jarinder had met with the motorbike man at the recovery centre and two days before he'd contacted Strathen. The assault on her fitted with that dire warning. The family were also familiar with the stretch of coast Jarinder had mentioned in his letter to Strathen and where Larroc had been killed. It was interesting to learn that Jarinder still had a yacht, which was kept in Mayflower Marina. Could he have left anything on his boat that could give them some idea what this was all about?

It was just over a mile away. Marvik made it comfortably in half an hour. He asked at the marina office for the berth number of Jarinder Vaidya's yacht, showing his veteran's card and his ID, and explaining that he'd been asked to check it over following his death.

'He was a lovely man,' Trevor, the marina employee, said sorrowfully. 'Although he didn't come here often we shall miss him, as will his patients.'

Marvik agreed, saying how he had worked with Jarinder on ops in the Royal Marines. 'When was he last here?'

'I'm not sure. I saw him about a month ago but he could have been on board since then.'

They chatted briefly for a few moments longer, Marvik revealing that he owned a boat and was currently on a friend's at King William Yard Marina.

'You should move it here. It's a much nicer marina, but then I am biased,' he added with a smile.

Armed with the berth number and a security code to get onto the pontoon, Marvik set out for the southernmost part of the large marina. The wind was growing in strength, with an edge of autumn freshness about it. He didn't pass anyone, which added to that end-of-season feeling in terms of summer boating.

Oyster Catcher was an older boat than he had expected, built sometime in the 1980s. It was a good solid Westerly Conway, the largest cruising yacht the now defunct company had made, with a seven-foot-long cockpit and two cabins, three if you counted converting the seating and table in the saloon into sleeping accommodation. He thought of Nishan's comment about them sailing this when they were younger. The boat had been in the family a long time.

He wasn't here to admire it though, or to take an inventory, and he could see that something was wrong. The blue cover across the helm and cockpit was unfastened and flapping in the breeze. That alone didn't mean anything — Jarinder could have forgotten to fasten it, or the wind could have loosened it — but Jarinder certainly wouldn't have left the hatch padlock dangling and the hatch slightly open.

He waited for a moment before boarding, in case he could pick up the sound or movement of anyone below. There was nothing. Nevertheless, he stealthily climbed on board, noting that the lockers either side of the cockpit had been opened and one was left ajar. What greeted him in the saloon and galley was an unholy mess. The seating had been upended, lockers and their contents strewn across the deck, the galley cupboards gaping. Swiftly, he checked the cabins aft and for'ard and found the same sad state of affairs. Jarinder's clothes were scattered about; even the meagre toiletries in the heads had been tossed aside. Whoever had done this had been in a hurry or a rage. Maybe both. But what had they been searching for?

He returned to the galley, to the right of which the instrumentation and radio were mounted. Below them was a small table used for laying out sea charts, underneath it a drawer. He opened it not expecting to find the logbook, but it was there. Before he could examine it, he caught movement on the pontoon and footfall on the deck. Quickly, he thrust the logbook inside his bomber jacket.

Remaining still, he waited out of direct sight of the steps. First a pair of trainers appeared, followed by jeans, a jacket and a shapely woman in her early thirties, with long dark hair tied back. On seeing him she gave a startled cry, followed by, 'Who the hell are you and what are you doing on Jarinder's boat?'

'I'd like to ask you the same.'

'Did you do this?' she hotly demanded, her eyes taking in the devastation. 'I'm calling the police.' She turned to leave.

Quickly, he said, 'I found it like this. I've only just come on board and you can confirm that with the marina staff. I'm Art Marvik, a friend of Jarinder's. We met when he was a surgeon commander in the services, hence this.' He pointed to his scar.

She glared at him, her brown eyes full of suspicion.

Rapidly, he continued. 'I'm saddened and sickened by Jarinder's death and I'm trying to work out what was worrying him so much that he had that accident. I know there has to be something, because he'd never have crashed the car. He was a very careful driver, and Nishan, his son, told me the post-mortem found no evidence of illness or of drink or drugs.'

'So you thought you'd ransack the boat,' she scoffed.

'I didn't do this,' he repeated. 'Nishan told me his father still had the boat and I came to look at it and found it open.'

'Huh!'

'OK, go ahead, call the police if you think I'm a thief and they can search me. Nishan will confirm who I am and so too will Amanda Nightingale. She's a consultant surgeon who worked with Jarinder. I can wait.'

She pulled a dubious face and narrowed her eyes. 'I haven't got time to waste while the police plod about.'

'Is that because you shouldn't be here either? How do I know you haven't come to rob the place?'

'I've come to *clean* the boat and, yes, I know there's little point with Jarinder dead, but he was a Hindu, and if you know anything about that religion you'll know that cleaning comes into it big time. It's a Hindu belief that when someone dies everything has to be cleaned.'

Marvik wasn't at all convinced by her excuses. She wouldn't look at him as she spoke and she had no cleaning items with her, unless they were in the cockpit.

'But why should you?' he asked. What connection did she have to Jarinder?

'Because I want to, all right?'

'Fine by me. I'll help you straighten up the place.'

'There's no need,' she snapped. 'I'd prefer to do it alone.'

Marvik shrugged indifference. 'I've told you who I am, but you haven't told me who you are.'

'No, I haven't. I'm Debbie McCleary.'

CHAPTER EIGHT

It took Marvik a few seconds to recover from his shock, although he hoped he hadn't shown it as much as he'd felt. 'Pleased to meet you, Debbie.' His head was spinning, but he moved slowly into the saloon.

'You said that as though you know me?'

'Did I? Maybe I heard Jarinder talk of you.'

She studied him closely. 'He might have done.'

'How did you come to know him?'

'That's none of your business.'

'No, I guess not. Where's your cleaning stuff? I'll fetch it.'

'I can manage.'

'Of course. You have a key to the boat then? I mean, you weren't expecting the hatch to have been open.'

'I wasn't, and to save you asking twenty questions: yes, I have a key. And I'll tell you why, seeing as you're bursting to know: Jarinder and I were lovers.'

He hoped he looked suitably astounded. She'd changed her mind quickly enough from refusing to tell him how she knew him one minute to declaring they were lovers the next. 'I didn't know. I had no idea.'

She tossed her ponytail and gave what Marvik thought was a malicious smile. 'No one knows. We usually met here.

It was more private than his house — too many nosy neighbours and we had to be careful.'

'Why? He was a widower. Are you married?'

'No, and I don't have a jealous partner either. But it was difficult, with him being a medical man.'

'I don't see why it should be.' Marvik hoped he looked suitably baffled. 'Doctors are allowed to marry and to have affairs.' He'd given her a lead and she took it.

'Yes, but not with their patients.'

'I see.'

She sighed and tried to look abashed, but she simply looked smug. 'We fell in love while he was treating me and that is unacceptable. Jarinder said we had to be very careful or he'd get struck off, and he was such a skilled doctor it didn't bear thinking about. I tried to end it, knowing it wasn't right and could only do harm, but he was besotted with me. He wouldn't accept it.'

'He pursued you.'

'If you like.'

'And now he can't anymore,' Marvik said sadly.

For a moment her head came up, then she looked away and moved to the other side of the cabin.

'What was he treating you for?'

'I had reconstructive surgery on my neck for a sarcoma. Successfully removed. I'm fine now.'

It was said glibly, as though rehearsed, and she wouldn't look at him. He'd have liked to have seen that scar but she was wearing a polo-neck T-shirt under her jacket. 'I'm glad to hear it,' he said pleasantly.

Her head whipped round and her brown eyes flashed suspicion.

'Are you going to report this break-in to the police or shall I?' he repeated, wanting to gauge her reaction.

'There's no point. They won't do anything anyway. And I don't want the police traipsing all over the boat and spoiling it. Jarinder's soul would hate that.'

'Looks as though someone's already done that.' Marvik didn't think she cared a damn about Jarinder's soul, or anyone else's come to that, save her own.

She picked up a cushion and placed it on the bench. 'If you didn't do this, then who did? It's not as if there's anything to steal.'

'There's the instrumentation. But that's all in place.'

'You know about boats then.'

'I said I was in the Royal Marines.'

'Yes, you did.' She moved around the cramped space, idly plucking at items and putting them on the bench seats and table. Marvik thought she was trying to consider what to do next and how to treat him.

'You don't think this is connected with his death?' he asked, keen to hear her answer.

'How can it be? He was killed in a car accident. This must be the work of some lowlife who probably thought he could see what he could grab.'

Marvik looked suitably bewildered. 'I don't think the press or social media have mentioned Jarinder had a boat. How would they know it was here? And how could they have got onto the pontoon without the security code?'

A flash of annoyance crossed her round face. 'Could be someone who works in the marina office, or a visiting engineer, someone like that. It could be another boat owner or visitor. How should I know?'

'I just can't see why anyone would ransack the place. It strikes me they were desperately looking for something. Have you any idea what that could be?'

'No. Now, I'd like to get on.' She stepped forward but Marvik ignored her request. He blocked the way up to the cockpit.

'Did Jarinder say anything to you about his concerns?'

She licked her lips. 'Only that he didn't want to end our affair. I came here last weekend to tell him we had to finish it, but he didn't like it. Maybe that was why he wasn't concentrating and had the accident. I'd hate to think I was the cause of it.'

'I'm sure you're not. But it would be tragic if your affair were to come to light. You'll want to protect his reputation, having once been his lover.'

Her eyes narrowed. 'Yeah, well, I'll try.'

But not very hard.

'There were emails between us. The health authority might find them.'

Yes and you damn well know they have.

'They'll see that I tried to end the relationship.'

'I'm sure they will.'

'What's that supposed to mean?' she flashed.

'I'll leave you to your cleaning.' He made to go, noting the relief on her face, then stalled. 'Unless you'd like me to stay and help?'

'No!' she almost screamed. 'No. I can manage.' She corrected her panic. 'I want to be alone. Memories and all that.'

'Of course.'

He alighted and made his leisurely way down the pontoon, in case she was watching him, which he was sure she was. It had started raining. There were only a handful of people about and only a few vehicles in the car park. One of them had to be Debbie's. She hadn't asked him how he had got on to the pontoon, where he lived or where he was staying — was that because she already knew? Or maybe she had assumed the marina staff had given him the code. She had been singularly lacking in curiosity about him.

He found a secluded spot and settled down to wait. He didn't have long before she crossed the concourse and climbed into a Skoda. She hadn't spent much time cleaning, he thought sardonically. Marvik memorized the registration number and returned to the boat. It was as he had left it. She hadn't locked it.

He studied the exterior a moment longer, then made his way to the marina office and said that he would be bringing his boat *Sea Fever* into the marina that evening. He paid for a visitor's berth for one night in advance, saying he wasn't sure how long he would be staying, and set off back to *Sea Fever* at King William Yard Marina, just over a mile and a half away. His reasons for changing marinas were twofold: one, he wanted to be close to Jarinder's yacht; two, no one would know he was in the marina, including Amanda, who might take it into her head to turn up personally to give him an update on her findings. He postponed the many questions swirling round his head until he could run them past Strathen, who greeted him with the news that he'd had no visitors.

'We're moving the boat to Mayflower Marina, or at least I am. You stay below decks, they're expecting me. Meanwhile, cast your eyes over that.' Marvik unzipped his jacket and put the logbook on the table. 'It's from Jarinder's yacht.'

'And it's kept at Mayflower Marina?'

'Correct.'

Strathen made no further comment. Marvik cast off. It didn't take long and soon he had moored up and was seated across the table from Strathen in the saloon.

'I also had a nice little chat with Debbie McCleary on Jarinder's boat. And if her real name is Debbie McCleary, then I'm Jason Bourne.'

Strathen's eyebrows shot up. 'Tell me.'

Marvik relayed what had happened at Jarinder's house, his visit to the marina office and his decision to take a quick look at the boat, only to find it had been broken into and ransacked. He ended with the gist of what Debbie had told him.

Strathen listened intently and without interruption. 'Interesting timing on her part.'

'Isn't it? I can't see the marina staff member I spoke to alerting her. Someone could have been watching the boat from one of the quayside flats, but I can't imagine they would sit there all day with binoculars primed on it just in case someone showed up.' Marvik had been giving this consideration while waiting for Debbie to appear in the car park. 'My best guess is that Jarinder's boat is fitted with a surveillance device. I didn't see one but then I don't have your scanning equipment. Debbie was summoned to hurry on board and pretend she was going to clean it for Jarinder's soul. Not in order to discover who I was, because she didn't seem that curious, but to tell me about the affair. Her paymaster could have given her instructions when he saw me board the yacht, which if he did means Debbie lives or works close by. But there is an alternative: Nishan could have told her. There's certainly something troubling him. And he told me about the boat and where it was kept. But I can't see him being involved in discrediting his father and killing him.'

'Is the house bugged?'

'We spoke outside — admittedly only a short distance from the front door, so it's possible someone picked up our conversation. I also spoke to Rohan, but briefly. He was in a hurry to get away, and not all that pleased to see me. Whoever is behind this has gone to a lot of trouble. Whatever Jarinder uncovered must be big.'

'How believable was she, Art? If you hadn't known Jarinder, or had prior knowledge about the alleged affair, would you have believed her?'

'Not unless I was slow on the uptake or gullible, and sadly there are plenty around who are both. For a start she wasn't upset enough and secondly she was contradictory. First she said she'd call the police, then she said she didn't want them wasting her time and they wouldn't do anything anyway. She said she'd come to clean the boat according to the Hindu custom of bereavement — so she'd been primed about that, and it was a good excuse — but as I said, she hadn't brought any cleaning gear. Then she said he'd relentlessly pursued her even though he knew it was wrong to have an affair with a patient, and she'd tried to break it off but he wouldn't. And if she had been halfway uncomfortable with the relationship and had insisted on ending it, then she wouldn't have been on that boat intending to scrub it down out of love and obligation. Her story and reaction were all over the place. But she could easily fool others who want to believe it, the no-smoke-without-fire lot. Not to mention the trolls on social media who would jump on it and believe every single word.'

'Will she go public though?'

'If she's paid enough, I think she'd shout it from the roof-tops. And she won't only be paid by whoever's running this. There'll be media who would cough up a nice little sum for an exclusive expo. And she'll file for compensation from the health authority. She'll play the exploited vulnerable patient. I'd say she's clever enough to change her story if she needs to, but the authority will check out her patient record—'

'Which will have been created and entered onto the system by our black-hat hacker.'

'But the records would surely show who assisted in the operation for her alleged sarcoma.'

'Those who did won't remember her or the exact details. Some will have moved on or left the NHS. Or they might think they recall something when it's suggested to them.'

'False memory syndrome. And no doubt she'll have scars to show them, courtesy of good make-up. That wouldn't get past a medical examination though, if it went that far. If it did she'd probably disappear before it could take place.'

'She might anyway when she's served her purpose, which is to tarnish Jarinder's memory and destroy his reputation. Dead men can't fight back.'

'I know.' Marvik knew the horrendous damage Debbie could do, but he worried that, when she was no longer of use to the mastermind behind this, she too would be eliminated. 'I'd like to know how she intended getting into the boat. She didn't appear to have a key — I think she knew the padlock had been forced.'

'She'd probably have said Jarinder had a duplicate made so that they could more easily meet there. They're pretty basic keys, unless Jarinder had a special padlock fitted.'

'He didn't, and no alarm. It's an old boat and he probably thought it wasn't worth it.'

'Then if she did have a key, it could have been bought at any locksmiths if someone had the number to the original.'

'And they'd get that if Jarinder had loaned his key to someone, or if it was stolen. When I returned to the boat, she hadn't relocked the padlock, which indicates she didn't have a key. I don't think she ransacked it earlier and then returned but it's not impossible. I'd like to search it again, especially for any surveillance devices.'

'She could have removed them.'

'Maybe that was why she was told to go there. Give me your scanner, Shaun.'

'I'll get Debbie's address from the DVLA and take a look through the logbook.'

'I'll see if there's anything on his chart plotter.'

Marvik was glad of the rain and gusting wind. It meant he had the pontoon to himself. He rapidly discovered there was no surveillance device on the hull or in the cockpit. There was, though, as Strathen had said, the possibility that Debbie had removed it.

He climbed down into the saloon and again did a sweep with Strathen's equipment. Nothing. Debbie hadn't done any tidying, save putting a couple of cushions back on the bench seat. So exactly why had she come here? Had it been to bump into him and back up the email smear campaign against Jarinder?

He switched on the navigational aid and saw that Jarinder had plotted a trip to Salcombe in late August and another to Falmouth on the weekend of 9 and 10 September. But what really caught his interest was the trip that was plotted to Cork the weekend before, that of 2 and 3 September. What had Jarinder written in his logbook about that, he wondered?

As he began a thorough search of the boat, he turned his mind to some of the points that were nagging at him. Why had it been ransacked? Not for valuables. This boat hadn't been randomly targeted by any lowlife. Had it been a mistake? Had Debbie been sent here to clean it to cover up the mistake? No one had expected him to be on board. But as he had been, there was now no point in setting things straight. Had Debbie been sent to look again for whatever had been missed the first time? Or had another party searched it? Someone else who had wanted Jarinder silenced?

Marvik straightened up. He'd found nothing. He would search the lockers on deck before leaving, but first the engine. The boat had an inbuilt diesel one and he lifted the cover and fiddled around. He wondered when the ransacking had taken place. Shortly after Jarinder had left for Strathen's or after his death?

His fingers froze. Yes, there was something lodged there. He twisted his fingers round until he could get a grip. He couldn't see what it was but it felt like a padded envelope with something hard inside. With his heart beating a little faster, praying it wasn't an explosive device, he teased it out.

He was staring at a small, square brown package that looked remarkably like the one Elaine had described — the one she'd seen motorbike man trying to hand to Jarinder in the recovery centre's grounds. It could still be booby-trapped. But he couldn't see why anyone would want to blow up the boat. Strathen's boat maybe, and make it look like an accident if they knew they were on board, but not this one now that Jarinder was dead. And not here. Perhaps to be on the safe side though, in case someone was banking on him finding it and wanting to eliminate him, he would take it back and let Strathen run his explosive-detecting equipment over it.

He stuffed it in his jacket pocket with a wry smile, hoping he'd reach Strathen in one piece.

CHAPTER NINE

'His logbook makes interesting reading,' Strathen greeted him, before Marvik could tell him of his discovery. 'He made a trip to Falmouth the weekend before he died. It reads, *"Sailing to Falmouth to hopefully ease my mind,"* and before that he went to Salcombe at the end of August.'

Marvik sat opposite Strathen. 'The chart plotter bears that out.'

'He anchored overnight at Salcombe and returned on Sunday. Saturday's entry reads: *"The sea state is calm. It's a clear beautiful day, with little wind, a good sail to Salcombe. Salcombe Bay, always so lovely, does not seem to be so now. It is tainted, as is everything."* Then on his return on Sunday he writes, *"A pleasant sail, or it would have been if my heart wasn't so heavy."* He's also written it in Hindi underneath that entry.'

'And that's it? No mention of a trip to Cork?'

'No, why?' Strathen studied him closely, then added, 'The chart plotter.'

'Yes. According to that, he plotted a course to Cork via stopovers at Falmouth and Milford Haven. This was on Friday the first of September. And the absence of an entry in the logbook means he didn't want any written record of it, *if* he went.'

'Oh, I think he went all right, and with a passenger.'

'Larroc.'

'Yes, a good way to get into Ballycotton under the radar. That way he'd have avoided the border patrol and showing his passport.'

'I'll ask in the marina office tomorrow if they can give me dates of when Jarinder's berth was vacant. Meanwhile, look what I've found.' He reached into his jacket pocket and produced the jiffy bag. 'It could be booby-trapped. I found it lodged under the engine.'

Strathen rose and within moments had swept a handheld scanner over the envelope. 'It's OK. Shall I do the honours?'

'Go ahead.' Marvik watched fascinated as Strathen withdrew a DVD.

'Nothing written on it. Perhaps it's what the intruder and Debbie were searching for.'

'It looks very much like the packet Elaine saw motorbike man trying to give to Jarinder.'

Strathen inserted the disk into his computer.

'It was hidden in an obscure place,' Marvik added.

'And that's probably why.' Strathen nodded at the contents on screen. 'Is that Debbie?'

Marvik cursed. 'I haven't seen her without her clothes, only her face, and that's certainly her. Whether the rest of that body is, I have no idea. The build is about right, and that's Jarinder's face, but I doubt the other body parts are his. In fact, I'd swear they aren't.' Marvik was tense with fury. 'They have the colour right, but the skin doesn't look the right age even if I was inclined to believe it — and I'm not. The hand shots are possibly Jarinder's because they could have got pictures of him off the net.' He sat back, shaking his head in disgust. 'Jarinder could have been told this disk existed by the man who accosted him at the centre. He'd never have had an affair with Debbie. Those pictures, like the whole sordid tale, have been manipulated.'

'I agree. A filthy piece of manipulative artwork. And if these pictures are on a DVD, you can bet your life they're on Jarinder's home computer, if he has one.'

'Nishan said there was a laptop in the house but I didn't get any indication from him that he's managed to get on it, or found anything like that or the phoney emails. God, I hope they're not on the hospital's emails. And what's to stop these popping up on social media?'

'I'll make this bastard swallow that bloody DVD before I'm through. And I'd like to thrust it in Debbie's face.'

'I'll see to that. You're dead, remember.'

'Then maybe it's time I came back to life and to hell with hiding from danger. If this bastard wants me, let him come after me. He'll soon see who can get nasty, even with a handicap. I'll thrash the living daylights out of him.'

'I know. But he's cunning as well as dirty and whatever he's behind is dirty too. We'll get him.'

'Too bloody right we will.' Strathen ran a hand across his eyes. 'I'm sick of sitting behind screens. I want—'

'Action, yes, I know, but you might find the reason why this has happened behind a screen. I can't do what you do, Shaun, and I need you.'

'Just don't cut me out at the end, if there is one to all this.'

'There will be and the right one, and no, I won't cut you out. We owe this criminal big time for Jarinder.'

After a moment Strathen took a breath and nodded. Marvik continued. 'I think Jarinder needed to be seen either taking or refusing to take that disk at the centre. I'm not sure why — possibly to back up the claim that it is him in those pictures and to further incriminate him. He told this guy to go to hell, even after Tarina was attacked. But then he fully realized how deadly their game was. He didn't care about the threats to himself, but to his children, and his daughter in particular, he did. He could see no way out of this alone and contacted you.'

'But why plant the DVD on the boat if it's on his computer and possibly the NHS system?' Strathen said, puzzled.

'Perhaps it isn't on the system. Maybe Debbie's been doing a bit of freelance work. She doesn't have the hacking experience to put those pictures on Jarinder's laptop and certainly not on the hospital's system, so she thought she'd put them on a DVD and tell the family where they could find it, and that she also had a copy.'

'Blackmail.'

Marvik nodded. 'She either planted the DVD on the boat after I left, or she was there to remove it now that Jarinder is dead but she didn't know where it had been put by an accomplice, although I'd have suspected he or she would have told her.' He rubbed a hand across his eyes. His head was thumping. He reached into the pocket of his jacket, took out some tablets and swallowed them without water. 'There is another option,' he continued. 'Jarinder put it there.'

'He took it from motorbike man.'

'Or he was sent a copy. Horrified, he hid it on the boat until he could discuss the whole thing with you. It would explain why the boat was ransacked. Someone was searching for it, either Debbie's accomplice, if she has one, or the motorbike man. Or his paymaster ordered someone else to find it who failed.'

'Maybe Debbie was then despatched to look for it, but got scared with you there so left before really looking. You can ask her when you see her. And I think I know who her accomplice is. The Skoda is registered to Lee Barker and he lives here in Plymouth.'

'This calls for an evening visit. Do you have a blank DVD?'

Strathen fetched one. 'I'm leaving tonight, as soon as it's dark. I'll get the 21.25, which will get me into Hamble after two changes tomorrow at 7.43. I'll slip off the boat without being noticed. If someone is watching, let's hope they think it's you. I'll keep my head low and covered. I don't think my prosthetic will give away my gait. When I get to Hamble I'll leave my car in the marina and slip into the house by the hatch, courtesy of our American Marine cousins.'

Marvik knew Strathen would easily achieve that.

'I'll monitor my flat on the way there,' Strathen continued. 'My surveillance device is still operating and so far no one has attempted to visit the apartment. I'll enable a jamming device to take out any additional surveillance equipment, if it's there.'

'Won't that alert them you're back, if someone is monitoring it?'

'They'll probably think it's gone on the blink, but I don't think they will be watching the flat as they believe I'm dead. They're keener on seeing what you're up to now that they have a good description of you, courtesy of Debbie. I'll leave you the surveillance monitoring equipment, and the explosive detector — I'd hate to lose my boat.'

'Thanks.' Marvik smiled.

'Update me on what you get from Lee Barker when you can. I might be gone by the time you return.'

Marvik requested a taxi to meet him at the marina entrance as soon as possible. One would be with him in five minutes. As he hurried there, Amanda called him.

'I can't find anything on Daniel Larroc on the hospital system. He's certainly not a patient. He might have been previously but Heather doesn't recall the name, and she has an incredibly good memory. I asked Human Resources if he was an employee — they wanted to know why I was interested. I fobbed them off with some tale but again I drew a blank. He hasn't worked for the hospital, although he could have worked, or works, for one of the agencies, and I don't know all of them or have the time to ask them.'

'I don't think it's important,' Marvik lied. 'Jarinder could have met him anywhere.'

'How did you get on with the family?'

'Drew the same result as you. Never heard of Larroc, but Nishan told me the family used to sail to Ireland and in particular to Cork and Ballycotton when they were younger.'

'Could Jarinder have been going back there to meet this Larroc? Maybe he's Irish. Or perhaps this Debbie McCleary is. It has an Irish ring to it.'

'Possibly.'

'Anything on Shaun?'

85

'No.'

There was a moment's silence before she spoke. 'Are you sticking around here?'

'For another day. I want to go to the crematorium tomorrow to see Jarinder off. Then I'll decide after that.' He wasn't going to mention his visit to Lee Barker; the fewer people who knew what he was doing, the better. The taxi pulled up.

Amanda said, 'If I pick up any news, I'll call you. Art, don't leave without telling me.'

'I'll phone you tomorrow evening and give you an update.' Although what he would tell her would be selective — not because he didn't trust her but because he didn't know if he would have anything new, and even if he did he would keep it between him and Strathen, not wishing to put her in danger.

'Better still, I'll buy you dinner,' she said. 'Which marina are you in?'

'Mayflower.' Strathen would have left by then, so no danger of her, or anyone else, paying the boat a visit.

'Then we'll eat in the restaurant there. I'll meet you at eight.'

'I'll call or text you if I can't make it.'

'Are you on the trail of something?'

'I can always hope.' He rang off and gave the driver instructions to Barker's address. It was half an hour off sunset. If he got no answer he'd return tomorrow.

It took the taxi only twenty minutes to reach the fairly modern estate and Marvik asked to be dropped off at the corner by the busy superstore. From there he walked into the residential area to a T-junction, where he faced a row of four-storey modern buildings with double driveways and garages. Outside his destination was the Skoda.

He rang the bell to flat one. There was no answer. He assumed it was a video doorbell and that Barker, and possibly Debbie, were inside and determined not to answer it. He pressed the bell again and hammered on the door.

At last he could hear movement. The door was flung open and an irate Debbie with a large towel swathed around her hair and neck glared at him. 'For fuck's sake, you'll break the door down. I was washing my hair.'

If her hair was wet, then Marvik was Queen of the May. He pushed her aside and marched in, to her vehement protests.

'Hey, you can't storm in like that. How did you find me? You followed me. That's stalking. I'll report you to the police.'

She chased after him as he strode down the narrow hall and into a kitchen at the rear while his ears strained for movement in the other rooms. He detected something. He spun round. 'You said that once before.'

'What do you want?'

'A word about Jarinder and you.'

'I've got nothing to say to you.'

'Oh, I think you have, Debbie, or whatever your name is. I think you have a great deal to say.' He waved the blank DVD in front of her. She stared at it wide-eyed, before trying to snatch it from him.

'Now, now, where's your manners? Or did you leave them on the boat along with this? Don't worry, I haven't come for the same thing that's on here. You're quite safe with me. How much were you paid for these pictures?'

'I don't know what you mean.'

'Then let me rephrase the question. Who paid you to pose for these and who is the other man in them? And I mean the body parts, not the face. I know who that is.'

'You're talking rubbish.'

Marvik moved closer. Alarmed, she stepped aside, as he knew she would. He tucked the DVD back inside his jacket. He was in the doorway now and a soft footfall was coming from the hall. Marvik's keen hearing picked out the sound of breathing. 'Am I? Then perhaps your friend will enlighten me.' In a trice, Marvik had his hand around the neck of a man, and his arm halfway up his back. The heavy torch that had been in the attacker's hand clattered to the tiled floor.

Debbie screamed and stepped forward, but one look from Marvik made her recoil. Her skin went white, while the man in Marvik's grasp, tall and skinny, cried out.

'Let him go,' Debbie pleaded.

'So that he can bash me over the head with that torch? I don't think so.' Marvik again gave the twisted arm a jerk. The fair-haired man with a rabbity face cried out and tried to extricate himself, resulting in Marvik applying more pressure on the arm to cries of pain.

'If you tell me what's going on with Jarinder, then I might consider not breaking his arm.'

'Tell him nothing, Dawn.'

'So that's your real name. Dawn what?' Marvik tugged at the man's arm, resulting in another scream.

'Snell!' she yelled. 'It is. Honest.'

'And this, I take it, is Lee Barker. Where's the motorbike, Lee?'

'What motorbike? He hasn't got one. Just who the hell are you?'

Marvik studied her for a moment, then thrust Lee onto the floor. His build didn't fit the description Elaine had given him, and, although leathers could make a man look bigger than he was, he was practically certain this wasn't the one he was after.

'You've broken his arm,' Dawn cried, aghast.

'No, just dislocated his shoulder. But I'll break something if you so much as move a muscle.' He glared at Lee on the floor and picked up the torch. Then to Dawn he said, 'Now, tell me what's going on with Jarinder Vaidya, and it had better be the truth.'

CHAPTER TEN

'Lee's a photographer. He was approached by a man about a job.'

'Name?'

'Paul Webb.'

Had she just made that up? 'Address?'

'I don't know. I don't.'

Lee was incapable of moving.

'Get Lee's mobile phone,' Marvik commanded.

'Webb's not on there.'

'Get it.'

She bent down, the towel slipping off her head to reveal her dry, shoulder-length hair. She handed the mobile nervously to Marvik, who pocketed it while spinning her round. She cried out.

He pulled down the collar of her shirt. 'The hospital did a good job on that sarcoma,' he said sarcastically, letting her go. 'Where's Webb?'

'I don't know.' She straightened her collar, looking glum. 'It's the truth. Can't I take him to hospital?'

'No. I've got plenty of time. Not sure about your boyfriend though. I think he's either about to throw up or pass out.' Marvik leaned back against the work surface.

'Please.'

'When you've answered all my questions. And the quicker you talk, the quicker you can get lover boy to the hospital. When did you meet this man, Webb?'

'Lee met him when he was taking some photographs at the marina for a client. He asked Lee if he was up for doing some freelance glamour shots. He was paying good money. Webb didn't have a model, so Lee suggested me.'

'Try again, Dawn,' Marvik said in a bored manner.

Lee groaned and through gritted teeth said, 'For fuck's sake, Dawn, tell him the truth and stop pissing about, I'm in agony.'

'All right.' She sulked. 'I've got these glamour shots of me on a website, it's one where you post provocative poses, you know the sort of thing.'

'I don't but I'll take your word for it.'

'Lee's good at that sort of thing.'

'I've seen some of his work. Go on.'

'I got this message from a guy, Paul Webb, who liked the way I looked and asked if I would like to earn some money. He—'

'When did he contact you?'

'Beginning of September. I thought he meant in porno films and I said I wasn't interested.'

Marvik doubted that.

'He said it involved a bit of acting if needed but he doubted it would come to it. All I had to say, if anyone asked me, was that I'd had an affair with this bloke. I told him I didn't want to get into any trouble with the police. He said there would be nothing like that. It was for a divorce case. He was a private detective.'

'And you believed him?' Marvik scoffed.

'Why not? He said he'd pay generously and I needed the money. I can't get a job, except boring dead-end ones, and I'm not going to do them.'

No, thought Marvik, work of any kind was not really Dawn's forte. 'You spoke to him?'

She looked at him as though he was mad. Speech was for the elderly or old-fashioned.

'Of course not. It was all done by message through the website. He told me this bloke was a plastic surgeon called Jarinder Vaidya. I was to get five hundred pounds.'

'For shit's sake, get on with it, Dawn,' Lee hissed.

'I said I wanted a hundred up front. He could have been anyone spinning me a tale. He told me he'd put the money on a boat that this bloke Jarinder owned. He gave me the code to get onto the pontoon and the name of the boat. The money was there.'

'The boat was open?'

'Yeah, and tidy then.'

'When was this?'

She remained silent.

'I've got all day.'

'Monday before last,' she grunted.

'You mean the eleventh of September?'

'If you say so.'

Marvik stepped closer to Lee.

Dawn shouted, 'Yes!'

Four days before Jarinder was killed. 'Where on the boat was it?'

'In the kitchen, stuffed in a mug,' Dawn answered.

The killer had known Jarinder was unlikely to visit his boat before that fateful Thursday night. Or he'd taken a chance on it.

'I took the money, came back and told him I was up for it. He told me what to say if anyone came asking. You're the only bugger who has.'

'So you went to the boat today to collect your four hundred and thought I might have taken it. Then you remembered what Webb had told you to say, that you'd had an affair with Jarinder, which you then told me because you wondered if I was Webb or someone trying you out.'

'You might be, for all I know.'

'For Christ's sake, Dawn, I'm dying here,' Lee cried.

'You're not,' Marvik tossed at him. 'But I can arrange it.'

Dawn quickly continued. 'I told you about the affair, as Webb had instructed me, then came back here and messaged him to say you'd come asking and I'd done what he said.'

'You gave him my name?'

'Yeah, I said you were called Marvik, you were a friend of Jarinder's, and I described you. You're not easy to forget.'

'Did he reply?'

'Not yet.'

Marvik knew he wouldn't. 'I don't think you'll see the rest of your money.'

'Then I won't carry out my part of the deal.' She tossed her head.

That would at least mean the matter would fizzle out, but not before Jarinder's reputation had been damaged.

'Has Webb contacted Lee?'

'No, why should he?' she answered, surprised.

'Because he was also paid to hack into Jarinder's computer and plant those false emails to back up your claims.'

'Don't be daft.'

'I never. I'm no expert at hacking. I just take pictures,' Lee protested vaguely. His eyes were beginning to have trouble focusing.

'Wrong answer.'

'All right, I've done a bit of hacking but not the hospital, and nothing to do with this,' Lee gabbled.

'Where?' Marvik barked.

'Just some companies. Their systems were asking for it.'

'And you sold the information on the dark web?'

Lee groaned and nodded.

'Have you got a criminal record?'

Lee seemed incapable of answering.

'Have you?' Marvik repeated.

'Yes, but I didn't go to prison, just community service.'

'What about you?' Marvik swung to Dawn, glaring hard at her.

'Yeah. Only theft.'

92

'Only!'

'Look, we haven't done anything wrong,' she protested.

'No, only lied,' he mocked, 'and I can add blackmail threats to that. When you learned Jarinder was dead, you decided to go into business on your own account. The explicit pictures were your own and lover boy here's invention. You thought you'd blackmail his family. I should pull your arm off,' he snarled at Lee, who cowered. 'When did you make them?'

'After we saw his picture on the internet saying he was dead,' Lee muttered. 'We didn't think Dawn was going to get the four hundred pounds. We thought we were entitled to something.'

Marvik could have rammed his fist into his face but steeled himself against it. They weren't worth it. He turned on Dawn. 'So you weren't on the boat to see if the balance of the filthy money had been left, because you'd already sussed out that, with Jarinder Vaidya dead, Webb no longer had any use for you. You were there to plant a copy of that disgusting DVD, which you did after I left. Then you'd tell a member of his family where to find it. If you've already done that, I'll—'

'We haven't, I swear,' Dawn gabbled.

'Why not?' he rapped.

'We were waiting.'

'For what?'

'The right time.' She glanced at Lee, who was turning grey.

'Just tell him, for fuck's sake.'

'His family have got plenty of money. The media said that one was a doctor in London, one a barrister and the other a financial investor, and we all know they're stinking rich. It said they were Hindus and they deal with bereavement differently to us.'

Marvik felt disgusted with them. They were completely without feeling or compassion. 'So as part of your hateful plan you read up about funeral and bereavement rites, which included the cleaning ritual you tried to spin on me when you found me on board and had to think quick. And the plan was that after the funeral you, or this scumbag, would phone one of them and tell them what you had got and where they could find it. And I bet you'd have sent them a small taster by email.' Thankfully Marvik had got to them first. 'Which of them were you going to target?'

'Does it matter now?'

'Which one?' Marvik demanded, moving closer to Lee.

Dawn quickly said, 'One of the sons, both have got email addresses on their company websites and Lee can hack into them anyway.'

And threaten to spread those filthy pictures to all the staff and possibly their clients. Only just controlling his fury, Marvik rounded on Lee. There were a few more questions he needed answers to. 'Why did you approach Jarinder direct at the recovery centre?'

'I didn't. I don't know what you're talking about. I . . . I'm going to be sick.' He promptly threw up.

Dawn sprang back. 'Bloody hell. Now can I get him to hospital?'

'Not finished yet.'

'Lee's telling the truth, he never went where you said,' she gabbled. 'We don't even know what it is or where.'

Marvik knew that was the truth, not only because the timescale was wrong but also because Elaine's description of the man accosting Jarinder in the garden did not fit Lee. It had to be this Paul Webb, but what was he trying to foist on Jarinder to blackmail him into silence? Not the DVD. And silence over what, for Christ's sake?

If what she said was true and neither of them had trashed the boat, then who had and why? Fingerprints and DNA might give him some answers but he didn't have the authority or resources to take either. Crowder would, but that would mean police intervention, and this had to be resolved before Jarinder's reputation could be further damaged. Marvik was sick of the pair of them.

'Give me your phone,' he demanded of Dawn.

'You can't . . .' Reluctantly she handed it over.

'I want your computers. Now.'

'Lee's is in the other room. I haven't got one.'

'Show me.'

Lee was beyond doing anything. He was on the verge of passing out. Marvik followed her and found one laptop.

'Hey, you can't take that.'

He silenced her with a glare. 'Any other devices?'

'No.'

He conducted a rapid search anyway. Then, in the garage, he found only cobwebs, dust and a few empty boxes. No motorbike.

On leaving he said, 'Give me your passwords.'

She hesitated, then reluctantly gave them. He tried them on their phones. They were genuine. He didn't try the laptop one. If he couldn't get into it, then Strathen would be able to. 'And your log-in for that website you told me about, Dawn.'

She relayed it.

'Now you can take lover boy to hospital, and if I were you I'd move out pretty quick and go a long way from here, because if Webb comes knocking, I don't think he'll be as gentle and polite as me.'

CHAPTER ELEVEN

Strathen had gone when Marvik got back to the boat. He called him on the mission mobile. 'I know you can't talk.' He also knew Strathen wouldn't use the internet while travelling by train or in a public place unless it was for something completely insignificant, knowing how easy it was to be traced and hacked. 'I found Debbie McCleary, who is really Dawn Snell.' He gave Strathen the digest of the conversation, adding, 'Dawn claimed not to have seen or spoken to Webb, so I didn't get a description of him. That could have been a lie but it had a ring of truth about it. Barker is not the man who accosted Jarinder at the recovery centre. I believe it was Paul Webb, who made sure to keep his visor down to prevent being described. I expect it's a false name.'

'I'll look for him anyway tomorrow when I'm back in the flat.'

'I have their mobiles, a laptop and their passwords. I'll see what's on them. If I don't get anything tomorrow from Jennings at the centre, or from Amanda in the evening, I'll bring your boat back to Hamble on Saturday.'

He made himself something to eat and drink, and with the wind whistling around the boat he turned first to Dawn's phone. He easily found the website she mentioned, and trawled through her page with all its provocative imagery. He also found the record of her messages with Webb. It was as she had said. There was no picture of him, and only a holding page. Strathen would possibly be able to burrow down and get more. But Webb had been suitably cautious. Marvik doubted they would pick him up this way.

He sat back, considering how and why Webb had selected Dawn. His criteria had been to find someone who lived in Plymouth who was greedy, had no scruples about lying, and would be easy to manipulate and bribe. She probably wasn't the only Plymouth female on that website; Webb could have tried others before striking lucky with her. She, by her own admission, had a criminal record, demonstrating that she was perfectly happy to work outside the law, and Webb had discovered that. He might have found references to her crime on the internet, reports of a court case, perhaps, or other media coverage. Marvik would leave that to Strathen to discover.

Barker's mobile didn't yield anything in connection with Webb, nor did his laptop, although Marvik found the file of the despicable images of Dawn with a fake Jarinder, which made him want to smash the screen before a wave of despondency fell on him. He switched it off. He'd leave any further computer interrogation to Strathen.

His head was pounding like a piston. The headaches seemed to be getting more frequent and intense. Perhaps because he had been working nonstop on operations for Crowder for some time, some of them personally painful. There had been the death of innocent people like Sarah Redburn, a marine archaeologist. Sarah had been mercilessly killed in order to protect his mother's murderer. Fury and sadness combined as he recalled Sarah's gentle manner and smiling enthusiasm. She should never have died.

Then there had been the recent people-smuggling assignment for Crowder, which came immediately after the frantic and dangerous personal mission to discover the truth behind his parents' deaths after the only evidence he'd had was stolen. That had been an emotional rollercoaster and he'd barely had time to catch his breath before Crowder had pitched in and sent him over to the continent on the recent operation that could have and nearly did cost him his life. Now this. He swallowed more tablets.

He wondered if Dawn would somehow manage to get a message to Webb, perhaps using a public computer in the library or an internet café. Could Webb have picked up a trace of him while he'd been accessing her phone and pinpointed the internet address as being that of the marina? Would he have a nocturnal visitor? He sincerely hoped not. He wasn't sure he was in a fit enough state to encounter a man who could beat someone to death as he had Daniel Larroc. But he had to be. He couldn't let Webb win.

He set up an alarm sensor on the boat that would warn him of an intruder and retired to his bunk fully clothed, wondering if his days of action were behind him. He couldn't keep going like this for ever. Helen flashed before him with her purple-streaked hair and her outspoken manner. He and Strathen had at least saved her from being killed, twice. The first time was when Marvik met her on an assignment that was linked to the murder of her sister some years previously, and the more recent time was on a mission for Crowder in East Sussex when someone had wanted to frame her for the murder of her then boss. Now Helen worked for Crowder on deskbound intelligence analysis. Marvik smiled whenever he thought of her. He liked her courage, her intellect and her personality, but he thought her affections were drawn to Strathen and not to him. Thank goodness she didn't know about this. She was currently working in Sweden with the Swedish Security Services, in what capacity he didn't know.

He rose and went on deck, wanting the wind to blow away his maudlin thoughts and the rain to keep him alert. Maybe it was time to find some other way of earning a living, not that he needed much to live on. His parents had left him wealthy but money was not the issue. He needed purpose and action and this gave him both, so he needed to pull himself together. He shook himself mentally. He was all in and, intruder or not, he needed sleep.

He applied the mental techniques learned and utilized in the Special Boat Services to switch off, letting his body relax from the legs upwards, gravity pulling them down. He took deep breaths and, clearing his mind of everything, focused it instead on the rhythm of the sea. It worked and he was able to get five hours of uninterrupted sleep and no sight nor sound of an intruder.

Strathen sent him a text just after eight to say he was back in his apartment. At nine fifteen Marvik set out for the recovery centre, where he located Alan Jennings and offered to buy him a coffee. It was Elaine's day off. He explained that he was trying to trace a man Jarinder had been seen talking to on Wednesday 13 September in the gardens and wondered if his visitor, Gary Reide, had seen this man. 'I'd like to ask him.'

'I'm sure he'll help you if he can, but I didn't see any man in motorbike leathers and I don't think Gary did either. He was my commanding officer in the Royal Logistics Corps. He's in the reserves now. If you give me your number, I'll pass it on and ask him to call you.'

'Thanks.' Marvik sent it over to Jennings.

'You said you're ex-Royal Marines. Is that how you know Jarinder?'

'Yes.'

'Bloody shame he's dead. Good man like that. He didn't operate on me but I know those he has done. This is a spinal injury.' Jennings indicated his wheelchair. 'Not the result of conflict or a training exercise but a bloody stupid sixty-five-foot jump off a bridge into a river that I was forced into doing by my commanding officer despite my reluctance. Because the men had done the jump, he thought us officers should. It would look cowardly if we didn't. It was probably my reluctance that made me bend my legs when I should have jumped with my body straight. This is what I got. Confined to a wheelchair.'

'Bad luck.'

'Yes, wasn't it?'

Marvik didn't blame him for being bitter.

'I'm suing the MOD on the grounds that my commanding officer was negligent. He didn't consider all the evidence
of the jump, the height and speed of impact, he failed to
take into account the risk of serious injury, and, although he
didn't order me to jump, he put pressure on me to do so and
I felt I had no option. Hope we win. Not that the money
can compensate for being a cripple, but it will make my life
a bit easier. Got a good barrister working on it, but then so
has the MOD and they won't give up without a fight. Nor
will I. Sorry I can't help you about this motorbike guy. Hope
Gary can. Emily might have seen him,' he added, smiling
at a woman in her twenties approaching them, wearing the
uniform of the centre's physio team.

'I might have known I'd find you here, Alan. You're late
as usual,' she said brightly.

Marvik stood up. 'My fault. I kept him talking.'

'Marvik asked me if I'd seen a guy who visited the centre, about Marvik's height, wearing a black motorcycle helmet, leathers with a red stripe and motorcycle boots, did you
see him? This was on the Wednesday before last.'

She brushed a hand over a stray strand of her brunette
hair that was swept back off her clear-skinned face. 'I did,'
she answered, surprising Marvik. 'I'd popped outside to send
a message to my partner and I saw a man get on a motorbike
and ride away. I looked at it specifically because my partner
has a motorbike and I thought he'd give his eye teeth to have
one like that. It was a powerful BMW. I've learned something about bikes since being with Michael.'

Marvik could have hugged her. 'I don't suppose you
remember the registration number?' he asked hopefully but
not expectantly.

'No, sorry.'

As he'd thought. 'I'll leave you to get on. I hope I hav-
en't delayed you too much.'

'Not at all,' Jennings answered cheerfully.

'Good luck with the litigation.'

'And good luck with finding your man.'

'I might need it,' Marvik muttered to himself as he headed out. He now knew the make of bike, but not the model, and without the registration number it was practically useless unless Reide could enlighten him, and he doubted that.

He gazed around. There had to be CCTV cameras about the place and on the base — one of them could show him the registration number of that motorbike, *if* the images had been kept. Accessing them though would be difficult, even for Strathen, who probably wouldn't be able to get into the Ministry of Defence systems. Crowder could request access though, but being police he would have to apply to the necessary authorities and explain why. And Marvik hadn't even told him what he and Strathen were working on. Even if he did, it wasn't Crowder's unit's investigation. Maybe they'd have to use that route as a last resort. Marvik decided to give the main gate security officer another go, and hoped a different man would be on duty who would be more cooperative than the previous one.

He was in luck. Furthermore, Marvik's reading of the fit, upright officer, with a face that showed restlessness, convinced Marvik he was ex-service. He very quickly discovered, by direct questioning and divulging that he was a veteran, that the officer was ex-Royal Marines like him. They immediately struck up a bond. Marvik revealed how he had got his scar and head wound on ops, and confided that he'd found it difficult to adjust to civilian life and was still finding it so — not strictly a lie, especially after his thoughts last night. He still missed being with the men though. As far as Dellow, the security officer, was concerned, Marvik had pressed the right button. He did too. Most veterans experienced that sense of loss and regret at leaving military life and missed the camaraderie.

'I often wonder what the heck I'm doing here,' Dellow confided. They were in the small office by the main gate, his colleague having left to investigate an incident elsewhere. 'Didn't want to leave but a bout of post-traumatic stress and the wife giving me an ultimatum made it a no-brainer. What are you doing these days?'

'Private security work, mainly for individuals who want protection on their luxury yachts.' He had started out that way but his foray into close protection hadn't been successful. The wealthy boat owner he'd been protecting on his luxury yacht in pirate-ridden seas had died and he'd incurred a bullet in his shoulder before he'd managed to overpower the pirates.

'Nice work if you can get it.'

Not always. That had been before he'd teamed up with Strathen again, and before Crowder had enlisted their help.

'Not many luxury yachts in here.' Dellow grinned. 'Though possibly a few in the marinas.'

'But not the one I'm on. I'm trying to find a man who visited the rehabilitation centre on Wednesday the thirteenth of September. He met a friend of mine, a former Marine like us, who's gone missing. He's believed to have taken his own life. I thought if I found this man he might be able to help me by telling me what they talked about.' Marvik stretched the truth.

'Another one who couldn't adjust,' Dellow said solemnly.

'My friend was in the centre here for some time, an amputee, lost his left leg above the knee in combat.' That much was true.

Dellow nodded his head knowingly. 'What's this man he met look like?'

'All I know is that he was wearing motorbike leathers with a red stripe and was riding a powerful BMW.'

'We won't have kept the CCTV images but we keep the ANPR records — don't suppose you know the registration number?'

'No, but it was around 11 a.m.'

Dellow called up the day and time, and swivelled the screen round to show Marvik. There were three vehicles registered around that time. One caused him to start with surprise. He'd seen it as it had driven up to Jarinder's house — Nishan's Mercedes. What had he been doing here? Was he the barrister representing the MOD that Jennings had told him of, or perhaps he was representing Jennings? If so, he would hardly have met Jennings here but more probably at his home. Had Nishan seen his father? Had he seen motorbike man?

'Have you got a corresponding signing-in log, the old-fashioned kind?'

'No. We run the numbers though the DVLA and confirm the ID of the vehicle owner as they come through the gate, and check their authorization, although we don't keep a record of who they've come to see.'

'Can you do those three for me?' Marvik wondered if he'd refuse but he didn't. One was confirmed as Nishan Vaidya's, another as Gary Reide's and the third as Paul Webb. Bingo!

'Looks like that's your man — motorcycle registration,' Dellow said.

Marvik memorized the number, an easy task for him with his photographic memory. 'Have you got the address?'

'That's my phone.' Dellow turned away. There was no phone call.

It was an address in Battersea, London. Again he memorized it. 'Thanks.'

'For what?' Dellow smiled. 'I haven't done anything. Hope you find out what's happened to your mate and it's not bad news.'

'Me too.'

Marvik shook Dellow's hand and called for a taxi to take him to the crematorium. He was early. Using his phone, he searched for Webb's address, and gave a soft whistle. It was a new apartment in an exclusive complex. He called Strathen and relayed what he'd learned.

'Could be a false address,' was Strathen's verdict. 'In fact, given the planted emails and our belief we're dealing with an expert hacker, I'd say it is.'

'Nishan was also in the base at the same time as Jarinder. He could have been there in a professional capacity. Jennings told me there was a barrister representing the MOD in the case he was bringing against the army.'

'I guess he could have been. Or he was there in relation to another case. He specializes in clinical negligence and serious injury. According to his profile on his chambers' website, he studied preclinical medicine and biological anthropology at Cambridge University, graduating with a first-class degree.'

'Having met him, that doesn't surprise me.'

'He then took a law degree and was admitted as a solicitor for a practice in Leeds. He was a higher courts advocate before being called to the Bar at Inner Temple, and joined his current chambers the same year. He acts for claimants as well as defendants, including some health authorities.'

'Devon?'

'Possibly. He also acts for healthcare insurers, government bodies and defence organizations. He was, as he told you, in Cork six years ago on a product liability case, a faulty medical implant used to deliver low dosages of medication. The pharmaceutical company, based in Cork, settled out of court.'

Some cars began to arrive. Jarinder's relatives. In one vehicle, though, Marvik saw a white man dressed in a dark suit, white shirt and black tie, in his late fifties with short greying hair. Perhaps he was there for the next funeral and had arrived early.

'I've also found the police notice on the Met's website about the assault on Tarina, asking for witnesses. It doesn't go into much detail, as you'd expect, but it confirms what Nishan told you. The attack happened just off Clink Passage, by Clink Wharf, and the police are appealing for witnesses and any sightings of a man wearing black leather motorcycle clothes running off.'

'Webb? Who reported that? Tarina?'

'It doesn't say. I'll see what I can get on Paul Webb, although I suspect there'll be hundreds of them around the country. He picked a good name.'

Marvik looked up to see the cars slowly pulling into the crematorium. 'The hearse has arrived.'

'Say "bon voyage" to Jarinder from me.'

'I will.'

CHAPTER TWELVE

Friday

Marvik made his way closer to the chapel but not too close. In the Daimler following the hearse were Nishan, Rohan and two other older men whom Marvik took to be Jarinder's brothers or cousins.

'Such a tragedy.'

Marvik turned to find a grey-haired man beside him. He had remarkably blue eyes that were mournful and a square-jawed, rugged face that held deep lines around his mouth and forehead.

'I'm Steven Lingfield. Jarinder was a long-time, valued friend. We met at medical school before he joined the navy. I take it that, like me, you've come to say farewell.'

'I have. Art Marvik, ex-Royal Marines.'

'Hence the scar and your relationship with Jarinder?'

'Yes. Are you in plastic reconstructive surgery too?'

'No. I became a clinical consultant pathologist. I have a medical laboratory in London, Horizons. We specialize in gastrointestinal, skin, breast and autopsy pathology to the medical profession and patients direct.' He fell silent.

Marvik looked over to where the coffin was resting in the hearse. He caught the deep throb of a motorbike slowly drawing to a halt. His head whipped round. It had stopped some distance away, to the left of the car park, but even from where he stood Marvik was certain it was a BMW, and on it was a man dressed in black leathers with a red stripe and a dark visor over his face. His heart quickened. It had to be Webb, but from where he stood he couldn't make out the registration number.

The engine purred. The rider made no attempt to alight. Marvik wanted to leave Lingfield and race across to the bike, but he realized that would be a waste of time and energy because he could never reach it before Webb would swing round and race off. He'd be gone before Marvik could take even two paces. Or perhaps he'd play with him and wait until he was very close, then rev up and speed off, giving him a two-fingered salute. Catch me if you can. Well, he would.

As his eyes flicked back to the coffin, his blood curdled at the thought that the man involved in Jarinder's killing had come to the cremation to crow over it. Lingfield was saying something but Marvik had no idea what it was because it struck him that perhaps Webb had come here to intimidate Nishan or Rohan. Yes, that had to be it. Was Webb, not content with threatening and killing Jarinder and Larroc, now targeting Rohan or Nishan, or both? Was his appearance here a warning that, whatever they knew about Jarinder's death, they should remain silent or the same treatment would befall them? Had Nishan been coerced into going to the naval base the Wednesday his father was there because Webb had also wanted to see him to show him what was in that package? And if that didn't contain the pictures Dawn Snell and Lee Barker had taken, then what? And Webb being here could mean that he'd also paid a visit to Dawn and Barker. A deadly visit.

Rohan turned to look in their direction. Marvik saw him start and hastily glance away while Nishan, following his brother's glance, glared at the motorbike then across to Marvik.

Lingfield said, 'It doesn't look as though they're pleased to see us.'

'I think it's the man on the motorbike they're not pleased to see.'

Lingfield turned. His brow creased. 'I hadn't noticed him. Who is he?'

'No idea.' Marvik wasn't going to air his opinions on that. Nishan and Rohan were being gently urged by the funeral director and their uncles to lift the coffin. Marvik said a silent 'bon voyage' as the coffin and mourners filed into the chapel. He turned away and fell into step beside Lingfield.

'I find it hard to believe Jarinder was killed in something as pointless as a car accident,' Lingfield said. 'But then it happens, and sadly all too often. I'd liked to have paid my respects at the house, but I only got back from Germany last night. A medical conference. Did you go?'

'Yes.'

'How are they taking it?'

'As you'd expect.'

He nodded. 'This was the closest I could get to saying farewell. I'll get in touch with some of his colleagues at the hospital and the British Association of Plastic Reconstructive and Aesthetic Surgeons to see if anyone is arranging a memorial service.'

Marvik wondered if he'd learn of the accusations surrounding Jarinder. He hoped not and he certainly wasn't going to give them airspace. 'When did you last see Jarinder?'

'The weekend before last. I have a holiday place in Falmouth. Jarinder sailed there. We had a lovely couple of days.'

That fitted with the logbook entry.

'I'm divorced and live alone,' Lingfield went on.

'So you were close?'

'We kept in touch from time to time when work commitments permitted it.'

'Did he say if anything was troubling him?'

'No. Why do you ask?'

They halted by Lingfield's car.

'He told a friend of mine, shortly before the car accident, that he was worried about something.'

'Was it a medical matter?' Lingfield looked uneasy.

'I don't know, my friend isn't a doctor and he's no longer around for me to ask.'

'You mean he's also dead?' Lingfield's brow knitted.

'He's missing, believed suicide.'

'That's dreadful. It surely can't have any connection to Jarinder's car accident?'

'Shaun was a patient of Jarinder's and, like me, in the Royal Marines. We both saw how hard Jarinder worked when on ops and had nothing but admiration and respect for him. Shaun's an amputee and he and Jarinder were very close. Maybe Shaun was struggling emotionally. Maybe Jarinder did tell him something upsetting before the car accident. Maybe I'm seeking reasons for random happenings, but I'm left with a lot of maybes that I'd like some answers to.'

'A natural reaction to bereavement.'

'I know, and the answers aren't always forthcoming.'

'And you got no hint from your friend before he went missing what this was about?'

Marvik shook his head. 'Do you know of any colleagues or friends Jarinder might have confided in?'

Lingfield looked distant as he considered this. 'If it was a medical matter then those on his team would be my first option. If not them, then the other consultant surgeons he worked alongside. I'm not familiar with any of them. Jarinder and I tried not to talk shop. There was someone he used to be close to — Julian Boyce, an orthopaedic surgeon. I'm not sure if he's still around though. Jarinder hadn't mentioned him for a long time. He used to live at Salcombe.'

That possibly explained Jarinder's sailing trip there.

'I'll miss him.' His expression darkened. 'Can I give you a lift anywhere, unless you have a car here?'

There was no other vehicle in the car park except a van displaying the name of a gardening company.

'Thanks. If it's not out of your way, you could drop me back anywhere in the town centre.'

'Climb in.' Lingfield started up the Audi. 'Are you staying in the city?'

'Not for much longer. I brought my friend's boat here. It was found off the coast of Ireland not far from Ballycotton Harbour. It's where he took his own life. I'm taking the boat to Hamble Marina, where it's usually moored, but thought I'd stop off here and make some enquiries about Jarinder to see if I could learn anything more about why Shaun should have taken his own life, and in Ireland. Did Jarinder speak to you of Ballycotton or Ireland? Shaun must have gone there for a reason.'

'But it might not be connected with Jarinder — in fact, I can't see how it can be. I've never heard him speak of the place.'

'He didn't tell you that he'd sailed to Cork recently?'

'Did he?'

'I don't know. He used to sail there with the family when they were younger. Nishan told me.'

'But that still doesn't answer why your friend went there,' Lingfield said, puzzled.

'No.'

'Maybe he had past connections there as a child, fond memories, that sort of thing.'

'Possibly.' Marvik didn't see the need to tell him the truth. 'How did Jarinder seem when you saw him?'

'Fine. As I said, we talked over old times, the state of the nation, sailing, a bit of work chat but not much. He said how well his children were doing and that was more or less it.'

Marvik wasn't so certain about that. There was something uneasy in Lingfield's manner. He seemed edgy, as though he wanted to tell him something but was holding back for some reason. Maybe he didn't trust him, and why should he? They'd only just met.

'Will this do?' Lingfield pulled into the railway station car park.

'This is fine. Thanks.' Marvik stretched out his hand. 'I hope we meet at the memorial service. And if no one is going to arrange one, I will.'

Lingfield had explained why Jarinder had sailed to Falmouth and possibly Salcombe. But neither had any bearing on the fact that Jarinder had been threatened. And now possibly Jarinder's sons, too, judging by Webb's appearance.

He hurried towards Barker's flat, wanting reassurance that they were safe. There was no BMW bike outside it but Webb could have been and gone. There was also no sign of the Skoda. Thankfully the building was still standing. He'd half expected to see a burned-out shell.

There was no answer when he rang the bell. They could have taken his advice and cleared out. Lee's shoulder would have been reset at the hospital and he would have been discharged. Marvik disabled the video doorbell by taking down the Wi-Fi. As he manipulated the lock, he hoped he wouldn't find them dead inside from carbon monoxide poisoning or with a bullet in their heads.

He stood in the hall, listening. All was silent. He ran the scanner to pick up any surveillance system. There was nothing. Expertly and swiftly, he searched the ground floor. He was surprised to find washing in the machine. It was slightly damp, indicating that they had left in a hurry and earlier that morning. Or perhaps they had just popped out for some shopping. The kitchen cupboards revealed tins of food and packets of biscuits, and the fridge was stocked with milk, cheese and eggs, so perhaps they had gone out for the day and would return later.

He climbed the stairs and came out onto a small landing that gave onto two bedrooms and a bathroom. One bedroom didn't contain any furniture. He'd already scoured the house earlier when seizing the computers. Everything looked the same. But in the main bedroom he found their clothes had gone and there were limited toiletries in the bathroom. He hoped they had taken flight, this was not the work of Webb clearing out their things to make it look that way and a report would eventually surface of two bodies being found in a car wreck. Even though they had been involved in trying to discredit Jarinder, he didn't wish them dead. They were greedy, selfish and stupid, without any conscience, but he knew they were no match for Webb.

He returned to the boat, wishing he could make for Hamble and then for London to check out Webb's address, but he was to see Amanda that night and she might have something for him. And he wanted to speak to Nishan and Rohan again in light of Webb's appearance at the crematorium and discover what Webb was threatening them over. Nishan had said their mourning period would end on Sunday. He'd catch them hopefully before they returned to town. And before then Strathen could have some news on Paul Webb from his searches.

He toyed with the idea of going to the hospital to speak to some of Jarinder's colleagues, but he doubted he'd be able to. They would be busy with patients or in theatre. That side of things was best left to Amanda. He decided a change of scenery might prompt some fresh thought, and cast off. He made for Fowey in Cornwall, moored up at Penmarlam pontoon at Mixtow, had lunch in the café and had just returned to the boat with no new ideas when Strathen rang him.

'How did it go?'

Marvik knew he was referring to the crematorium. 'An unexpected guest showed up on a motorbike.'

'And?'

'He sped off. No chance of seeing his face, but neither Nishan nor Rohan looked very pleased to see him.'

'Well, I've found several Paul Webbs, including the one who lives at that exclusive apartment in Battersea. I couldn't find his ownership listed on the Land Registry, but there is a time lag between purchase and listing, which suggests he bought it recently. That's also borne out by the fact that the complex was only finished a year ago, although he could have bought off-plan. The cost would have been anything from three million pounds upwards, depending on the size, so he's certainly not short of money.'

'Earned, inherited or gained illegally?'

'Looks like the latter because none of the Paul Webbs I've found have the profile to fit an upper-bracket earner or billionaire.'

'False ID then.'

'I'd say so. I could keep digging, but this guy is clever enough not to have left a trail, or has masked it thoroughly, so it'll be a waste of time.'

'I'll return to Hamble after my meeting tonight with Amanda. I can catch the train up to London on Saturday or Sunday, ask around at that address and see what I can pick up. I can also see Nishan and Rohan in London if I don't catch up with them here. They'll be back at work on Monday.'

'You won't, because tomorrow you're going to Salcombe.'

'You've found Julian Boyce.'

'Who's he?'

Marvik forgot he hadn't mentioned meeting Lingfield to Strathen, or their conversation. He did now.

Strathen said, 'Boyce might live there but it's not him you're going to visit. I've been re-examining Jarinder's logbook — something was bugging me about that entry in Hindi. I flicked back through the other entries. There's nothing written in Hindi for any other sailing trip. So why that one? I translated it and got something very interesting. It's a contradiction of his English entry. Jarinder's English account says the sea state was calm, it was a clear beautiful day with a little wind, but he had a good sail nonetheless. The weather reports for that day and the sea state confirm that, I checked. The entry in Hindi goes completely against that. Translated it reads: wind force ten, waves high, cloudy, sea state rough.'

Marvik sat forward. 'A code?'

'Yes. It took some imagination, a consultation with an anagram website and a bit of guesswork, but this is what I got. "Windforce" is written by Jarinder as one word, and although not a true anagram it could be interpreted, according to the website, as "confide". I next took "cloudy, sea state rough" again all as one word. I got a number of permutations for that, but the one that struck me as the most appropriate was the word "courageously". However, playing around with the lettering I also got "guardhouse" or "schoolyard". Then there is "waves high". "Waves" could be "save" or "sea", but I couldn't get anything from "high" except perhaps "hi" to say hello, so perhaps he went to Salcombe to say hello to someone who he wished to confide in who had acted courageously and ended up in the guardhouse.'

'A former navy colleague.'

'Patience. I looked at "waves high" again as one word and got "Wes Haigh", but there's no one of that name on the electoral roll. I stared at it for ages seeking inspiration and then wondered if the "v" was in fact a "u". A "u" in Hindi is obviously a different symbol than a "v", but if I transposed them I could get the name Hugh Sawe from "Waves High". Yes, it was a bit of a stretch, and maybe I just wanted it to fit, but my hunch paid off. I found a Hugh Sawes — with an extra "s" — who lives at number ten, the Schoolyard, Salcombe. He's eighty-four, British.'

Marvik was puzzled. He'd expected someone younger or Jarinder's age. 'Any idea of his background?'

'None. I haven't been able to access the Department for Work and Pensions database or HM Revenue and Customs. I might be able to hack into them, eventually, but that would take some time and skill, and their systems are fairly robust, although not foolproof, nothing ever is. So the best method is for you to ask him.'

Marvik made his way back to Mayflower Marina and had just moored up when his mission mobile rang again. Strathen had more news, he thought. He was wrong. It was Crowder.

Marvik's heart sank. He sincerely hoped he wasn't going to be pulled off this and put on another case.

'What's this about Strathen taking his own life?' Crowder launched in without preamble.

'How do you know about that?' Marvik said, startled. His head spun with possibilities.

'Is it true?'

'No.'

'Good, although I never considered it possible. Is he in hiding or with you?'

'He was with me. He's back in his apartment and in hiding. You haven't tried to call him?'

'He's supposed to be dead,' he answered wryly.

Marvik knew that wouldn't have stopped Crowder from checking Strathen's mission mobile, but he wouldn't have wished to do so in case it was in the hands of someone it shouldn't be, or that it would alert someone who could be holding Strathen.

'OK, so tell me what's going down.'

Marvik brought him up to date while Crowder listened in silence, then said, 'Now tell me how you know about Strathen's alleged suicide, or maybe I can guess. The body at Ballycotton has been found.'

'Yes.'

'And I bet I know who reported it. It's got to be either Tom Gilley the publican or John Walsh the fisherman.'

'The former. He claims he was concerned about the man with one leg asking after a stranger in the village and then another with a scar on his face following on from him. He decided to go to the cottage and investigate and found the body. He reported it to the Garda, who are now looking for the scarred man. They believe the man with one leg killed himself after killing the man in the cottage. But they also have a theory that the second man — you, Marvik — killed the man in the cottage because you believed he had driven your friend to commit suicide.'

'The post-mortem will reveal that Larroc — that's who we believe the dead man to be — was killed some days before either of us arrived.'

'We'll let the pathologist report that to the Garda. I'll liaise with the Hampshire and Isle of Wight Police. They're looking for you, Marvik. I'll inform them that you're working for my squad, which both you and Strathen now are, and they are to do nothing.'

'You have intelligence on this?' Marvik asked, surprised.

'No, but the fact that two of my operatives are involved makes it a squad matter.'

Marvik wasn't sure he believed Crowder. He had to know something more. 'How did you get notified of this?'

'When both your names were flagged up in a police report, it was brought to my attention.'

'Does Daniel Larroc have connections with the intelligence services?'

'Not that I know of, but I'll check.'

'Gilley will have told them Strathen had asked about Daniel Larroc and me about Giles Milton, who I made up on the spur of the moment.'

'Then we'll let them think the deceased could be either for the time being.'

'Have they checked their records for them?'

'I believe so, and neither man has shown up as residing in Ireland. And neither is on our police records. Strathen will have been searching for evidence of Larroc.'

'And hasn't found any.'

'Could be a false name given to Jarinder.'

'Yes, which makes me think this could involve MI5 or MI6.'

'I'll let you know what the post-mortem finds.'

'Keep this from Helen,' Marvik said.

'I've already told her that you and Strathen are working on an assignment, which she doesn't have access to from Sweden.'

'Thanks,' Marvik said warmly.

'Keep me informed.'

He called Strathen and reported his conversation with Crowder.

'I'm glad he's on board,' was Strathen's verdict. As Marvik hurried to his engagement with Amanda, he was too.

116

CHAPTER THIRTEEN

He was late but Amanda wasn't there either. She had reserved a table, though, and ten minutes later she breezed in looking good in a short, smart tailored skirt suit and high heels. A few heads turned as she crossed to him.

'Any news of Shaun?' she asked, shrugging off her wet jacket.

'No.' He felt a bit of a heel for lying but he couldn't confide in anyone. He asked her what she'd like to drink.

'Mineral water. Boring but necessary, don't want the scalpel slipping. I'm on call,' she said lightly.

'I hope your partner doesn't mind me buying you dinner.'

'How do you know I've got one?' she joked.

'Must have, an attractive woman like you.'

'Corny but nice, even though some would accuse you of being sexist and patronizing.'

'Because I paid you a compliment!'

'Not permitted these days,' she teased. 'But yes, I have got one, so it's no dice, Art, if that was what you were fishing for.'

Had he been? Perhaps. 'Pity,' he said not entirely in jest.

'Yes. Maybe it is,' she answered, studying him contemplatively.

He was rather glad the waitress arrived at that moment. He ordered their drinks, opting for the same as Amanda, wanting a clear head — not only for his morning interview with Hugh Sawes, but there was still the possibility that Webb could pay him a visit.

'And another thing,' she continued, picking up the menu, 'I'm buying you dinner and my boyfriend is in Frankfurt probably wining and dining countless frauleins.'

'He's not in the medical profession?'

'No, high finance.' She glanced at the menu. 'I'm not really hungry but I'll have the lasagne.'

Marvik would plump for the same. 'Have you heard any more about these phoney charges against Jarinder?' he asked.

'No, despite my best efforts. His medical team have picked up on the rumours, although none of them believe it and they're all still in shock over his untimely death. I tried to pump the clinical director but he ducked and dived the issue so many times that my admiration for him went up. I think he's wasted in medicine; he should have gone into politics. I also spoke to someone in IT but I might just as well have been speaking Greek. The idiot said it was impossible for the system to have been hacked. I told him that perhaps someone didn't believe in that word "impossible" and was smarter than any of them. He just looked smug and pitying. Good job I didn't have my scalpel on me.' She smiled, then more seriously added, 'But I can see you've had more success.'

'I hope I'm not that transparent.'

'Maybe not to everyone, but I know that face — intimately, you might say.'

'You didn't operate on it.'

'No, but I've studied your medical records.'

'Talking of which—'

'Are you ready to order, sir?' The waitress placed their bottle of mineral water on the table.

Amanda promptly gave her order, forgoing a starter. Marvik followed suit. He was ruminating on how much to tell her. He had to give her something for her to continue to cooperate, working on the inside of the medical profession. Crowder and Strathen could get a lot but not the gossip and hints.

'Do you know a Steven Lingfield?'

'The name is familiar but I can't place it for the moment.'

'I met him at Jarinder's cremation.'

'They didn't let you inside the chapel, did they?'

'No. Lingfield and I stayed outside. He'd come to say farewell to Jarinder, as had I. He's a clinical consultant, runs a laboratory in London called Horizons. They provide pathology testing for the healthcare sector.'

'Of course, that's how I know the name. Yes, we use their services at the private hospital. Although I don't know him personally. I've met him a couple of times at seminars.'

'He might be in touch with you and other of Jarinder's colleagues to see if anyone is arranging a memorial service.'

She drank her mineral water and pulled a face. 'Would much prefer a large red wine. I hope we can clear up this mess about an alleged affair, otherwise there might not be a memorial service. Did you get anything else?'

'Jarinder had a boat.'

'Yes, I knew that. He keeps it here. He enjoyed sailing, but how is that relevant?'

'It's been broken into and ransacked.'

'Really! Not good. Why?'

A group on the table closest to them broke into raucous laughter over something. She scowled at them, although they didn't notice.

'It gets worse,' Marvik continued. 'I found a DVD hidden on board. It contains explicit pictures of Jarinder and a woman.'

'What?' She almost choked on her drink. Her expression darkened with fury. 'I don't believe it. Was it this bloody Debbie?'

'The images were manipulated. And Debbie is in reality Dawn and she admits she was paid to lie about an affair with Jarinder.'

'You found her?' Amanda sat forward eagerly.

'Yes, and her boyfriend, Lee Barker. He took the pictures of Dawn and computer-enhanced and manipulated them to include body parts that are not Jarinder's, but it's his face.'

'Tell me where she is and I'll slap her until she squeals for mercy — the boyfriend too.'

'They're not important anymore. I've dealt with them.'

'How?' Her eyes widened.

'Told them to clear out and fast. Dawn admits she was paid to lie about the affair if anyone asked her. The DVD was her and the boyfriend's idea. They'd decided to branch into blackmail.'

'So who paid her? Have you found him?'

'No. The name he gave Dawn was false. And no, I don't know that for certain but it's bound to be. She can't describe him either because she never met him.'

'Then how the blazes are you going to find him?'

'I might not. And he might not be important anyway,' he lied. 'He was probably paid to enlist Dawn's help. The situation regarding the phoney relationship will peter out because she won't be around to reiterate it, but I know what you're going to say, the stigma will last.'

'Then we should hand it over to the police. They'll haul in Dawn and her boyfriend and prosecute them. And clear Jarinder's name.'

'That will mean the family will be told about the pictures and the emails, unless they already know about the latter?'

'They don't, according to the clinical director. That was one thing he did tell me, because they're still in the mourning period. That might change when it's ended.'

'And that's Sunday night, Nishan told me. See if you can hold the clinical director off for a few days.'

'How much do I tell him? I can't say you're onto it, because you don't have any official authority to investigate and he's bound to point that out to me. He'd say if you've got any information then the police need to be informed. And please don't tell me to use my charm,' she joked. 'Because the director has been inoculated against that. And yes, I have tried it once or twice when absolutely desperate. He's an iceberg of a man, or maybe he just doesn't fancy me.'

'Is that a cue for me to pay you another compliment?'

'Careful, Art, people will start talking about us,' she teased. 'But seriously, what do I say?'

Marvik thought rapidly. 'Tell him that you might have some new information that could clear up the whole matter. Say that one of the family has confided something to you about someone out to ruin Jarinder's reputation, and that you should have evidence of this within a few days. It would be in everyone's interest, including the hospital's, to hold back a while. Can he stop the head of IT going to the police?'

'Yes, but he might have already asked them to instigate a full investigation in conjunction with a cybersecurity consultancy.'

'Fine. They'll discover the emails were planted, and they might pick up the trail of who's behind it. In fact, if that hasn't already been actioned, suggest it to the director. It might save me time and help me find this man who paid Dawn to lie.'

'OK. I'll let you know how it goes. Do you think Jarinder was so upset about the blackmail that it caused him to crash?'

'Yes, and he was on his way to confide in Shaun, believing him to be the only person who could help him handle it, and to ask his advice.'

'But that wouldn't have sent Shaun off to Ireland to take his own life,' she insisted.

'I still can't find out why he went there.' As much as he wanted to tell her the truth, Marvik had to continue to play along with the story that Strathen was dead. 'Perhaps he had happy memories there as a child. And perhaps he really couldn't cope with life anymore.'

'Rubbish and you know it.'

'I'm not sure I know anything much these days, Amanda.'

She eyed him critically.

'You never really know anyone, do you, even though you think you do,' he said pensively, meaning it. Not Shaun

— they knew each other inside out. Perhaps he was thinking of himself. 'There's always a part of us that we don't disclose to others, or we camouflage. We project to another person the image we think they need to see, or want them to see. Maybe that's because we don't really know ourselves.'

'You're getting into psychology now, or is it philosophy?'

'And I haven't even had a drink.' He smiled. 'Dawn and her boyfriend depressed me.' That was true to a degree. 'I'm going to speak to Jarinder's family Monday morning.'

'And over the weekend, what will you do?'

'Take a boat trip.'

'Do you good. Anywhere special?'

'Probably along to Salcombe. It's a nice place.'

'I'd come with you if I wasn't on call.'

He was relieved about that. It saved him making excuses.

'But nothing to stop you showing me over Shaun's boat after our meal. You can make me a coffee.'

He smiled. 'Aren't I supposed to ask you to come back for coffee?'

'Marvik, you're living in the past.'

Now with Strathen safely back at Hamble, there was no need for him to refuse. But he would. Firstly, it wasn't his boat and it felt wrong to make love to her on board Strathen's — because he knew that was what they would end up doing, despite her having a boyfriend, which he could tell didn't bother her. Secondly, because sex would change their relationship and to him it would ruin it. And thirdly, he didn't want to take the chance of his mission mobile going off and having to pretend it was a wrong number or missing the call. What excuse should he make?

He was saved from answering as their food arrived at the same time as her phone rang.

'Damn, I've got to go. Road traffic accident.' She rose and grabbed her coat. 'Some other time, maybe?'

'Yes,' he replied, disguising his relief.

He sent back her meal and ate his, feeling the sooner he could return to Hamble, the better.

CHAPTER FOURTEEN

Saturday

It was mid-morning when he moored up on a pontoon in Salcombe Harbour, twenty-five miles to the east of Plymouth by road and much the same in nautical miles by sea. Although not as frantically busy as it was in the summer months, there were still plenty of craft bobbing about in the dank, breezy morning, while clouds hung over the green rolling hills surrounding the picturesque harbour town.

It took him a good hour to locate Sawes' bungalow, number ten, the Schoolyard, squashed in among a residential area of semi-detached and detached houses in Kingsland Road. It hadn't shown up on any of his internet searches. He thought Strathen must have got it wrong until a local estate agent pointed him in the right direction — they had the neighbouring property up for sale. He could see the board outside the large house next door that was falling into a state of disrepair, and the bungalow looked none too clever either. Weeds were strewn across the poky driveway. The double-glazed windows and ledges were filthy and the curtains pulled across the only window the same. The occupant took a long time to answer Marvik's persistent finger on the doorbell and he was about to give up, thinking Sawes must be out, when the door screeched open.

Marvik found himself looking down on a man in a wheelchair with long scraggly white hair and an equally unkempt white beard on a face so pale, with deep sunken watery eyes, that it looked sepulchral. He also had one leg and a tube running from his nose into a portable oxygen cylinder.

'Thought you were the carer,' he wheezed, scowling at him. 'Whatever you're collecting for, or selling, I don't want it.' He made to close the door.

'I've come to talk to you about Jarinder Vaidya,' Marvik quickly interjected.

'Who? Never heard of him.'

Oh, but he had — Marvik could see that in those bloodshot eyes. 'He was a plastic surgeon based in Plymouth. He was killed in a car accident eight days ago.'

'So? Lots of people die in car accidents.'

'He came to see you on Saturday the twenty-sixth of August.'

'Who says? You're nuts. I've never seen nor heard of him.'

'A dark-skinned man, six feet, slender.'

'I don't know anyone by that name and I haven't seen any dark-skinned men unless you count one of the carers, who's here now.'

Marvik turned to see a man pull up in a car. 'How did you lose your leg?' he asked, turning back to face Sawes, wondering if it had been in combat some years ago and Jarinder had operated on him.

'None of your bleeding business!'

Did he detect an accent there under the slight Devon burr? If so, from where? Did it matter? Marvik remained silent and stared at Sawes. He was elderly and frail but he was far from stupid. Behind the grey skin, scarred face, dirty clothes and unshaven, dishevelled state, Marvik saw a hard, calculating man. Not someone he'd have thought Jarinder would naturally contact or confide in. Maybe Strathen *had* got it wrong — not that Jarinder had come here, but that

124

he had come to confide in this embittered man. Marvik just couldn't see it. Nor that Sawes had been in the Royal Marines, or any type of armed service, come to that. Perhaps illness had made him like this — bitter, hard and sloppy over his appearance. Perhaps he was having a particularly bad day. His health was failing, obviously, and he was fighting against it in the only way that he knew how and remained to him, with anger and acrimony. Marvik had never feared death but he did illness, and being incapacitated and dependent.

Quietly, Marvik said, 'I know Jarinder Vaidya came here but I don't know why you're so afraid of admitting that.'

'Afraid! I've done more dangerous things in my life than you have, despite your scars.'

'Except you're too scared to admit to speaking to Jarinder Vaidya.'

The eyes narrowed. The lips tightened. 'Fuck off.' He spun his wheelchair round and disappeared from sight.

Marvik made for the carer. 'I've upset your client.'

'That wouldn't be difficult,' the carer replied brightly. 'He's a tetchy old sod at the best of times. Still, it can't be much fun being stuck in a wheelchair panting for breath and having to rely on others to do everything for you. We get used to all sorts in my job, which certainly makes it interesting and at times challenging — as well as rewarding.'

'How did he lose his leg and gets those scars? Bit like mine.'

'Car accident in Birmingham. Sued the hospital for medical negligence on account of the fact he shouldn't have lost his leg. Won the case and with the compensation bought the bungalow.'

Marvik could see Sawes watching them from the window. 'I think you're going to be in for a hard time being seen talking to me.'

'I'll cope.'

'Does he have any friends or relatives who visit him?'

'Not that I've seen, met or heard of. I'd better go.'

'Just one more thing, have you seen an Indian man, six feet, slender, visiting Sawes at any time?'

'No, sorry.'

Marvik walked back to the harbour, mulling over the interaction with Sawes. The link with Jarinder could go back to the Birmingham hospital where Jarinder had worked for four years before moving to Plymouth three years ago. He could have operated on Sawes. But why did he come here in August? Marvik felt certain Jarinder had, despite the denial. Was it fear that made Sawes deny it? He was old and helpless. He couldn't defend himself. Jarinder would never have harmed him, though. So what and who could he be frightened of?

But the more Marvik considered that hard expression, the more he didn't think it was fear. His experience told him that behind that sickly pallor and oxygen mask was a nasty piece of work, and a liar. And there had to be a reason why Jarinder had written his visit here in code. Sawes was the key to unlocking that. He'd return tomorrow. By then, Strathen might have some background on the man. If not, Crowder, because Marvik would update him.

Back on the boat he called Strathen on the mission mobile and told him about Sawes.

'The accident compensation will be easy to trace,' Strathen said. 'It'll be listed on the national register. And I can check with the Land Registry when he bought that bungalow, which will give me an approximate timescale. Also, despite his claim, it's more than likely it occurred when Jarinder was working at the Birmingham hospital, so the medical negligence case could have been brought against them. Although I don't think it was against Jarinder, or I would have known. I can't find much else on Sawes — no wife, widow or siblings. And no employment record, but then he is eighty and has probably been on invalidity benefit for years. But it would be interesting to know his previous occupation. I guess he could have suffered an industrial injury.'

Marvik flicked on the kettle. 'Any luck in finding Julian Boyce, the surgeon Steven Lingfield told me lived in Salcombe?'

'Yes and you won't be able to speak to him. Died four years ago.'

'Suspicious?'

'Death certificate says heart attack but that could have been induced. I think it's unlikely he has anything to do with this, though.'

Marvik did too. 'We'll concentrate on Sawes for now, and I'll wait to see if Crowder has any intelligence on Daniel Larroc. I'll head back to Mayflower Marina for the night and have another chat with Sawes in the morning.'

'I'll see what I can get in the meantime.'

Marvik thought one more crack at Sawes, then he would speak to the Vaidyas before they, and he, made for London. He was eager to see Paul Webb's apartment. The concierge could give him a description of the man and the bike. And he'd like to talk to Tarina about the attack on her.

As he motored back to Plymouth, though, he increasingly got the sense that he'd missed something vital about Sawes. That he'd made a mistake leaving him. He should have marched in as he had done with Lee Barker and Dawn Snell. But how could he threaten a dying elderly man, even if he was malicious and involved? And he had the feeling that Sawes had recognized that. Yes, there had been a gleam of triumph as well as evil in those watery eyes.

He moored up and looked over to Jarinder's boat. With surprise, he saw Rohan pressing the security code onto the pontoons. That was a stroke of luck. He didn't feel so bad now about leaving Sawes. He hastily locked up, and reached Rohan as he drew level with Jarinder's boat. His unshaven chin had darkened and thickened with bristles. His eyes had sunk deeper in their sockets and heavy bags dragged them down further.

'I didn't expect to see you here,' Rohan said with a flash of irritation. 'Did Nishan tell you I was coming?'

'No. I was on my friend's boat and saw you. Do you have a moment to talk? Can I come on board?'

Rohan shrugged as if to say, *Please yourself*. Marvik watched as he extracted a key, went to open the padlock, then found it broken. Puzzled, he glanced back at Marvik, then, pushing back the hatch, drew up with an exclamation at the devastation before him. 'Who did this?'

'It looks as though someone was searching for something.'

'Like what? There's nothing of any value.' He ran a hand through his hair.

'A diary, perhaps, or the logbook.'

'Why would anyone want that?' His restless eyes roamed the wreckage.

'Your father might have written in it what was disturbing him.'

'I doubt that. He wasn't one to pour his heart out on paper or to anyone.' He spoke harshly, not with sorrow or pride.

'Then you don't know what was troubling him?'

'He wouldn't confide in me,' he said with an edge of bitterness.

'In Nishan then?'

'I doubt it,' he scoffed. 'And he certainly wouldn't have burdened Tarina.'

'No, he wouldn't.'

'You knew him well?' He scrutinized Marvik with a slight air of trepidation.

'Yes.'

'Is that why you were at the crematorium to say your farewells? I thought you'd done that at the house.'

'Who was the man on the motorbike?'

'What motorbike?'

'The powerful BMW.'

'Probably someone for the next funeral. I didn't notice.'

A lie. Rohan was definitely uneasy about that motorbike. He turned away and opened the navigational drawer.

'No logbook.'

Was that what he had come for? 'Could it be in your father's safe?'

'Ask Nishan, he's in charge of that.' He flopped onto the bench seat. 'I should be at the house but I can't stand being cooped up. I've got to stay until Monday. Nishan insists.

He's very strict on the Hindu faith — when it suits him,' he added acerbically. 'His preaching about it gets on my nerves.'

Marvik sat opposite him. It seemed Rohan needed someone to confide in, and Marvik was only too pleased to be that person.

'There's nothing I can do at home,' Rohan continued. 'I've got to get back to work. I'm in the middle of a major investment deal.'

Marvik wondered if he had been about to add that his father's death couldn't have come at a worse time.

'I'd forgotten about this old boat, so had Tarina. It was only when Nishan said we would sell it that it occurred to me no one had cleaned it. Tarina's already done enough cleaning. And she's worn out with grief. I said I'd do it, but Nishan frowned on that. It's not a man's job in our culture. I said, all right then, Anika, his wife, could do it.' He gave a twisted smile. 'That didn't go down too well. Nishan thinks he has authority over Anika, but that's in his dreams. Nishan thought he'd made a good marriage to a woman who would do as he asked, but women in the Hindu tradition also have the power to take control of situations, which Anika does.'

'They don't get on?'

'They do if Nishan does what Anika says.' He smirked. 'She's a lawyer with a large firm in London. It's partly why Nishan moved to London from Leeds, where he worked as a solicitor before being called to the Bar. His was a traditional Brahmin marriage. Anika's father, also a lawyer, proposed Nishan as a suitable husband for his daughter and both families agreed, as did Anika and Nishan. That's not going to be my way.' Rohan gazed around the upturned interior. 'I loved this boat. Although Nishan wasn't so keen. He and Dad were always arguing even when Nishan was young. We used to sail along the coast, we even got to France and the Channel Islands.'

'And Ireland?'

'Yes. Dad loved it there.'

'Did you put into a place called Ballycotton?'

Rohan looked taken aback for a moment. 'Yes, why do you ask?'

'A friend of mine's boat was found just off there. It's believed he took his own life.'

Rohan's shock seemed genuine. So Nishan hadn't relayed their conversation outside the house.

Marvik let the silence hang between them. Rohan broke it. 'I told Nishan I'd buy the boat off the estate. He said it doesn't exactly fit with my image — fast cars, women, expensive tastes. I like to have fun, and why not? I work damn hard. My job's a gamble, all investments are. Seeing it like this, though, has spoiled it somehow.'

'It can be set right.'

Rohan's head came up. 'You're right. I shouldn't give in. It'll give me something to do. I need some physical exercise, no gym for ten days. We have one in the apartment block where I live in London. Tarina lives with me.'

'Nishan said your sister was attacked on her way home on Tuesday before last.'

Rohan's expression darkened. Marvik noticed how his knuckles tightened. 'She was on her way to have a drink with me and George Ferrer. He owns the apartment above mine. He's rather taken with Tarina, not sure she is with him though. He thinks he's in with a chance now her cowardly boyfriend has ditched her. Poor Tarina's had so much to put up with. George was late as usual and in this instance it was a good thing because he scared off the attacker. The police said it wasn't racist but how do they know that? My father was awfully upset over it. She came home here after it happened, although she wanted to carry on working to take her mind off it. She sees people in a far worse physical and mental state than she was, and said it was her duty to help them, but she came nevertheless. Nishan insisted. He drove her down. You know she's a doctor at St Thomas' Hospital, don't you?'

'Yes.'

Rohan pulled himself up. 'I'll make a start on this. No need for you to stay.'

Clearly he wanted to be alone. But Marvik had a parting question to ask him. He rose, saying, 'Have you heard your father speak of a man called Hugh Sawes?'

'Doesn't ring a bell.'

Marvik wasn't so sure.

CHAPTER FIFTEEN

Sunday

'Sawes didn't lose his leg in any accident,' Strathen said the next morning. Marvik was on his way back to Salcombe on the boat. 'There's no record of him having received compensation from the Birmingham Health Authority. And he has never brought a case against them, or anyone else, for medical negligence.'

'He lied to his carers. That could have been to save face for some reason, or he just didn't see why he should tell them the truth.'

'I could try and hack into his medical records, or those at the Birmingham hospital — I still think he was treated there when Jarinder was a surgeon — but that would take a lot of time. Crowder could access them, only he'd have to apply for a warrant, and he won't want to do that and alert them or anyone else that it's connected with his unit.'

'I'll ask Amanda to check them after I've seen Sawes. You never know, he might be in a more forthcoming mood today and tell me his life story,' Marvik said cynically.

'Huh!'

The day was bright, and as he made steady progress he again mused over his conversation with Rohan the previous day, much as he had done during the evening. Rohan had shown no reaction to his mention of Sawes. Perhaps he wasn't naturally curious. Perhaps he was too preoccupied with his grief. He was obviously deeply upset, and seeing the boat like that after losing his father so tragically would be enough to distract anyone. But why wasn't he more concerned about the missing logbook? He had lightly dismissed it. And why hadn't he asked why his friend had taken his own life off Ballycotton Harbour? Most people would have done, either out of curiosity or sympathy. Had Rohan really shown up there to get away from the house, or had he come for the logbook . . . or something else? Surely not the DVD, unless a copy of it had found its way back onto that boat courtesy of Dawn or Lee — or Webb even.

Last night, Marvik had returned under cover of darkness and conducted another thorough search, but hadn't found anything. He postponed his questions regarding Rohan and turned his thoughts to Sawes. Hopefully Sawes would throw some light on this, and he had to find the right way of getting him to do that.

The coastal town looked pretty in the morning light. He took his time mooring up on one of the pontoons and strolling up to Kingsland Road. When he arrived outside the bungalow, he found the grubby curtains closed, despite it being almost eleven o'clock. Perhaps the carer hadn't turned up to assist Sawes, he thought, pressing the bell. Or maybe Sawes didn't want the curtains opened.

There was no answer. He knocked. Still nothing. He peered through the letterbox. The place appeared empty. There was a narrow path to the right of the bungalow that led around to the back. He was about to take it when a voice hailed him.

'He's not here.'

Horton turned to find a man in his early seventies address-ing him from over the low wall of the house to Marvik's left.

Marvik tried a reassuring smile at the man's suspicious expression. 'I came yesterday and said I'd return to have a chat with Mr Sawes today.'

'Well, you're out of luck. He's dead. Died in the night. Carer found him this morning.'

Marvik cursed silently. This was no natural death — he should have expected it. He was dealing with a professional who had no hesitation in killing to hide his dirty secret, and this meant that Sawes knew what that was. Whoever was behind this had known that he'd been to see Sawes yesterday, and that meant either the bungalow was being monitored or someone, possibly Sawes himself, had told them, because no one else had known he was coming here. He discounted the estate agent and the carer.

Then he rapidly reconsidered. There was one other person he'd mentioned the name to, who had also pointed out that Jarinder's logbook was missing. Rohan, yesterday. Had he really been on the boat for a trip down memory lane, or had he been there waiting to be seen by Marvik so that he could find out what he had learned so far? But it was he who had asked if Jarinder had spoken of Sawes. Had that been enough to prompt this? Had Rohan reported back and instigated it? But maybe he was imagining things and Sawes *had* died from his illness.

'I knew he was in bad shape,' Marvik said, 'but I didn't expect this to happen so quickly.'

'Don't think any of us did, not that we knew him well. He made it quite clear he didn't want any help, pity or company. He was a touchy devil — sorry if you're a relative or friend, but he was very bad tempered. We made allowances for that because of his poor health.'

'Do you know how he died?'

'No. The carer called the ambulance but the old man was already dead, so they buggered off and along came the police. I suppose they had to in case there was any funny business, but I expect his lungs gave out. Emphysema.'

Or his oxygen did. Marvik's suspicious mind was going into overdrive.

'Did you see or hear anyone here last night?'

'Only the carers.'

'How many does he have?'

'Four usually. Breakfast, lunch, tea and one to put him to bed.'

'You said usually — was it any different yesterday?'

'Don't think so.' He looked puzzled.

'No strange cars or motorbikes?'

'Should there have been? Hey, you don't think someone helped him on his way?'

Marvik was certain someone had. 'No, just wondered if he might have had a visitor, aside from me, and it overexcited him.'

'Would have taken a lot to do that, although he did like to grumble when he spoke to me and my wife, which wasn't often. We'd have been only too pleased to help him with shopping and a bit of cleaning and gardening, but he made it quite clear he didn't want us nosing around in his business. That was how he put it. You should see the back garden, looks like a jungle. It's all I can do to stop the weeds and brambles coming over to my side. It's a good job this front is paved over, although as you can see the weeds are coming through the cracks.'

'And it looks like the trees at the back of his garden need pruning.' Marvik was fishing to get the lay of the land, glad he had a talkative person.

'Too right they do, and the ones the other side.'

'The house that's up for sale . . .' Marvik asked conversationally, glancing to his right. He'd seen the board yesterday. 'Have they got fed up with the weeds?'

'Theirs is just as bad. Although it wasn't when the couple who rented it lived there. But they've been gone for three months and the landlord decided to sell up. Used to belong to an old couple. She died, then he did. Biggest house in the street, and detached. That's because the original owner was the builder of all these houses on this side and built one for himself, years ago. It also had a large garden, and when the old couple died they left it all to a nephew, who sold it to a couple who got planning permission to put this bungalow

135

in part of the garden. My wife and I were only too glad it wasn't another house. You can see how it's sort of squashed in. They gave it a fancy name — the Schoolyard. God alone knows why, perhaps it was some kind of secret joke. Anyway, after the bungalow was built, they sold up having made lots of money, and the current landlord bought it and let it out.'

'And Mr Sawes bought the bungalow brand new.'

'Yes.'

'That was when?'

'Must have been eight or nine years ago now.'

'Was he an invalid then?'

'Yes, but his lungs weren't shot to pieces.'

'I wonder why he moved to Salcombe,' Marvik mused, thinking that at any moment the neighbour was going to ask him why he was being so nosy.

'We asked him that, being friendly like, and he told us to mind our own business. Upset my wife, it did. We tried a couple more times but he was just as rude, so we thought sod him, if that's the way he wants it. We thought he might have been from these parts or had relatives, but he's not a Devon man.'

'No, he didn't have a nice burr, like yours.' Marvik smiled.

The neighbour laughed. 'No, but you could hear something. I thought Irish or Scottish but then I'm no expert, and he wouldn't tell the carers anything either, except to shut up and do what they were paid to do.'

'Did he fund his own care?'

'Reckon so, never saw anyone from social services. We'll probably find out he left a fortune. Misers are like that, live like they're destitute and count their money every night before they put it to bed. There's been interest in the old house, as my wife and I call it, but I don't know if there have been any offers. Probably not, given the state of this bungalow on their doorstep. It probably put people off. And now Mr Sawes' bungalow will be up for sale. Whoever takes it on will have a job on their hands, and I don't just mean the jungle of a garden. I don't think it's been cleaned in months, years probably. You can see that by the filthy curtains and windows. He was a hermit, only left the place to go to the hospital.'

'How did he get there? It was Plymouth, I take it,' Marvik asked lightly.

'No, South Hams Hospital. It's the nearest, at Kingsbridge. Patient transport, and woe betide them if they were late. We could hear him moaning. I pitied the poor doctors and nurses.'

'Did he say how he lost his leg?'

'Told me it was none of our damn business, but we heard though the various carers that came and went that he'd been in the army.'

That wasn't what the carer yesterday had told Marvik, but then perhaps Sawes had told different helpers different tales. At the age of eighty-four, if he had served a full complement of years in the army — say, twenty-two — and had joined at twenty-two, that meant he had left the services approximately forty years ago. That was a long while back.

The neighbour said, 'He could have lost his leg in action.'

'Like me. My scar, that is. Royal Marines, in combat. I'm a civilian now.' Marvik thought he'd volunteer a bit of chat to keep things on a friendly basis.

There were plenty of conflicts between the 1960s and 1980s that could have caused the loss of Sawes' leg — the Indonesian Confrontation, the Aden Emergency, the Troubles in Northern Ireland, and the Falklands.

'There aren't any pictures of him in uniform, according to the more friendly carers who have come and gone over the years. Still, not everyone keeps photos. Maybe he didn't like to be reminded of it.'

'Did he have any relatives?'

'Might have done but none of them came here. Might now he's dead, if he's left them any money.'

Yes. Marvik wondered who would inherit. Had Sawes left a will? Maybe he'd died intestate. Maybe he didn't have much to leave and was in debt.

Marvik thanked the neighbour and said he'd contact the police for further information. He wouldn't. There would be an autopsy. Would that find someone had helped Sawes on his way? Or had the death been artfully staged to avoid detection?

Marvik walked slowly down the road and turned left into the street that he believed backed on to Sawes' bungalow. He strolled along it, casually looking around. The houses were a mixture of semi-detached with a couple of detached ones thrown in here and there. It was relatively quiet with only a handful of people about, some getting into their cars, others cleaning them.

He thought of how Sawes could have been killed. It would have been quite simple to have pulled out the oxygen tube and then leave the oxygen cylinder out of the man's reach. And easy to have held him by force from reaching his lifeline until he had died. That might have taken some time, so perhaps he'd been helped on his way by a blow to the head. If the autopsy found a head contusion, it could be assumed that Sawes had fallen while struggling to reach his oxygen supply.

Marvik could see the trees that backed onto Sawes' bungalow, and those of the empty house next door. They were swaying in the wind. He made for the harbour. He had some hours to kill before he returned under the cover of darkness to the bungalow, his aim to get inside and search it.

He bought some water and sandwiches and, after consulting his Ordnance Survey map, decided to set out on the South West Coast Path to Torcross, a little over twelve miles away and slightly challenging, depending on how fit you were. For him it was a stroll. He'd once trodden this path with the Marines when on a training exercise.

Soon he was on a rugged upward incline and the views were spectacular. He phoned Strathen and told him what had happened and his action plan. Strathen would investigate if Sawes had a service record.

Marvik's mind often turned to Sawes' death and the disturbing thought that it could have been connected with him mentioning the name to Rohan. Surely Rohan wasn't involved in his own father's murder? Perhaps he had relayed his meeting to Nishan, but again Marvik couldn't and didn't want to believe that either brother was involved in murder.

As he trekked on, he tried to remember if he had given his own name to Sawes. No, there hadn't been time. But after his visit, Sawes could have called someone to say he'd been snooping around asking about Jarinder and given a description of him. Strange that Rohan had shown up in the marina at the same time as he had returned by boat. Sawes couldn't have called Rohan and Nishan though — how would he have their number? Whatever the situation, it strengthened his view that Jarinder had visited Sawes.

Had the killer searched the bungalow and removed any evidence? Marvik suspected he was too late to find anything that could help him, but he had to try. As he passed the sandy beaches and rugged rocks, he thought of that stretch of coast in Ireland and the body of Larroc in that house, wondering what the post-mortem would find.

He took the steep climb to Torcross at a pace and ate thinking of the coastline around Ballycotton. Who did Tom Gilley report to? How deeply were he and his wife involved in this? The fishermen too. Did the answer to this lie in Ireland after all? If Jarinder had taken Larroc there — which seemed highly probable by the entry on his chart plotter — then how had he known of the existence of the cottage? Did that cottage in fact belong to Jarinder? Or perhaps Larroc had known of it. Amanda had suggested he might have been Irish. Was that the reason they couldn't find a link to Larroc in Great Britain?

It was gone four when he began his return journey to Salcombe. Strathen called him to say that Sawes was not a former veteran. He might have lost his leg in an accident. Perhaps it had been the man's own fault. He'd ferret around again.

Marvik completed the walk and snatched an hour's sleep on the boat. At midnight he made his way to Kingsland Road, and was pleased to see that the council turned off the street lights at one. It was easy to keep low and skirt the side of the bungalow next to the empty house. Soon he was in the wilderness of the garden looking for the easiest way inside.

The rear door was double-glazed but the lock was easy enough to pick. Marvik stepped into a filthy kitchen with dirty dishes piled up on the grimy work surfaces and sink. He'd have thought the carers might have washed up but perhaps Sawes didn't want them to. Perhaps that would have cost him extra money, and, as the neighbour had said, he'd been a skinflint.

The house smelled of dirt, urine and sickness. His torch picked out the shabby lounge with its worn and grubby sparse furniture. The dirty wheelchair was pushed to the right of an ancient sideboard that was caked in dust, as were two ornaments and a clock whose dial was barely visible through the grime. He could just make out it had stopped at 2.43, though on what day, morning or afternoon was anybody's guess. The oxygen cylinders were beside the wheelchair, and some of Sawes' clothes sat on a table in front of a lean-to conservatory that extended from the lounge. There were no photographs, as he had expected. He felt a twinge of pity for the man, then recalled those cold, hard eyes. But then his illness and incapacity could have caused his bitterness.

Swiftly, Marvik checked out the two bedrooms. One was practically devoid of furniture, the other was Sawes' room. There were no books but a pile of newspapers, including the local one, had been left on the filthy, threadbare carpet. Marvik lifted the top one and saw immediately that it was open and that someone, most probably Sawes, had put a ring round the news item on Jarinder's death. Now that was interesting.

He tore out the page, folded it and stuffed it inside his jacket and rapidly went through the other local papers to see if Sawes had marked any other news items. He was in luck. There was a much fuller article on Jarinder, including his time spent in the navy and as a surgeon at the Birmingham hospital before moving to Plymouth. There was a quote from the hospital's chief executive on the tragic loss and how Jarinder would be hard to replace. Sawes had written something underneath it. Marvik couldn't quite make it out but he'd study that later. He again ripped off the page and tucked it inside his jacket, then searched the drawers and cupboards. They revealed only clothes, some badly in need of washing and repair. There were no mementoes of a former life.

On returning to the lounge, Marvik stood for a moment and listened. Only the wind greeted him. He wondered if Sawes had owned a mobile. There was a landline. With gloved fingers, he lifted the receiver. It was operative, so perhaps he had only used that. There was no computer. The killer could have taken it, if Sawes had owned one. Marvik was convinced this was murder even though there was no evidence of it. And he was equally convinced the killer would have searched the place and taken away anything vital. Except he hadn't found the newspaper articles. That gave Marvik hope.

The top drawer of the sideboard was ajar. He suspected it had been open like this when Sawes' body had been found on the floor and no one had thought to push it back. If Sawes had had something to hide then he would have been canny about it, and he wouldn't have fallen out of that wheelchair if whatever it was had been pushed inside the drawers. But Marvik's pulse quickened as he rapidly considered this. Sawes could have been reaching for it and fallen or been struck before he could manipulate it.

He pulled out the drawer. It was heavy and crammed full of utility bills, scraps of paper, leaflets and flyers. There was also an NHS medical card, and letters from the DWP about his state pension. He took the medical card and turned the drawer round. There was nothing on the back, but as he ran his fingers underneath it he smiled. He couldn't believe his luck. If Sawes had been killed then his killer had slipped up in his search. Was that Webb? Perhaps his job wasn't to look for anything, just to make sure Sawes was eliminated and his death made to look like an accident.

Tipping the contents onto the table, Marvik stared at the passport stuck to the bottom of the drawer. Eagerly, he ripped off the faded yellow sticky tape. He opened it, nodded, stuffed it inside his bomber jacket pocket and made his way out. There was no need to stay any longer. On the boat, he called Strathen. It was almost 3 a.m. but Strathen answered promptly.

'Hugh Sawes' real name is Peter Shoulter, according to the passport he'd hidden. He lived in Hong Kong from 1964 to 1983, when the passport stamp says he returned to the UK. That's far too long a period to have been stationed with one of the armed forces there. I don't know when he became Hugh Sawes but he's put a ring round two articles in the newspaper on Jarinder's death and underneath the fuller one he's written, *Crewe*. Has Jarinder ever worked in Crewe?'

'Not that I'm aware of. I've never heard him speak of it. I'll get working on Peter Shoulter.'

'And I'll see if Nishan, Rohan or Tarina can tell me more about him and Crewe.'

CHAPTER SIXTEEN

Monday

Marvik was outside Jarinder's house Monday morning just before nine. Nevertheless, he was too late. Neither Nishan's Mercedes nor Rohan's Porsche were outside the garage; they had already left for London. There were no other cars parked and it was highly likely that Tarina had returned to London with one of her brothers. He was intending to go there anyway. There was no longer any need for him to remain here. He wanted to follow up on Webb's Battersea apartment. He could always speak to the Vaidyas in town. He'd return the boat to the Hamble and from there travel to London tomorrow. As he was here though, he might as well try the bell.

He rang, not expecting an answer, but the door promptly opened and there stood Tarina. She looked exhausted, with heavy shadows under her deep-set brown eyes. He could see a packed rucksack behind her in the hallway.

'I thought you were the taxi.' She peered behind him, looking for a car.

Quickly he introduced himself, in case she didn't recognize him from his previous visit. Her expression softened.

'I remember how kindly you spoke of my father when you came here to pay your respects. Nishan said you thought something was troubling him before his death.' Her voice faltered and she turned her head away. 'I'm sorry, forgive me. What is it you want? I was just leaving to catch the train to London.'

'I won't keep you long. I'd like to talk to you about your father — but I don't wish to distress you,' he quickly added. 'I think he stumbled on something that someone wanted kept secret.'

Her brow furrowed. 'You can't mean he was killed?' she whispered incredulously.

He hesitated to tell her that was exactly what he believed, because it looked as though it might be a burden too heavy for her to carry in her bereavement. And if she didn't know about the non-existent affair then he wasn't going to enlighten her. Rohan and Nishan, maybe, although he'd reserve judgement on that. There was no need to add to their grief, or to Tarina's. Perhaps he was being overprotective — maybe she could take it — but he didn't see the need to make that decision. Instead, he said, 'I think he might have been so anxious and distracted that he came off the road.' Marvik didn't believe this was the truth, but he couldn't reveal that.

'He was very upset about the attack on me. Do you know about that?'

'Yes. Both Nishan and Rohan told me.'

'It shook me up but I'm fine now.' She looked far from it.

A car swept into the drive. 'Would you mind if I come with you? We can talk in the taxi.'

'Not at all.' She locked the front door almost with an air of finality, Marvik thought. He took her rucksack and the driver placed it in the boot. 'Why didn't you return with one of your brothers?' he asked when they were seated in the back and on their way.

'Because Rohan left on the stroke of midnight and Nishan about five minutes after with Anika, his wife, and I couldn't bear to sit with Anika and Nishan in their frozen silence. I could have gone with Rohan but I wanted to be alone in the house. There's always been someone there since Father died. I wanted to say my own quiet goodbye. I also prefer to be alone with my thoughts on the train journey.'

Marvik could understand that. 'Did your father have a desktop computer or laptop?'

'He had a laptop, why?'

This confirmed what Nishan had told him. 'I wondered if he had put something on it to indicate what was disturbing him.'

'He might have done but Nishan hasn't mentioned it. He's taken Father's laptop to London. He has all of his papers. I can ask him if you feel it's important.'

'No, please don't, but if he tells you anything that could help me would you let me know? I'll give you my contact details.'

They swapped numbers.

'When was the last time you saw your father?' Marvik asked. The taxi driver had earphones plugged in and was jigging his head about as though listening to music, which suited Marvik fine.

'The Wednesday before he died. He was quite depressed but that was on account of being overworked and worried about me.'

'The assault must have been terrifying.' He liked her gentle manner and her soothing voice. He thought she would be calm in a crisis, much like her father. There was nothing pretentious about her as there was with her brothers. She was dressed casually and not extravagantly. Her eyes were soulful and intelligent. He suspected she was a good doctor with a tender approach to her patients, empathetic and reassuring. The complete opposite to Amanda, who although an excellent surgeon was devoid of bedside manner.

'It could have been a great deal worse if it hadn't been for George scaring off the man,' she said. 'George Ferrer — he's a neighbour of Rohan's, and I was on my way to have a drink with him and Rohan when it happened.'

That was what Rohan had told him. 'Do you remember anything about the attacker?'

'Only that he was dressed in black. It all happened so quickly.'

'Was he big or small?'

'Biggish, I seem to recall, or at least that's my impression. And he smelled of leather. I didn't want to come here after the assault, we're so short-staffed at the hospital, and I only had a few cuts and bruises. I thought work would take my mind off it. There are plenty of people far worse off than me, but Nishan insisted, although Rohan disagreed. But then they disagree over everything,' she added sadly. 'Nishan drove me down.'

'Did he stay?'

'No. He drove straight back that evening after speaking to my father.'

'And your father went to work as usual on Thursday?'

'Yes. But the last time I saw him was the night before. He didn't wish to wake me on Thursday morning and he didn't come home after work.' Tears welled in her weary eyes. 'Was he on his way to see your friend?'

'Yes.'

'Nishan told me he too is dead. Is that true?'

'He's missing, believed dead, off the coast of Ireland near a place called Ballycotton.'

'Oh yes, Rohan mentioned it to me yesterday after he'd been on the boat. He said he met you there.'

'You used to sail there as a family.'

'We did.' A smile lit up her face. Her beauty sent his blood pumping.

'Have you heard your father speak of a man called Hugh Sawes or Peter Shoulter?'

'No. Who are they?'

'Just people he might have known when working at the Queen Elizabeth Hospital Birmingham. Did you know your father sailed to Cork recently?'

'I knew he'd been there but I don't think he sailed there. He's been settling Uncle Alex's estate. He lived in Cork. He's not really an uncle, but we always called him that. He was a close friend of my father's and a colleague. They worked together at Birmingham hospital. Before he retired to Cork he used to take holidays there. So did we as children, in the place you mentioned — Ballycotton. Uncle Alex had this old stone cottage above the harbour.'

Marvik threw her a surprised glance. His head spun, but before he could ask her any questions the taxi drew up at the station. The driver retrieved Tarina's rucksack and she made to pay, but Marvik intervened.

'No,' she insisted. 'I called the taxi and it's my fare. But thank you for offering, that was kind.' She again gave him that smile that made his heart skip a beat or two.

'Was Uncle Alex a plastic surgeon like your father?'

'Yes, a brilliant one. His wife was seriously injured in a hit-and-run some years ago, so he retired to look after her and moved to Cork. He died six months ago. My father was executor and sole beneficiary. The estate had just been granted probate. But with my father dead, Nishan said the original grant has to be revoked and reissued in the name of the new executor, him. It's called the chain of representation. Nishan is our father's sole executor. Uncle Alex's estate will come to us.'

'How did he die?' Could this be another victim to add to Webb's hit list?

'Brain haemorrhage.'

A natural death then, it seemed.

'He was a kind, gentle, wise man. I was surprised he didn't retire to Jersey, which was where he was from. He had such a lovely, grand-sounding name, it always made me smile.' And she did again. 'Alexander Le Grewe,' she said softly.

Marvik look at her astonished. 'Le Grewe?'

'Yes, you knew him?'

'No, it was just the name sounded familiar,' he quickly covered.

'I'd better go. I don't want to miss my train.'

'No. Thank you, Tarina.'

'I don't know what for. Will you keep in touch with me, and tell me if you discover anything about my father?'

'Of course.'

She turned away and then back. 'And even if you don't, will you keep in touch?'

'You bet.' He leaned forward and kissed her lightly on the cheek. He watched her go through the ticket barrier, then, with thoughts swarming around his head like tormented bees, hailed a taxi outside to take him back to the marina. On *Sea Fever*, he picked up the crumpled newspaper he'd founded in Sawes' bungalow. The word the elderly man had written on it wasn't Crewe but Grewe. Alexander Le Grewe.

CHAPTER SEVENTEEN

Tuesday

'It explains quite a few things,' Strathen said. They were in the operations room in his apartment, and by his appearance Strathen hadn't slept or shaved, and probably hadn't eaten for some time. It was almost 1 a.m. Marvik had made good time on the boat and had had plenty of time to think through what this latest news meant. He wasn't tired; he was too keen to hear what Strathen had to say.

Strathen continued. 'Firstly, the reason why Jarinder took Larroc to the cottage — he knew who owned it and that it had been neglected for years.'

Marvik's conclusion. 'And Sawes wrote "Grewe" under that article on Jarinder's death because Jarinder had visited Sawes and they'd spoken about Le Grewe. You translated the coded message in the logbook as possibly being "someone who he wished to confide in who had acted courageously and ended up in the guardhouse". I don't have Sawes down as a courageous man but I could be wrong. Perhaps he got that injury by acting courageously but hadn't been given any thanks or payment, which made him bitter. Jarinder discovered something about the incident that had caused

149

the loss of Sawes' leg from Le Grewe's papers, and that was why he went there. Jarinder would have gone through them, being the executor and a beneficiary. Nishan must know about it, he has the paperwork. But why did Jarinder put it in code?'

'I'll come to that in a moment, or you'll get there when I tell you what I've discovered.'

'Sorry. Go on.' Marvik grinned and swallowed some coffee.

'Le Grewe was an orthopaedic plastic surgeon.' Strathen confirmed what Tarina had told Marvik. 'And there is a connection between him and Peter Shoulter aka Hugh Sawes — Hong Kong.'

Marvik raised his eyebrows.

'Le Grewe's background was easy to trace. He was a renowned surgeon. There was a great deal about him in the professional media over the years, and full obituaries. He worked overseas for a medical charity in underdeveloped countries helping to train their surgeons, but it was his stint in Hong Kong from 1964 to 1969 that caught my eye.'

Marvik's brain was working rapidly. 'The height of the Hong Kong riots.'

'Correct. They began as a minor labour dispute and escalated into full-blown protests, demonstrations and bombings against British colonial rule. Many of the protesters had sympathies with the Chinese Communist Party, who further stirred them up, and who also gave a hand with bomb making and planting. Sawes' passport shows he was in Hong Kong from 1963 until 1983, when he returned to England. Now, what did he do there all those years?' Strathen smirked. 'And he wasn't in the armed forces.'

'Do I get three guesses?' Marvik said lightly.

'You might get it in one.'

Marvik thought of those cold, hard eyes and that bitter manner. He didn't think it was charitable work. 'He was in prison. The guardhouse! So Jarinder visited Sawes to reveal to him that he knew he had carried out a risky act that had landed him in prison. Jarinder had read about it in Le Grewe's papers.'

Strathen nodded. 'I delved into the court and criminal records for that period, which took a bit of ferreting. I discovered that Peter Shoulter, aka Hugh Sawes, was convicted in Hong Kong of planting a bomb that injured three people, including himself. He was acting on behalf of the Chinese Communist Party and was found in an underground hospital when the Royal Navy despatched a helicopter from the aircraft carrier HMS *Hermes*, along with the army bomb disposal experts and police. The helicopter landed on the roof of a building that was found to contain bombs, weapons and a leftist hospital with a dispensary and operating theatre.'

'I knew he smelled wrong,' Marvik crowed, glad his perception of people hadn't failed him.

'Sawes was tried, convicted and sentenced to serve twenty years in a Hong Kong prison. He served just over fifteen and was released in 1983. On his release I'm assuming he returned to Northern Ireland, where he was born, and I'll tell you why in a moment. I know what you're thinking. He could have been a member of the Irish Republican Army. Not because he had any political persuasion or strong religious beliefs, although he might have, but because he was a professional terrorist — a mercenary, if you prefer that term.'

'You'd have thought he'd have learned his lesson in a Hong Kong jail.'

'Probably made him even more embittered and rebellious. As Le Grewe worked at the Hong Kong hospital from 1964 to 1969 it's perfectly feasible that he operated on Sawes there.'

'Did Sawes lose his leg in Hong Kong?' Marvik's mind was in overdrive.

'No. But he could have done in Birmingham before he moved to Salcombe, and I don't think Sawes' injuries were from a car crash or industrial accident. So, we ask ourselves, what could have caused it? What happened in Birmingham at that time that resulted in the loss of his leg and his scarred face?'

'A bomb?'

'And I found an incident that matches. Further interrogation of the internet and the media confirms it.'

'The IRA?'

'No. The Real IRA. They were formed in 1997 by disaffected members of the Provisional IRA who rejected the IRA's ceasefire that year. There are other groups, any one of which Sawes could have been acting for, but it's not such a leap of faith that Sawes was working for the Real IRA given he was from Northern Ireland and lived there before Birmingham, although I haven't been able to confirm that for certain. Crowder would, though, through the DWP and other government databases. The intelligence services might also have files on him. You can check with Crowder.'

Marvik would. He hadn't spoken to him since asking him about Larroc. Perhaps Crowder hadn't yet got the information he'd requested. Or he was being delayed or urged to be silent.

'The Real IRA mounted bombing campaigns and shootings, primarily in Northern Ireland, but Sawes could have been active over here. There were attempted bombings, which were thwarted, and one in particular about the time Sawes was injured. There is considerable archived coverage of it on the internet. And yes, he's named as an innocent victim who happened to be walking past a derelict shop near an army recruitment office when a bomb exploded in October 2010.'

Marvik scoffed.

Strathen gave a twisted smile. 'I agree. It's much more likely that it went off too early after he'd planted it — I'd stake my reputation in intelligence on it. My theory is that Sawes was taken to Birmingham hospital, where Le Grewe operated on him. His medical records would confirm that.'

'Jarinder was still in the navy then.'

'Yes, but he could have been assigned to work at the Birmingham hospital with Le Grewe.'

Marvik was racing to pull the threads together. 'Jarinder went to see Sawes — why? The operation wasn't botched, was it? Did Jarinder feel he owed Sawes an apology? But that doesn't account for Jarinder being taken out and the smear campaign. And would Sawes still have had contacts who would be willing to take Jarinder out after thirteen years?'

'If Sawes could name some prominent people orchestrating terrorist campaigns back then, who are either still active or would have a lot to lose by that information becoming public, then yes. When you told Sawes that you believed Jarinder had been to see him, Sawes made a telephone call to the same person he did after Jarinder's visit.'

'Webb.'

'He might be the muscle rather than the brains behind this. The paymaster thought Sawes was a liability and had to be silenced.'

Marvik sat back. 'Jarinder wanted to expose Sawes as a former terrorist and a phoney.'

'Yes. And reading up on Le Grewe, I think we can put more meat on the bones of what happened. Le Grewe, being a plastic surgeon, recognized Sawes when he was taken into Birmingham. Le Grewe would have known that face and recognized his handiwork. But he was puzzled about Sawes' new ID. He'd been taken to the Hong Kong hospital under the name of Shoulter. Perhaps he tackled Sawes about it when he was recovering. Le Grewe wasn't stupid. On the contrary, he probably realized Sawes had set that bomb. Sawes would have denied it, of course, but Le Grewe could have requested the medical records from Hong Kong. They confirmed it was the same man and he threatened to go to the authorities with his information and his suspicions that Sawes had planted the Birmingham bomb.'

'Then his wife had an accident and Le Grewe took early retirement and moved to Ireland. Why there?' Marvik asked. 'Especially if the Real IRA were after him. I'd have thought that would be the last place he'd want to live, there or Northern Ireland.'

'Maybe his wife was Irish.'

'And maybe the hit-and-run wasn't an accident.' Marvik thought of Tarina's mugging. 'It was a warning for him to keep his mouth shut.'

'And he did. But Jarinder refused. When Tarina was attacked he wanted to ask for my help, but didn't make it.'

Marvik scratched his scar. 'Then why would Larroc hide out in Ireland? He'd have been an easy target there for Real IRA operatives and sympathizers.'

'And he was. The latter could be the Gilleys or the fishermen. Webb did the deed and buggered off. We might be able to trace his ferry crossing and border crossing, but I somehow doubt it. Or perhaps a local assassin was deployed. After I came sniffing around, the Gilleys — or one of the fishermen, Walsh perhaps — had to wait for instructions on what to do about me. Suicide was considered the best option, until the killer could take care of me, only he didn't, for reasons we've previously theorized. He was delayed, lazy or misled into thinking he could easily catch up with a man with a disability.'

'But what has Larroc got to do with Sawes, Le Grewe and the Real IRA?'

'I don't know.' Strathen rubbed his hands across his eyes.

Marvik exhaled. 'You need rest, Shaun. And so do I. We've got a little further forward.'

'It's not enough.'

'We'll get it. I'm going up to town tomorrow — today,' he corrected. 'To see Nishan. I'd like to know if he found a note of all this in his father's safe. And if so what he's going to do about it.'

'Nothing, if he has any sense. He'd be next in line to be taken out.'

'Surely he'd want to avenge his father.'

'Maybe he's not that emotionally strong. Perhaps he's too ambitious and doesn't want to rock the boat for himself.'

'I'll ask him. And I'll speak to Crowder tomorrow. He could get more for us on Sawes.'

That agreed, they retired for the night. Marvik could hear Strathen asleep in the adjoining bedroom, while his mind refused to shut down. Over and over it went, replaying the events that had occurred since that first phone call from Strathen seventeen days ago. It seemed like an age. It was too long, and the longer they took to get to the truth the harder it would be. The perpetrators would make sure they had covered their traces. He felt, as Strathen had voiced earlier, that they hadn't got very far with establishing the truth behind Jarinder and Larroc's deaths. And although this new information could be a breakthrough, it threw up more questions that they didn't have answers to. It could also be a blind to the real reason both men were murdered, though what that could be he simply didn't know. Someone did, though, and he was determined to find that person. The elusive Paul Webb. But he was clever. Then he and Strathen had to be even cleverer.

He turned over yet again, thudded his pillow and tried to engage his Marine sleep-training techniques. This time they failed him. He gave up just before five, showered, shaved and slipped out without waking Strathen. He caught the first train to Southampton from the small station of Hamble at 5.54 and the busy commuter train to London Waterloo at 6.30. He managed to grab some sleep on board, and after arriving at 7.47 stopped for breakfast in a café close to the station. Fortified, he walked to Battersea, to the address he had for Paul Webb.

It was as he had seen on the internet — a swish, exclusive apartment complex entered by a controlled gated entrance. He pressed the buzzer and said he had come to see Paul Webb. The disembodied voice bade him enter and the gate swung slowly and silently open. Marvik walked up the beautifully landscaped path with clipped yew hedges and a lawn so immaculate that it looked as though it had been cut with nail scissors. The tinted glass-fronted entrance was gleaming; not a smudge, fingerprint or remnant of last night's rain spoiled its surface. Somewhere there was a discreet camera system.

The door slid silently open and he stepped inside a grey-tiled lobby that smelled of wood, polish and money. In the far right-hand corner beside the lifts was a modern desk that resembled a sculpture by Henry Moore, and behind it a man in his early fifties with a military bearing, clean-shaven with bright hazel eyes, and whose maroon uniform was pressed to a knife edge with buttons so shiny Marvik could see his reflection in them.

'I'm trying to get in touch with a former Royal Marine commando colleague, Paul Webb,' Marvik said. 'And this is the address I have for him. I'm wondering if I've got the right place.' He stared around as though impressed and confused by the apparent wealth of the place, which wasn't entirely an act.

'You have the right address, sir, but Mr Webb is not here.'

'Do you know when he might be?'

'No. I'm happy to take a message for him, sir, if I see him.'

'If?' Marvik picked up.

The man gave a small twitch of his lips. 'Well, he's not here much. In fact, he's never here or hasn't been so far, sir.'

'No need to call me sir. I'm not in the Marines now, Sergeant.'

The concierge smiled. 'How did you guess?'

'I'd know that bearing and that look anywhere,' he joked. 'Army?'

'Yes. Came out after twenty-two years, that was three years ago. Been here a year since it was completed.'

'It's very exclusive. Must cost a fortune. I didn't know Paul had that much money. He must have come into a legacy or won the lottery.'

'If you say so,' he replied with that twinkle in his eyes.

'You don't believe that?'

'No.'

'I am trying to find out more about Paul Webb.'

'Who is not a friend or ex-colleague,' the concierge said knowingly. 'You in private security work?'

Marvik smiled.

'What is he? Drug dealer? Shady businessman?'

Marvik shrugged.

'Can't say, eh? Well, I can't help you because I've never seen him. And he's not the only one like that in this building. Half the apartments have been sold as *investments*.' He stressed the last word.

Marvik knew he meant money laundering, which could be Webb's act.

'Do you know when he bought it?'

'On completion, or possibly off-plan. His name was on my list when I started work here.'

'That's a long time not to have seen him. Could he have come in at night when you're off duty?'

'He could, I guess. But there's been no post or messages for him except for the motorbike.'

Marvik was all ears. 'A BMW?'

'Yes. It was delivered here. A BMW M 1000R. I was asked to sign for it.'

'By Webb?'

'Yes. He sent me an email and a text and said it would be delivered by Breckenridge of Park Lane. I was to sign for it and see that it was safely put in the underground car park, which I did. The next morning it was gone, so Mr Webb must have come here once in order to collect it.'

'It was him?'

'I didn't see who took it, but I got an email and a text from him to say he'd collected it.'

'That's odd behaviour.'

'Not for the seriously rich. They do things differently. You wouldn't believe the things I'm asked to do and arrange. Signing for a brand new motorbike seemed quite normal.'

Marvik didn't ask him what else he had been tasked with. 'When was the motorbike delivered?'

'Two months ago. Beginning of August.'

'Thanks.'

'For what?'

Marvik smiled.

Webb was shrewd and discreet. He was also seriously rich. Alternatively, Marvik thought as he made his way to Park Lane, Webb could be working for the intelligence services or some other undercover organization who was funding all this and had sent Webb to eliminate Jarinder, Larroc and Sawes.

He called Crowder on the street. 'Any news on Daniel Larroc?'

'He's not engaged by the intelligence services.'

'Are you sure?'

'I'm never sure. The autopsy confirms he was dead some days before Strathen's arrival. Killed by blunt-force trauma to the back of the head then bludgeoned a couple of times on the face.'

'Nasty.' Marvik reported on his visit to Sawes, and his real name, including the history Strathen had unearthed, along with their view that this could be linked to past terrorist activity that someone was keen to suppress.

'I'll leave you and Strathen to follow that up,' Crowder said. 'Any enquiries I make, discreet or otherwise, could jeopardize your operation.'

Marvik understood that. So he and Strathen were on their own on this, as they had been from the beginning.

He made his way to the motorbike dealers, hoping he might get a physical description of Webb, although he wasn't overly optimistic. If Webb had been at such pains not to show himself at the apartment, and to have someone sign for the bike and to collect it at night, then he'd hardly have walked into a showroom.

CHAPTER EIGHTEEN

'I'm working for a client who wishes to find a Paul Webb who recently purchased a BMW M 1000R from you,' Marvik said to the sales manager at the pristine, gleaming Breckenridge office some forty minutes later. The man wore an immaculate light-grey suit, as impressively pressed as the concierge's uniform. His dark eyes froze on Marvik's scars, then he quickly looked away as though embarrassed, focusing instead on his computer terminal, the sole item on his highly polished desk. 'I don't need any specific confidential information,' Marvik continued. 'I just need confirmation that he did purchase the bike and the method of the transaction. I already know how it was delivered.'

The manager looked uncertain. 'I'm not sure I can help you.'

'I understand,' Marvik replied pleasantly. Then, after a moment, 'My client would like to buy a BMW M 1000R motorbike, can you help me with that?'

'Yes, certainly.' The manager's expression brightened as he caught on.

'But he doesn't wish to have a test drive. He knows exactly what he wants and is very specific. In fact, he'd like to buy it without even coming into the showroom. Is that possible?'

'Oh yes. It happens more often than you would think. We've had a few of those transactions over recent years — we had one at the beginning of August.'

Webb's. 'So how does it work?'

The manager relaxed even further now he was on generic ground. 'A client emails or telephones us and requests a certain model. We supply it and deliver it to the address on the date and time specified by the client.'

'And the money is cleared through the bank before delivery.'

'Of course.'

'But it has to be signed for to ensure that delivery has gone to the right person.'

'Yes. It might be to the client himself — it has always to date been males. Or he might give specific instructions that it's delivered to a concierge. Sometimes it's a relative, perhaps for a birthday present. Other times it could be a housekeeper or butler.'

This was Park Lane, and their clientele was expected to be well-heeled.

'It might not be an address in London. It could be the Home Counties, the Cotswolds, Scotland even, if they have an estate there. And once we had to deliver it to a superyacht in Southampton.'

'And the paperwork? The logbook, for example.'

'We have the client's name and address. We fill in the necessary forms online, register the bike and tax it. It's all straightforward.'

'Sounds very efficient. Does anything ever go wrong?'

He looked a little hurt. 'Not to date.'

'You don't check out the ID of the person buying the bike, or where the money has come from?'

The sales manager squirmed and went a little pale. 'The bike could cost up to thirty thousand pounds, but that's not a lot of money in the scale of things. It's not in the same league as purchasing property or high-performance cars, or buying gold or diamonds, or art and artefacts.'

He'd got Marvik's drift — money laundering. Marvik rose, eliciting an expression of relief from the manager, who sprang up. 'I hope that answers some of your questions.'

'Yes, thank you.'

Oh, clever Webb, Marvik thought on his way to Nishan's chambers. This man probably had a few identities and spread his money around buying properties, and perhaps fast cars as well as motorbikes. And, as the sales manager had said, it could also include works of art from dubious sources, or diamonds or gold. If that were the case, then Webb was not from British Intelligence unless he led a double life.

The chambers clerk confirmed Nishan was at a trial at the Royal Courts of Justice in the King's Bench Division. The court would break for lunch, so from midday Marvik hung about inside the building. It was just after twelve thirty when Nishan emerged. Marvik quickly intercepted him. 'I need to talk to you in private.'

Nishan eyed Marvik with annoyance, then, glancing over his shoulder at his fellow barristers and a few people from the courts milling around, said tersely, 'I'm in the middle of a trial. I haven't got time. What is it about?'

'Hugh Sawes.'

His expression darkened. 'I'll meet you outside as soon as I've disrobed.'

Marvik stepped out of the impressive building, watching the growling traffic in the drizzling rain. He didn't have long to wait. He fell into step beside Nishan, who set off at a brisk pace as though the faster he walked the sooner he could rid himself of Marvik. They crossed the bustling Strand and turned into the quiet confines of Essex Street with its line of attractive listed houses, but Marvik wasn't here to view the scenery or take in the history of the area.

'Your father asked you what he should do about a man called Hugh Sawes,' Marvik began.

'How do you know about him?'

'Jarinder believed Sawes had been acting for the Real IRA when that bomb went off in Birmingham. He lost his leg and was treated by Alexander Le Grewe.'

'Did my father speak to you about this?' Nishan dashed him a look that was both apprehensive and hostile.

'He wanted to know if he could bring Sawes to court with the evidence he had and asked your advice. What did you tell him?'

'I can't see that this has any bearing on my father's accident.'

'You really believe it was an accident?'

'Yes.' But he wouldn't look at Marvik.

'What did you tell your father?' Marvik repeated.

'That he had no case to answer. He couldn't prove that Sawes was involved in planting that bomb or that he was—' He shut his mouth tight.

'Or that he was really Peter Shoulter.'

Nishan pulled up so sharply that a man behind him careered into him, and swore before marching on. 'How do you know that?'

'I also know that Sawes, as he became known, threatened Le Grewe that if he ever revealed his true identity he would regret it. His wife was involved in a hit-and-run and was left with life-changing injuries. It could have been coincidence or it could have been a warning. Le Grewe left his job to care for her, moved to Ireland and became a recluse. Your father was made of stronger stuff. He would not allow himself to be threatened into silence, but when your sister was attacked he knew the extent to which these people would go.'

They walked on. They had the street to themselves. 'I told my father that he would need evidence other than Le Grewe's diary and notes, which the defence would say were fiction, to bring a case to court with any possibility of winning.'

'Even though Le Grewe's wife had been injured?'

'An accident.'

'There seem to have been a few of them,' muttered Marvik grimly. 'Sawes would have to prove his identity.' Marvik wasn't ready to tell Nishan he was dead.

Nishan halted outside his chambers. 'Even if it was revealed he had a false identity, it doesn't prove he planted

162

that bomb, or that he was involved with its ignition, or the Real IRA, or any other terrorist organization.'

'Wouldn't his conviction for doing the same thing in Hong Kong acting for the Chinese Communist Party carry weight?'

'You seem to know a lot. How?'

'Maybe Jarinder told me.'

Nishan eyed him critically. 'I can't see how he did.'

'Then maybe you don't know everything about your father.'

'I'm sure I don't,' he replied somewhat acidly, leaving Marvik in no doubt that son and father had clashed as both Rohan and Tarina had intimated. 'I told my father that Sawes had already been tried for the Hong Kong bomb and served his sentence. That wouldn't be taken into account. The police would need to prove he planted the bomb in Birmingham and they would fail to do so. It was pointless to even think about it.'

'Even if he got a confession from Sawes?' Marvik could see by Nishan's expression that Jarinder had asked him the same thing.

'I doubt the Crown Prosecution Service would bother. No one else was injured aside from Sawes.'

'He got compensation. That's fraud.' Marvik didn't know that for a fact and Strathen hadn't found any evidence of it, but Marvik thought Sawes must have done to have bought that bungalow. He couldn't see how Sawes would have been paid by the Real IRA, or any terrorist organization, for failing. He could, however, have blackmailed the key person behind the failed bombing attempt, although Marvik thought Sawes would have been unlikely to have lived this long if that were the case. He wanted to test it out on Nishan. He didn't deny or confirm it.

'From what my father told me, Sawes is a sick, elderly man. By the time it came to court, if it ever did — which as I say is incredibly unlikely — then Sawes could very well be dead. I told my father to drop it.'

'Did he?'

'I have to go.' He turned to make into the building.

'You have your father's laptop.'

'Yes. And before you ask, there was nothing on it about Hugh Sawes or Alexander Le Grewe.'

Marvik wasn't so sure about that. 'Why were you at Devonport the day before your father was killed?'

'What has that got to do with you?' Nishan snarled.

'It's a simple question. I can't see why you're hostile about answering it.'

'I'm hostile about being questioned about my movements when it's none of your business.'

'Your father was there at the same time. Did you see him?'

'No.'

'Did you go there to meet with a man called Paul Webb who rides a powerful BMW motorbike?'

'Of course I didn't. I have no idea who you're talking about. But if you must know, I was there to see a represent-ative of the Ministry of Defence and a private engineering company relating to a negligence claim made by one of their employees. The claimant won a sizeable settlement from both, and I'm representing them to get that reduced because the claimant contributed to his own medical negligence. It's the trial I'm currently conducting and you can look it up on the King's Bench Division.'

The fact that Nishan was there at the same time as Webb was trying to foist something on Jarinder was a coincidence then. 'Did your father consult Rohan about Sawes?'

Nishan was looking increasingly angry. 'Rohan has no legal experience.'

'But he knows about Le Grewe's secret.'

'Yes.'

Then why didn't he recognize Sawes' name when Marvik had mentioned it at their meeting on your father's boat?

'And Tarina?'

'No.'

'Why not?'

'I am sole executor of my father's will and therefore Le Grewe's estate. I didn't and don't see any need to drag up the past.'

'You won't have to as they're all dead. Your father, Le Grewe and Sawes.'

It took Nishan a moment to register the third death. 'Then everything we've spoken of is academic,' he snapped. 'Sawes had nothing to do with my father's death. Nothing did. His car spun off the road, he was killed.'

'And the assault on your sister?'

'A random mugging.'

'Nothing was stolen.'

'Because the mugger didn't have time before he was scared off.'

Marvik held his gaze a moment longer before marching off. He headed down the steps under the ancient gateway at the southern end of the street, which once had screened it from Essex Wharf and its neighbouring wharfs beyond. Now he had two people who had known about Sawes — Nishan and Rohan. Which one of them had Sawes contacted after he had shown up at the bungalow? And which of them had killed him?

CHAPTER NINETEEN

The answer was neither, he told himself, staring across the river. He just couldn't see Nishan or Rohan as killers, not that it would have taken much to move the oxygen cylinder out of reach and take the feed from an elderly sick man's nose. Maybe they were both capable if it meant silencing Sawes, but then they had no reason to do so. Sawes wouldn't want his ID known and he had nothing to blackmail the Vaidyas over. Nor could either of them have summoned Webb to do the job, because the same logic applied. Sawes' death had to be accidental, or else connected with his past terrorist activities. Which brought Marvik's thoughts back to Ballycotton. He reached for his mobile and called Rohan. He wanted to know why he had remained silent over Sawes when he had mentioned the name.

'What do you want?' Rohan demanded with an edge of annoyance. Maybe Marvik had caught him at a bad time.

'I'll tell you that when we meet. I'm in London at Temple Place.'

There was a moment's silence. 'You've been speaking to Nishan?'

'Yes.'

'And he's told you a pack of lies about me, or rubbished me. Are you still pursuing your idea about my father's death?'

But before Marvik could reply, Rohan continued, 'I'll meet you at the Old Bell Tavern, Fleet Street, in twenty minutes.'

'OK.' It would only take him about twelve minutes to get there on foot. It must be close to where Rohan worked.

He set out, mulling over what Nishan had said. He envisaged Nishan arguing with his father, and Jarinder being disappointed in his son's stance, especially when it was his job to see justice done. But that was a narrow view and incorrect. Nishan's task wasn't justice; it was seeing if there was a case to answer and winning it on behalf of his client, guilty or not.

His phone rang. It was Amanda.

'I got your message. I assume you're in London.'

'I am.'

'No more has been mentioned about Jarinder's emails. It's gone very quiet on that score. Have you found out anything new?'

He was speaking on his usual mobile and what he said could be tapped at Amanda's end if it was being monitored. That was a possibility, given that she had been close to Jarinder and a former colleague, but he reckoned the paymaster couldn't go around tapping everyone who had worked with Jarinder. And it hardly mattered now. If it precipitated action against him, then so much the better. He'd be prepared for it. He told her that he'd found a message in Jarinder's logbook about his trip to Sawes at Salcombe, though he didn't mention it had been in code. There was no need to complicate matters.

'Jarinder inherited some documents from his friend and fellow surgeon Alexander Le Grewe about Sawes possibly being involved in terrorist activity in 2010,' Marvik said. 'Nishan says Jarinder discussed it with him and talked about taking his findings to the police but Nishan cautioned against it.'

'And you think those emails were planted on the system in case Jarinder did so. It wouldn't look good for him with the police, and could have been used as leverage to stop him from reporting it. But Jarinder wouldn't succumb to threats.'

'No, so Tarina was attacked.'

'Was she? Where? When?'

'In London just before Jarinder was killed.'

'Art, this is serious stuff, maybe you should go to the police.'

'I will when I get more information.'

'What about Sawes, what does he say about it?'

'Nothing. He's dead.'

There was a fraction of silence. 'Accident?'

'Possibly. He was in bad health. Amanda, can you get hold of the results of the post-mortem and his medical records?'

'Yes.'

'I'm on my way to meet Rohan in the Old Bell Tavern. I'd like to know why he lied to me when he said he didn't recognize the name Sawes.'

'There must be some straightforward explanation for all this. It seems to get more bizarre by the day.'

Marvik agreed. He rang off and some minutes later turned into a classic London pub with stained-glass windows, boasting the news that it served traditional pub food and real ales. Judging by the number of people inside, that was obviously an attraction. Rohan was at the bar with a well-built, fit man in an exquisitely tailored suit, and by their expressions and body language they weren't the best of buddies. Marvik wished he could lip-read, but he was well enough versed in human nature to know that the other man had the upper hand and was menacing in a slick, quiet way, while Rohan was attempting to placate him. His eyes caught Marvik and he quickly uttered something to the other man, who looked briefly in his direction, then dashed one more comment at Rohan before turning away. He brushed past Marvik with a stare that Marvik didn't much care for. He recognized a cruel man when he saw one behind the slickness and the suit.

Rohan was looking drawn, although well-groomed and fashionably and expensively dressed. By the dark circles under his eyes, it was clear he was still having trouble sleeping.

'A client whose investments are not performing as well as he'd expected,' he explained to Marvik.

Marvik thought it might be the other way around. Rohan's investments in whatever addiction had a hold on him were not going well, and it was payback time. Another explanation could be that Marvik had almost rubbed shoulders with motorbike man — Webb. The build and height seemed right and Webb wouldn't always be wearing motorcycle clothes.

'He looks familiar,' Marvik said, causing Rohan to look startled. 'Yes, I think he must have been the man on the motorbike at the cremation. I mentioned it to you on Saturday on your father's boat.'

'You're wrong. Jack Temperley wasn't there and he certainly doesn't ride a motorbike. He has a Ferrari.'

The Breckenridge sales manager's words occurred to Marvik regarding buying the motorbike for cash practically anonymously: *It's not in the same league as purchasing property or high-performance cars, or buying gold or diamonds, or art and artefacts.* But Ferraris were two a penny in the City.

'What does he do for a living?'

'Is that relevant? What did you want to talk about?' Rohan snapped.

Touchy. 'Can I buy you a drink?'

'OK. I'll have another of these.'

Marvik ordered a red wine for Rohan and a non-alcoholic beer for himself. A table in the far corner had become vacant. Marvik suggested they take it.

'What do you know about Hugh Sawes?' Marvik launched when they were seated.

Rohan looked puzzled. 'Nothing. Who is he?'

Marvik studied him carefully, looking for deception. 'Didn't your father tell you?'

'No. I've never heard of him. Hang on, though, didn't you mention him when we met on my father's boat?'

A quick cover-up. 'Yes. Your father paid Sawes a visit just before he died. Nishan hasn't spoken to you about him?'

'Nishan rarely speaks to me unless it's to preach and lecture.'

A lie? Or had Nishan lied? One of them had. 'But you know Alexander Le Grewe, and that he had a house in Cork and Ballycotton.'

'Of course.'

'Have you seen the papers Le Grewe left to your father?'

'No. Nishan takes his duties as executor very seriously and doesn't trust me,' he sneered.

'Why not?'

'He likes to feel important. He thinks he's the only one with a brain and business sense, though he has little of the latter.'

'Why don't you get on?'

'I think he's a prig and he thinks I'm reckless.'

'Are you?' Marvik sipped his beer.

'I told you before that I like to drink and womanize. But I can afford it.' His smile never reached his eyes. In them was fear.

'Did your father approve of your lifestyle?'

'What do you think? You knew him. Ever the hero,' he scoffed.

'You sound bitter.'

'That's because I am. I could never live up to his ideals. I tried by going to medical school but I was hopeless. Not like Tarina, who's a natural. Even Nishan managed to excel, but it wasn't for me. I was always a disappointment to him.'

'He told you that?'

'I could see it in his eyes and hear it in his voice.'

Marvik wondered if that were true. Perhaps Rohan saw and heard what he expected. Or he wanted someone to blame for things not turning out the way he had hoped.

'You seem to have done well, though, surely he was proud of you?'

Rohan swallowed some wine. 'If he was he never said. It wouldn't have hurt him. He was hardly ever around when we were young, he thought more of his career and his patients than us. He wasn't the sort to shower encouragement or emotions on us. Nishan is as cold as Father was. Whatever

Father said, Nishan would argue against as though he was in court. I couldn't stand listening to them. They didn't bicker, they debated, not good-naturedly either. Just coldly, neither giving way. It got on my nerves. I did my best not to be there when they were together, but the three-line whip meant I had to go to family celebrations.'

Yet Rohan had seemed genuinely upset when Marvik had seen him on his father's boat. Although he had admitted he wanted to get out of the house and away from Nishan and his wife.

'Well, you won't have to listen to them debating any-more,' Marvik said deliberately harshly, seeing what reaction he'd get.

'No, thank goodness, and I won't have to kowtow to Nishan and toe the family line. Once I get my inheritance, that's it. I'll cut off ties with most of them, except Tarina.'

Did he mean that or was it the drink talking? How many had he already had? His eyes seemed glazed, and his manner sulky now rather than hostile.

Marvik was about to speak when a figure loomed beside them.

'Rohan. And it's Marvik, isn't it?'

Marvik looked up to see Steven Lingfield beside them. 'Once seen, never forgotten,' he replied, rising and taking the outstretched hand.

Rohan seemed surprised. 'You know each other?'

Lingfield answered. 'We met outside the crematorium.'

Rohan must have seen them together, so why not say? Maybe because he was distracted by Webb, or Temperley, on that BMW motorbike?

'Any joy finding your friend?' Lingfield addressed Marvik.

'No. You had any with a memorial for Jarinder?'

'It's been hectic. I'll get on to it soon. Can I buy you both a drink?'

'Not for me,' Marvik answered, wondering what Lingfield was doing there and at such an opportune moment.

'Me neither. I've got to get back.' Rohan swallowed the remainder of his wine and rose. Marvik got the impression that he was keen to escape Lingfield.

'Any news on the deal with Ferrer?' Lingfield asked, stalling Rohan.

'I'm seeing him later tonight. I'll call you in the morning and set up another meeting before he goes to Germany.'

'Good.' Lingfield turned to Marvik. 'My medical laboratory is seeking investment to expand. George Ferrer is interested. Sorry to have interrupted you.' He made his way to the bar.

Outside, Marvik said, 'Did Lingfield know you'd be in the bar?'

'I go in there often.'

'But does he?'

'No. First time I've bumped into him there.'

Again Marvik wasn't sure he was getting the truth. 'I think your father was killed.'

'That's ridiculous. Who would want to do that?' Rohan blinked hard.

'Someone who didn't want him going to the authorities.'

'About what?'

'Sawes' history, perhaps.'

'Does he have one?'

Was it a good bluff? 'Oh yes. And if *you* don't know it then maybe you should talk to your brother.'

He stared at Rohan for a long moment before walking away. Rohan was in some kind of trouble, of that Marvik was certain.

He headed towards the South Bank, mulling over what he had learned from the meeting with him and Nishan. One of the brothers had lied about Sawes. Which one? Why? Why hadn't Rohan asked him more about Sawes? Was that because he already knew it from Nishan? Or from another source?

It was also clear that the brothers hated each other, and both had no real affection for their father. Their views shook

Marvik a little. He was seeing another side of Jarinder that he hadn't before. Nor, as far as he was aware, had Strathen. Marvik's views of Jarinder were that of a highly skilled surgeon, dedicated to his work, fearless under fire, cool and in control, perhaps too cool and too controlled where his family had been concerned. A man who didn't show affection to his children, at least not to his sons, whom he had pushed to achieve and who had disappointed him when neither had followed in his footsteps, although both were clearly successful. How had Jarinder been towards his only daughter? He didn't get the impression from her that he had been distant and cool. Maybe because she was female and had taken up medicine. He reached for his phone and called her, expecting to get her voicemail, but she answered.

'Are you free anytime soon?' he asked. 'I'm in London.'

'Have you some news about my father?'

'I've been speaking to Nishan and Rohan. And I'd like to see you,' he said evasively. That was the truth; his desire to talk to her wasn't purely to do with the investigation.

'I've got a twenty-minute break at three thirty, emergencies permitting. I can meet you at the Mary Seacole Memorial Statue. It's just behind the hospital in the St Thomas' Riverside Garden.'

'I know it.'

'Bear with me if I'm late, I might be with a patient. If I don't show, then you know I've been called away. I'll message or call you later.'

'Fine.'

CHAPTER TWENTY

He grabbed something to eat along the South Bank, then made his way to St Thomas' Riverside Garden. The weather had turned chilly. It had stopped raining some time ago but the air hung heavy and sultry with more to come. The river looked a sluggish grey, reflecting the sky. His mind felt the same. He ruminated on many of the elements of the situation, wondering how and where all the pieces fitted, *if* they did. Perhaps Amanda's report on Sawes' autopsy would throw up some answers, although he doubted it.

He stared across to the MI5 building. There could be files buried somewhere deep in there on Sawes and that failed Birmingham attack that could point to whoever was behind this. Then another thought struck him, one that he'd skirted over before but now examined in more detail. Had Jarinder been killed because of his knowledge of Sawes? Did the intelligence services want the whole sordid affair suppressed because it implicated someone high up in political circles or would expose a prominent person as a terrorist or agent, or perhaps a double agent? Le Grewe's wife could have been injured by that person or by someone acting for the intelligence services. And what of Le Grewe's death? Had it really been a brain haemorrhage?

Probably. He was looking for conspiracies everywhere. But perhaps Jarinder and Larroc could not be allowed to expose Sawes because of this person's prominence and the intelligence services' involvement. That was why Crowder couldn't get any assurances from them regarding Larroc. Larroc had discovered who was behind this and, realizing the danger he was in, had asked Jarinder for protection until they could both expose the truth. Jarinder had intended confiding in Strathen because of his background in intelligence.

Marvik's mind raced around these points, feeling that they went some way to explaining what had happened but got him no closer to who was behind it. Webb had covered his tracks so well that Marvik's suspicion that he was working for the intelligence services deepened. Crowder, as he had made clear, was leaving it to him and Strathen to get to the bottom of it.

He stared at the statue of Mary Seacole, a black woman who had overcome racial prejudice to forge a career nursing sick soldiers in the Crimean War, where she had visited the battlefields, sometimes under fire. Her military hospital near Balaclava had been much closer to the fighting than Florence Nightingale's. The name made him conjure up Amanda with a smile. No relation, she had once remarked, and Marvik suspected she had grown weary of repeating it to people over the years, given her chosen profession.

'Inspirational, isn't she?' Tarina suddenly appeared beside him. 'The first statue in the UK in honour of a named black woman. The funding of this came mainly through small donations after a twelve-year campaign.'

'I know. The armed services were one of those donors.' He indicated a seat that had become vacant in the garden. She looked strained.

'Do you know a contact or friend of Rohan's called Jack Temperley? He drives a Ferrari,' Marvik asked before he got into talking about Sawes.

'Yes. He and Rohan used to work together at FXL. They were good friends. He'd come to the apartment. Then

Jack got a job as an investment director with another wealth management company, one that specializes in the technology sector. He was headhunted to lead a new development fund in the healthcare tech sector. They seem to have fallen out recently. I haven't seen him for some months but I've heard Rohan on the phone to him and he's not chatty. Rohan usually shuts the door or walks away when he's speaking to Jack,' she said with a worried expression.

'Any idea why they fell out?'

'Sadly, yes. I think Jack loaned him money.'

It was as he suspected. 'Your brother gambles?'

'Yes. I've tried to encourage him to get help but he won't. I think that has more to do with Nishan nagging him about it. Red rag to a bull.'

'And when Rohan receives his inheritance, he'll be able to pay off his debts.'

She nodded.

Marvik wondered how much power Temperley had over Rohan. Also just how desperate Rohan was for money. Desperate enough to collude in his own father's death? Marvik noted the fact that Temperley specialized in the technology sector, where he'd certainly have access to experts.

'Do you remember I asked you about a man called Sawes, who I believe your father visited not long before his death?'

'I do.'

'Nishan says he found a reference to him in Alexander's papers and he told Rohan about him, but Rohan denies it. I wondered which of them was telling the truth.'

'They probably both are. Rohan will never agree with anything Nishan says and Nishan will always say things that will get Rohan into trouble or make you doubt his word. I just wish they'd get on but I gave up trying to appease them both and bring them together long ago.'

'How did they get on with your father?'

'Not well, I'm sad to say. It wasn't entirely their fault. Father needs to take the blame for some of it. He was rarely at home and when he was he was always distant both mentally and emotionally. Mother had to manage alone for a great deal of the time — the lot of a serviceman's wife. That and never knowing whether her husband would come home or, if he did, whether he'd be injured. You can understand that.'

Even though he had no wife, he could. He'd seen it with his colleagues. He'd had relationships that had suffered because of the danger of his occupation, as had Strathen, but there had been no complaints from either of them. Sadness, yes, when the relationships had ended, but both had been married to their jobs. Jarinder had, too but he'd had a family.

'Mother naturally favoured Nishan, being the eldest, and she turned to him when she needed advice, which inflated his ego and further shut Rohan out, making him resent Nishan even more. He didn't see why he should do as Nishan said.'

'And you?'

'Me being a girl, my mother didn't think my views counted, but she loved me. So too did Dad and both encouraged me to have a good career.'

'Was he pleased when you became a doctor?'

'Yes.'

'Did you become one to please him?'

'Originally, yes. But once I started my medical degree I found I loved it. I want to specialize in neurosurgery.' Her eyes flicked to his scar.

'I've had some of that, still get the headaches to prove it,' he said lightly. There was a moment's silence before he broached a subject he didn't want to but had little choice over. 'There's the possibility that what your father was concerned about was linked to a past terrorist act.'

She looked momentarily stunned. 'Do you think your friend discovered it and he's been . . . killed because of it?'

She was the only one of her family who had voiced that. Maybe because she was the only one who really cared. He didn't wish to lie to her, so said nothing.

'Art, you need to be careful.'

She was echoing Amanda's sentiments. But whereas with Amanda he had taken it lightly, with Tarina — looking at him with those deep, expressive eyes that sent the blood rushing through his veins — it was far more meaningful. He wanted to reach out and touch her hand.

'I will,' he said softly, then mentally pulled himself up and continued more briskly, 'I don't want to tell you anything more because the last thing I want is to put you in danger. I don't think the attack on you was random. It was a warning to your father to keep silent.'

'And he would have known that. Which explains why he was so angry and then so worried and overprotective when Nishan took me home, insisting I stayed in the house and didn't speak to or see anyone.'

'Tarina, can you give me George Ferrer's mobile? I'd like to talk to him about the assault, see if I can glean more from him about your attacker.'

'Of course.' She relayed it.

'I don't want anything more to happen to you, so please don't talk to anyone about what I've said. I'm not sure who can be trusted, so it's best to keep any concerns or fears to yourself, or better still talk to me.'

'I haven't got anyone else to talk to anyway since Daniel ditched me just under four weeks ago.'

Marvik did a mental pull-up. There were lots of Daniels in the UK but one blazed before his eyes. Daniel Larroc in Jarinder's letter. *I am in danger . . . It is my duty to tell . . . One man was on my side . . . See Daniel Larroc . . .*

'What's Daniel's surname?' he asked, trying to sound casual, but his expression didn't fool her.

'Corral, why?'

Wrong Daniel, or was it? He rapidly recalled what Strathen had said about that note — the words had tailed off, and it had been written with a fountain pen in Hindi. Had Strathen got the translation wrong? 'What happened?' he asked.

'I'm sure you don't wish to know that.'

'I do.'

'You think he's—'

'Tell me precisely what happened when he broke it off.'
He tried to keep the urgency and excitement from his voice
but knew she had detected it.

'He sent me a text saying he had to go away to think
things over, our relationship had got too serious for him. He
was sorry and he'd be in touch, but he hasn't been. I tried
calling him because it was so unlike him. Daniel was always
up front and honest about his feelings. I must have read him
wrong. Maybe being from different backgrounds began to
worry him. It didn't me or my father, although Nishan didn't
like it. Rohan's not at all bothered. He and Daniel got on
really well and Rohan's had lots of white girlfriends. Daniel
is ten years older than me — maybe he thought I was too
young for him. He didn't answer my calls. I left a message.
He didn't get back to me. I tried again but still no answer.
And he didn't reply to my texts or emails. I wasn't going
to grovel. I thought we had something good between us.
Obviously I was wrong.'

'How was he before that?'

'Quiet, preoccupied, as though he was building up to
telling me it was over.'

Marvik knew that not to be the case. He was betting
that Daniel Carrol was Jarinder's Daniel Larroc and he was
disturbed because he knew Tarina could be in danger and he
wanted to protect her.

'I thought the accident must have shaken him up more
than he'd let on, but he—'

'What accident?' Marvik asked sharply.

'The weekend before he broke it off.'

'That would have been the end of August?'

'Yes. He was cycling to the shops in Woking, where he
lives, when not far from his apartment a motorbike shot out
from nowhere and caused him to swerve in front of a car,
which miraculously managed to stop in time. He had some
cuts and bruises but thankfully nothing broken. He could
have been killed.'

And I bet Paul Webb hoped he would have been. That had been no accident. Daniel had seen the lengths these people would go to. He'd told Jarinder and left for Ireland.

'Did you mention this accident to anyone?'

'I told Rohan and my father. He was in London that week, attending a seminar, and stayed overnight with us.'

'When exactly was this?'

'The Wednesday before. Daniel sent me the text on Thursday.'

And the immediate Friday after this, Jarinder had sailed to Cork. 'Was the seminar held at St Thomas' Hospital?'

'Yes.' She looked bemused at his questions.

So Jarinder could have made arrangements with Daniel then. 'Going back to the attack on you, Tarina, did you tell anyone of your movements?'

'I mentioned to a couple of colleagues that I was going to have a drink with my brother. They'd asked me if I wanted to go for a pizza.'

Marvik couldn't see how they could be involved.

'I also told Nishan.'

'Why?'

'He said he'd been trying to reach Rohan, who wasn't answering his phone. He gave me a message to pass on to Rohan to tell him not to be so stupid and to answer his phone.'

'What was so urgent?'

'It was just some silly argument, probably over nothing. Neither of them would say. As it was, I never gave Rohan that message. Nishan showed up at the hospital. Rohan or George must have called him.'

Marvik shelved that for a moment and returned to his concerns over Daniel. He didn't have much more of Tarina's time before she was due back on duty. 'Tell me how you met Daniel.' He was convinced it was his body in that cottage. He could ask her if Daniel wore the crucifix with a small stone in it that Strathen had taken off the body, but that would require explaining.

'He's a clinical scientist at the hospital here,' she said.

'What does that mean?'

'His role is to ensure that bioinformatics data is analysed, interpreted and used efficiently, as well as looking into researching and developing new opportunities.'

'You've lost me. Bioinformatics?'

'The NHS captures masses of information both of a medical and personal nature and all this needs to be handled. Bioinformatics combines computing science, that's the study of computers and computational systems, with information science, the management of information in any form — for example, storing, retrieving, describing, organizing, representing or providing information to others, and also brings in biology and medicine. It's a very fast-growing area of research.'

Marvik thought of the black-hat hacker he and Strathen had previously discussed. Could it have been Daniel, and now that he had performed his role for the paymaster he'd been eliminated? But Jarinder had trusted him. Had he been duped by Daniel?

He also recalled what Strathen had said about the black-hat hacker who might never have made it to the top of a medical profession and had turned to cybercrime to get even. The two hadn't seemed compatible at the time to Marvik, but Strathen had scotched that by saying that both needed a brilliant analytical, diagnostic brain and a high intellect. Daniel could have been targeting others as well as Jarinder, blackmail over something. Maybe Daniel had planted those emails. Jarinder found out. He was furious. What's more, his daughter was in a relationship with the man who was threatening him. Jarinder took him to that cottage under some pretext and killed him. When that was known, Daniel's paymaster had ordered Webb to kill Jarinder. But that didn't square with the bicycle accident. Not unless Daniel had confessed all to Jarinder, maybe because of his love for Tarina, and was going to give evidence.

Marvik pressed on with his questions, hoping her pager didn't go. 'Does Daniel have a degree in medicine or a medical background?'

'He has a master's degree from Oxford in biomedical sciences. That focuses on how cells, organs and systems function in the human body. It's highly relevant to the understanding and treatment of human diseases. With his background and skills, Daniel's job is to analyse the data gathered and interpret it for certain departments in the hospital, and to explain what it means to colleagues and peers, and for patients. He also advises on data security, patient confidentiality, record sharing and access to records, as well as recommending further developments in telehealth and telemedicine.'

Daniel had access. He had the capability and the intelligence to get into the system. Did he do so willingly?

She looked sad. 'Daniel loves data, number crunching and looking at medical things from a techy point of view.'

And hacking into a system would be child's play to him. 'Have you tried to contact him at work?'

She stared steadily at him. He knew she'd been hurt. 'Once. I didn't want to be seen begging, or being needy, but thought I'd give it one more go, to try and get to the bottom of why he felt he had to call off our relationship. His boss told me that Daniel had sent her a message at the same time he sent me one—'

'Thursday the thirty-first of August.'

'Yes. He'd been called away on urgent family business. He didn't say what that was or where he was going. As far as I'm aware, he doesn't have any family except a distant cousin in Australia. He expected to be away for possibly a month and he'd let HR know. You think that was a lie, don't you?'

'Yes.'

'Do you think he's had a mental breakdown?'

I think he's dead. 'Do you have a key to Daniel's flat?'

'Yes. I haven't been there, of course. I'll give it back to him when I eventually see him.'

Not now, she wouldn't. 'Give it to me. I want to check it out.'

Her eyes searched his in horror. 'You don't think he's there ill or dead? My God, I never thought of that.' She rubbed her eyes. 'I'll never forgive myself if that's the case. I'll call the police. No, I'll come with you. But I can't, I'm on duty.'

'I'll go there and tell you what I find,' he hedged.

She handed over the key and gave him the address. 'You promise to call me?'

'Yes.'

'I—' Her bleeper sounded. 'All right. Thanks.'

There was no hurry to search Daniel's flat. There was nothing he could do for the man — he was in the mortuary at Cork.

But he did want to see where Tarina was attacked and if possible find out more about her assailant from Ferrer, and he knew he was in town because of the exchange between Rohan and Lingfield. He called him.

CHAPTER TWENTY-ONE

'I'm not sure I can tell you anything that I didn't tell the police,' came the guarded reply on the phone when Marvik reached Ferrer.

'Probably not, but I'm going to look over where it occurred anyway, and I wondered, if you were free, if you could meet me in Clink Passage. It might jog some memories over what happened.' Marvik had already explained that he was a friend of Jarinder's.

'I can't see what Tarina's mugging has to do with Jarinder — or you, come to that.'

Perhaps Ferrer was jealous. He thought Marvik was muscling in where he hoped to make progress now that her previous boyfriend was off the scene. 'I'll explain when I see you, but if you can't make it, that's—'

'I'll be there. When?'

'Say forty minutes?' It would take him about half an hour to walk it but he allowed the extra ten minutes to reconnoitre the locale before Ferrer showed.

He set out at a brisk pace. Clink Wharf was just over a mile away, situated between London Bridge and Southwark Bridge. It was a fashionable area, popular with both tourists and those living in the luxury apartments lining the Thames that had been warehouses when the Port of London had boasted cargo ships from every corner of the world. Now the area was crowded with glitzy apartments, glittering glass-fronted offices, hotels, eateries and museums. Across to the north, where more wharves had once stood, along with Old Swan Pier, Fishmongers' Hall and Billingsgate Market, there were yet further offices and luxury apartments. Rohan was obviously doing well, judging by his address. It seemed just as expensive as Webb's Battersea apartment.

He stood by the river and gazed around. To his left was a square that boasted a budget hotel and a motorcycle bay. Directly ahead of it leading into a cobbled thoroughfare was a sign indicating the direction of the shops, bistros and restaurants of Clink Wharf. He set off down it, dodging the walkers and a few pushing their bicycles. This was the direction Tarina would have taken.

According to the police notice on the website, she had been attacked during the lull between the after-work drinkers leaving for home and the night-time crowd emerging. Despite that there would have been plenty of people around, but no one except Ferrer had gone to answer Tarina's cries — and she must have screamed. Perhaps by now the police had some other witnesses who had come forward, although Tarina hadn't said. Nor had he asked her if she had heard anything more from the police.

It would have been growing dark by the time she had walked along here just before eight. Sunset had been at eight twenty. But there were ample street lights, as well as those from the eateries.

He turned into Clink Passage, noting the area with interest. There was nothing along here except fire exits of the apartments that faced onto the Thames and a large grille that gave onto the car park of the apartments above. The rest was solid brick walls. There were also only dim lights. Three bollards stretched across the entrance to the passage from the Thames end, prohibiting any car gaining access. He walked down it, and emerged on the pedestrian path that overlooked the river. After turning right and walking a short distance along it, he was back where he had started, in front of the hotel and motorcycle bay. Opposite him, straddling the corner, was the impressive entrance of the apartments where Rohan and Ferrer lived, and to the left of it a grille that indicated it was the car park for those flats. As he made to consult his watch, a tanned, fit man in his mid-thirties emerged, wearing trainers, Lycra gym shorts and a fitted T-shirt showing the contours of his muscles. He gazed around, scowling.

Marvik stepped forward. He didn't know for certain it was who he had arranged to meet but took a guess. 'George Ferrer?'

'Yes?'

'I'm Art Marvik.'

'Oh.' Ferrer stretched out his hand with an appraising look. Marvik wondered what he saw. He in turn assessed Ferrer. The clear toffee-coloured eyes were sharp and intelligent, the round face open and of a genial countenance. The short dark hair was damp with sweat, which emanated from his muscular body.

'Forgive my appearance, I got carried away in the gym, forgot the time.'

'I'm sorry to disturb you. And I won't keep you long. Can you tell me what happened on the night Tarina was attacked?'

'I'll show you where it happened.'

He struck out at a good pace. Marvik didn't enlighten him to the fact that he'd already been there.

'OK, so why the interest?' Ferrer demanded as they walked.

Marvik gave him the same story he had others. 'I'm probably wasting your time and my own, trying to make sense of Jarinder's accident and my friend's suicide, when there is no sense to it, but I feel I have to do something to discover what had been troubling Jarinder. There's the possibility that he told my friend what it was and it so distressed him, along with the accident, that he took his own life. They were very close.'

Ferrer listened attentively, his manner softening. 'As you are to your friend.'

'Yes, we were in the Royal Marines together.'

'And saw action.' He nodded at Marvik's face.

'Yes. My friend, Shaun Strathen, lost a leg in combat.'

'Shit. That must have been difficult to live with.'

'He coped, or at least I thought he was coping. Jarinder served alongside us when he was in the navy as surgeon commander.'

'He was a good man,' Ferrer said.

'You knew him?'

'Not closely, but I met him a few times, at Rohan's, when Jarinder was in town for a seminar or visiting one of the hospitals. We had some interesting conversations about the healthcare sector. He worked in it, I invest in it — drug manufacturers, digital health medical devices, diagnostics, care providers, health insurance companies. That's how I met Rohan, four years ago. He advises me on possible investments. The sector is forecast to enjoy strong growth over the next decade and beyond with ageing populations, rising incomes and higher expectations for quality of life, in both developed and emerging markets.'

Marvik could see his enthusiasm in his expression and hear it in his voice. They halted by the entrance to the passageway but didn't go down it. 'Have you always been involved in healthcare?' Marvik asked.

'One way or another. I started working behind the counter in a chemist as a sixteen-year-old failure and soon saw that automating their ordering and prescription delivery systems would give them an advantage. When they decided I was talking rot, I left and worked as a rep for a couple of pharmaceutical companies, made a lot of money and invested it, successfully. Found I had a talent for spotting opportunities in the healthcare sector. But you haven't come to hear my life story. I was walking along here on my way to Mario's, where we'd agreed to meet, when I heard a scream.'

He turned into the passage and halted a few paces down. He'd stopped at a small alcove, to the right of which was a solid, closed fire exit door.

'I had no idea it was Tarina. I just tore down here and saw the bastard leaning over a woman on the ground. I don't work out at the gym for nothing. I launched at him but he slipped my grasp and ran off, otherwise I'd have beaten the shit out of him. He might have been bigger than me, but I learned how to fight on the streets. I'd have chased after him but the woman was more important. Then I realized it was Tarina.'

'Can you describe him?'

'No, he had a motorcycle visor over his face.'

Webb.

'He was about my height though and bigger-built, I'd say, although it was difficult to tell as he was wearing motorcycle leathers and boots. I'd have caught up with him if I'd given chase. You can't run far or fast in those boots.'

'So his bike was probably parked in the bay by the hotel.'

'Yes. And there are cameras there and at the entrance to the apartments and our car park. The police must know this, but I don't know if they've examined them. They might have got the registration number of the bike, unless the bastard had muddied it to obscure it.'

'Don't you think it strange that he went to all that trouble to mug someone randomly?'

'I didn't think so at the time. I thought he must have been lying in wait at the entrance this end looking for a likely victim.'

'But far easier for him to wait on a public road on his bike, push a victim to the ground and snatch their phone, watch or bag and then roar off into the traffic. Instead he parked in a pedestrian-only area where there are lots of people about.' Marvik wondered if the police had considered this. But then they didn't know the background to the attack.

Ferrer ran his fingers through his hair. 'You're right. You think she was targeted. But why?' Then it hit him. 'Because of her father. Jarinder knew something, and, whatever it was, someone didn't want him blabbing. Rohan said his father was going around snapping at him and arguing with Nishan.

I took that as being normal family behaviour. It was in mine when my father was at home, which wasn't often, thank God. Long-distance lorry driver and the longer the distance, the better. Look, I'd offer to buy you a drink but I'm not really dressed for the bar. Have you seen what you need to?'

Marvik said he had. They walked towards the Thames. 'Are there any CCTV cameras?' Marvik couldn't see any.

'Not here. There are some on the approach road by the river. The police haven't come back to me to say they've picked up any men in motorcycle clothes, and I don't know if they've viewed the cameras by the motorcycle bay and hotel. But there would be no need for them to tell me if they had done. They might have told Tarina.'

They hadn't. 'The images could be too vague to get much from them.'

'Yes. And our concierge would have wiped any images by now, so would the hotel and restaurants on the approach road. If I hadn't arrived, what do you think he would have done?'

Marvik didn't like to think of it. 'Roughed her up a bit.'

'Bastard.' He scrutinized Marvik as though weighing up an investment. He must have passed muster because he continued. 'I wasn't sure what to make of you at first, which was why I was a bit on the cold side, but as you seem to be the only one interested, and on my wavelength, I'll tell you, Marvik. I haven't got a clue who the attacker was or why Tarina was attacked, but I agree it wasn't random. And I'll tell you why. I'd already considered your view that he'd have found a much easier target on a street corner. And despite not being able to see his face, I know he wasn't a yob or a druggie out to steal in order to fund a fix because his leathers were good quality, new, and I'd say cost a packet. If this guy didn't do it for money, then I thought it could have been sexual. Maybe he got his jollies from that kind of thing, but he'd have spent a hell of a lot of time taking his leathers off, and by then Tarina would have been up and running or someone else would have come along.'

They came out facing the Thames, which had grown even greyer in the misty drizzle. Ferrer didn't seem to notice the rain. He halted. 'And if it was a racist attack, then there would have been others who could have been targeted. The area is hardly lacking in ethnic minorities. That means he must have been lying in wait for Tarina at the entrance. He *knew* she would be there and when. The question is, who knew she would be? There's myself, Rohan and Steven Lingfield.'

'Lingfield?' Marvik said, surprised. Tarina hadn't mentioned he had been joining them for a drink. Nor had Rohan. Lingfield hadn't said anything about it, either, even when they'd first met at the crematorium.

'Yes. He runs a pathology testing laboratory. I'm considering investing in it.'

As Marvik had heard in the pub.

Ferrer said, 'We were having drinks before a meal to discuss the deal. I was late, thank goodness. Tarina was only joining us for the drinks.'

'Who suggested she did?'

Ferrer thought for a moment. 'Not sure. I didn't. Maybe Rohan. Tarina needed cheering up after that dopey boyfriend dropped her. More fool him. I didn't tell anyone Tarina would be there and I can't see why the others would have either. Nishan knew though. He came to the hospital where Tarina was taken after the attack and told her she had no one to blame but herself. Poor girl was in a state and all he could do was pour scorn over her and belittle her. It's a wonder Rohan didn't thump him. I felt like it.'

'What happened immediately after you found Tarina?'

'I called Rohan, who came running.'

'Did Lingfield?'

'No. I don't know where he went. Home, I suspect. Rohan took Tarina to A&E to be checked over even though she protested.'

'So who told Nishan?'

'Nishan called Tarina when she was in A&E, probably checking she wasn't out boozing. He disapproves of women drinking, especially his sister, but then Nishan disapproves of most things. She told him and he went haring over. He practically accused Rohan of causing the attack.'

'You don't like Nishan?'

'He's a snob and a prig. He disapproves of Tarina being a doctor, of having any sort of career except that of dutiful wife. He didn't like her relationship with Daniel, a white man and non-Hindu. He thought her place was in Plymouth looking after her father until he could arrange a suitable marriage. Thankfully, I don't have anything to do with Nishan. He's not my lawyer. Did you know he prosecuted Lingfield's company, Horizons? I can see that you didn't. I think that's why Rohan is even more determined to get funds for Lingfield to get back at his brother. And probably one of the reasons I'll provide it.' He grinned.

'What happened with Lingfield's company?'

'They were sued for medical negligence six years ago. They gave an incorrect result on a gastrointestinal pathology test that delayed cancer treatment for the patient. It was argued that if it had been correctly interpreted the patient wouldn't have had to go through the rounds of chemo and radiology. The patient won the case, and survived. Lingfield's company had to cough up a lot of money, and, although their insurance covered it, their reputation suffered. They lost some big contracts with the hospitals, both NHS and private, and have struggled ever since. Horizon's on the brink of collapse but I think they're a worthwhile investment.'

'Does that mean you'll be a majority shareholder?'

'That's still being negotiated. But with my capital they'll not only survive but will be able to expand into new fields, providing diagnostic services to the medical sector and to people direct. That's the biggest growth market as I see it — genetic testing and profiling.'

'Did Lingfield resent Nishan's involvement?'

'I doubt he liked it, but if it hadn't been Nishan it would have been another lawyer.'

'But with Steven Lingfield and Jarinder being old friends it must have made it awkward for Jarinder.'

'I think Jarinder did his best to dissuade Nishan from taking the case, but Nishan is ruthlessly ambitious.'

'Like you?'

Ferrer laughed. 'I deserved that. I don't mind Nishan making money or being smart — I admire that — but his tactics leave a lot to be desired.'

'What do you mean?'

'Lingfield was involved in a somewhat dubious activity when training to become a doctor. It was a long time ago and it never got to court but Nishan discovered it. I did wonder if Jarinder had told him, or he found out in some way from his father. It all came out during the negligence case. It shouldn't have done but Nishan has a way of getting these things in, or so I was told by Lingfield. I wasn't at court. He showed that Lingfield was a questionable medic and did a good job smearing his name.'

As someone intended doing with Jarinder. 'What kind of dubious activity?' Marvik asked, his mind working in overdrive as it reviewed several things he'd been told.

'He had an affair with a patient.'

'He wasn't struck off though.'

'No, he went into research instead.'

As Lingfield had told him at the crematorium, but not the real reason for his decision. But then they had only just met and Lingfield, not knowing Marvik, had no reason to divulge anything like that. Had he been bitter over it? Had Jarinder stood by him back then? Had they really been friends, as Lingfield had claimed? And was Lingfield behind the smear campaign to get revenge on Jarinder? If so, he'd taken a long time, even if he'd only made the decision after Nishan had won that court case six years ago. However, this smear campaign and murder would have taken some time to set up, and resentment can simmer for years before it erupts into hatred and revenge. Would Lingfield have killed Jarinder though? Or had he got Webb to do it? Perhaps he would have

192

done if Jarinder and Daniel had discovered something even more damaging to Lingfield.

Ferrer's phone rang. 'Got to take this. Good luck and let me know if you find out anything more.'

Marvik watched him stride off. He scouted the area a little longer before making his way to Waterloo station and the train for Woking.

CHAPTER TWENTY-TWO

It was a tall, futuristic apartment block, all glass and steel, looming over an aggregate yard and the main railway line half a mile from the station. It was handy for working in London but he wouldn't want to live there. For a brief moment, Marvik craved the solitude and peace of his cottage on the Isle of Wight. It seemed a long time since he'd been there. He'd chosen it to try to get himself together after leaving the Marines and his failed first job in private security. He'd also bought his boat not just as a means of getting around the coast but also for the solitude at sea it provided. He hadn't expected it to be useful in his role with Crowder's unit. And now that he was often engaged on a freelance basis for Crowder, did he still need to live in the cottage on the island? Should he try to integrate back into the human race?

He let himself in the main door with a wry smile. He was already integrating but he still didn't know what he really wanted. Time to navel-gaze later.

The place seemed deserted. He suspected most of the inhabitants were still at work or making their way home. The directional signs indicated a lift, but he took the stairs to the sixth-floor flat. There in the hush of the corridor, he

194

unlocked the door to Daniel's apartment and stepped into the small lobby.

The place had an empty, stale smell to it. He thought of that body in Ballycotton, if it was Daniel, and he was ninety-nine percent sure of that. If Daniel was the innocent party in all this, then he felt a wave of sorrow tinged with anger for him.

The lobby gave onto three doors to his left and one to his right. All were open. There was also a closed door, which he took to be a cupboard. Leaving that until last, he stepped into the room on his right and into an open-plan kitchen and living room giving onto a small balcony. Crossing to it, he could see but couldn't hear two trains on the railway below, one approaching the station, the other leaving. The triple glazing deadened all sound.

He turned to face the room. It was furnished in a contemporary, minimalistic style, and either Daniel had been an untidy person who never closed kitchen drawers and cupboard doors or he'd been in a hurry to leave, which was entirely possible if he'd feared for his life and was escaping a pursuer — Webb. Alternatively, the place had been searched.

He checked out the other rooms. One was Daniel's office with a desk and computer screen, and if Marvik wanted evidence that someone had been here and searched the place then he had it in the missing hard drive. Then he corrected himself. Daniel could have taken that.

In the bedroom, the chaos was more evident. Drawers gaped open, as did the wardrobe, and there were shirts, ties and suits flung on the unmade bed, along with some T-shirts and jeans. It had all the appearance of someone packing, or searching, in a hurry. He went through the pockets of a coat and two jackets. All were empty.

The bed was unmade and Daniel's toiletries and shaving gear were in the ensuite shower room. Would he have left them behind? Perhaps he had two sets. He glanced around and saw a crucifix on the wall above the bed. And in the bedside drawer he found a rosary, which he pocketed. That more or less clinched it for him, although he knew that many religious people had these in their homes.

Marvik returned to the hall, then entered the bathroom. The cupboards under the sink gaped open and bleach and toilet cleaner were haphazardly positioned inside. He didn't think Daniel had done that before leaving.

In the lobby, the large airing cupboard contained bed linen and towels, all tossed carelessly about on the shelves as though someone had searched between them. Shirts, pants and socks lay crumpled on the carpeted floor, beside them an upright vacuum cleaner and a pull-along suitcase. Daniel had probably tossed some things into a rucksack to take with him to Ireland and the killer had taken that.

He lifted out the vacuum cleaner. 'Well, well,' he muttered, reaching for the item hidden behind it in the dark recess. Even if the intruder had seen it, he might not have realized its significance. He carried it into Daniel's office, placed it on the desk and, lifting back the cover, found himself staring at a portable baby-blue Imperial 200 typewriter.

It looked to be in good working order, the ribbon new, and he confirmed this by running his finger over it. It came back blackened. Excitedly, he found paper in a drawer and rapidly typed out, *The quick brown fox jumped over the lazy dog*. The keyboard was responsive and the letters unbroken. The return worked smoothly. He withdrew the paper, folded it and put it in his rucksack.

Then he searched the desk drawers, but didn't find any paper. Perhaps Daniel hadn't kept any. Or Webb had taken it. He placed the portable typewriter in his rucksack. It fitted snugly. The wastepaper bin in the office was empty. He searched the others in the apartment but found only tissues and some discarded packets of food.

After taking one further swift look around the apartment and noting there was no landline and therefore no answerphone, he locked up and made his way to the railway station. He called Tarina on the way.

She answered promptly. 'What did you find?' she asked anxiously.

'Nothing.'

She gave a sigh of relief. 'Then he's not lying dead in his flat.'

No, but he is elsewhere. 'Daniel seems to have left in a hurry. Perhaps he was worried about the family crisis he told his boss he'd been summoned to.'

'Then why doesn't he answer his phone?'

'Because he doesn't wish to speak to you, Tarina. It would be too difficult for him,' Marvik lied.

'Huh. Then you try him.'

'I have. No answer, but then he wouldn't recognize my number, so there's no necessity for him to respond. And perhaps there's no signal where he is, or he's switched his phone off deliberately so as not to be disturbed. I'm sorry, Tarina, but there's nothing more I can do about Daniel.'

'I'm not sure I believe you.'

'You must . . . for now,' he added.

'I see,' she slowly answered. 'What will you do now, Art, regarding my father?'

'I don't think there is anything I can do. I just have to accept that Shaun took his own life and your father's death was an accident,' he lied again.

'I don't believe you,' she asserted.

'You must, Tarina,' he insisted. 'Please.'

Perhaps she picked up the intonation in his voice, or her instinct told her he was going to follow this through to the end and didn't wish to involve her, because she left a small silence. 'Keep in touch. I'd like to hear from you.'

He didn't need a second invitation for that.

* * *

It was after eleven thirty when he arrived in Strathen's apartment. 'Look what I found.' He placed the typewriter on Strathen's desk and told him all that had happened.

Strathen listened, a deep frown on his rugged face, nodding on occasion. 'Let's see if the envelope Jarinder used was typed on it.'

Marvik handed over the sample he'd taken at the flat. It didn't take long for Strathen to match it with the envelope, meaning that too had been typed on Daniel's machine. He retrieved the note written in fountain pen and scrutinized it for some minutes. Marvik looked over his shoulder. Finally Strathen said, 'The Hindi symbols for Daniel's surname aren't clear. But yes, I'd say I got the LA and CA wrong. It's Carrol, not Larroc. What an idiot,' he said, annoyed with himself.

'It's easy to misinterpret.' Marvik had given the matter considerable thought on the train to Southampton, and voiced his ideas. 'I toyed with the idea that Daniel could be our hacker — that he was working for the other side, then changed course after Webb almost took him out. He approached Jarinder when he was in town at a seminar at St Thomas' Hospital the Wednesday after the bicycle accident and admitted that he'd been paid to smear his name if he attempted to expose Sawes. After the bike accident, Daniel got very scared, not only for his own safety but also for Tarina's as his paymasters wouldn't be above harming her.'

'It's certainly possible. So Jarinder said he would get Daniel away to safety at Le Grewe's stone cottage. And it had to be that weekend because I'm assuming Jarinder wasn't on call and didn't have any operations or clinics arranged for the early part of the ensuing week, or he instructed Heather to cancel and rearrange his appointments.'

Marvik continued. 'After the seminar, Jarinder went to Daniel's flat. Daniel could have bought the typewriter that day, or maybe he had it anyway, not trusting any sensitive information to his hard drive. They agreed what to do. I'm only guessing but because the envelope was typed I think the original letter might have been too. Jarinder typed that envelope and a letter to you, as insurance in case anything happened to him. But he later destroyed the typed letter, worried it might be intercepted or found. He rewrote it in pen in Hindi, after the attack on Tarina, or when he returned from Ireland, in order to make it more difficult for someone to interpret. He stuffed it in the already typewritten and possibly stamped envelope.'

'He could have done so when he couldn't make contact with Daniel.' Strathen sat back, rubbing his chin. 'They'd agreed to keep in touch by phone. Daniel would have disabled the location setting on his phone and done the same with Jarinder's. The signal there though is non-existent. At first, receiving no reply to his calls, Jarinder thought that might be the reason for the lack of response. He only guessed what might have happened after Tarina was attacked. He called me and sent the letter in case he never made it.'

'And if Jarinder and Daniel's phones didn't give away their location, then someone knew Daniel was at that Ballycotton house, because he was killed very soon after Jarinder took him there, certainly the following week. Before Jarinder went to Falmouth and saw Lingfield.'

'Does that rule him out?'

'No. Jarinder could have phoned Lingfield, told him briefly his fears and that he'd got Daniel away to safety and asked to meet up that weekend, or Lingfield suggested it. Jarinder didn't realize that Lingfield harboured a grudge, possibly from their medical student days, exacerbated by the fact that Nishan won a court case against him six years ago.' Marvik told him what Ferrer had said. He could see Strathen considering this, but before he could comment Marvik pressed on. 'The alternatives are that someone read the letter Jarinder wrote to you, that person also went on board Jarinder's yacht and saw the chart plotted for Cork, and that person knew all about Le Grewe's cottage at Ballycotton, which means it could be Rohan.'

'Or he confided in someone else. Nishan?'

'I don't think so. Their relationship was and is strained.'

'Jarinder and Daniel could have been seen arriving by someone in Ballycotton,' Strathen considered. 'In particular, Tom Gilley and the fisherman, Walsh. If Jarinder had visited

Sawes before that sailing entry in his logbook and confronted him with what he knew, then Sawes could have tipped off his contact, who in turn alerted Gilley to be on the lookout and report back. This Gilley did, and an assassin was called in to deal with Daniel in Ireland, and Webb to deal with Jarinder over here.'

'But how does Daniel fit into that?' Marvik said, exasperated.

'Jarinder could have used Daniel to dig deep on Sawes. Once he learned from Le Grewe's diary that Sawes had threatened Le Grewe into keeping silent about his part in a terrorist campaign, Jarinder wanted more information on him. He was able to look up the medical records held by the Devon health authority but not the Birmingham hospital medical records. He knew Daniel's IT medical expertise and background through Tarina. He asked for Daniel's help. That triggered an alert somewhere down the line, or maybe I should say up the line.'

Marvik knew what Strathen was alluding to. It was the same thought that had occurred to him while staring across the Thames at the MI5 building. 'The intelligence services. They're protecting someone from back then, who could still be active now. A senior figure. Or an undercover operative? Webb could be working for the intelligence services.' Marvik rose and paced the operations room as he scrambled to think it through. 'Jarinder was tracked visiting Sawes and Sawes had to be silenced. I'm amazed I'm still walking around.'

'You might not be for long if they know you're close to the truth. Webb and his mates could still be working for an underground IRA cell or, as you say, for someone in the government or in another high-profile area. And Sawes knew exactly who that was. He was never investigated, even though someone must have been suspicious about that bomb. Le Grewe was warned off and Sawes ended up with a bungalow and a pension for life.'

Marvik silently digested this. 'He retired to Salcombe and kept his head down until Jarinder showed up with Le

Grewe's written testimony. So there are two factions who have an interest in this, and in keeping it quiet — on the one hand the intelligence services or anti-terrorism unit, and on the other the terrorists.'

'Alternatively, we could be seeing conspiracies and terrorism when this is about something completely different.'

'Such as?'

'Money.'

'How?'

'Perhaps one of the companies Rohan attracts investments to is non-existent.'

'Fraud.' Marvik frowned. 'Whatever the reason behind this, one or both of them, Jarinder and Daniel, were being watched and tailed. A tracking device on Jarinder's car would have shown that he drove to the marina, and there could have been another device on his boat. Daniel, too, could have been watched. He was seen leaving his flat and he was tailed on the train, or someone reported back that he was at Paddington. It wouldn't have taken much brain power to work out he was making for Plymouth.'

'Jarinder could have driven Daniel down on the Thursday after that seminar.'

'Of course. And even if Jarinder had decided to put in to Cork Marina and Daniel caught the bus or hiked to the cottage from there, the paymaster still might have known, or guessed, he was making for Le Grewe's cottage because of the paperwork Jarinder brought back after his death.'

'Does that bring us to Nishan?' Strathen said thoughtfully.

'Or to Rohan, if he lied about not being party to it. I'd say he's in debt up to his eyeballs — Tarina told me about his gambling habit. I think he owes money to a guy called Jack Temperley, who, according to Tarina, was a former work colleague and friend and now has a decidedly cool relationship with her brother. And I can back that up. Temperley and Rohan were having a set-to in the pub when I arrived. He drives a Ferrari.'

'Nice if you can afford it.'

'And he's an investment director in the healthcare technology sector. He might also be Webb, who has a luxury apartment that he's never stayed in and who bought a BMW motorbike online without making an appearance in the showroom.'

Strathen said, 'There is yet another way they could have tracked Daniel — someone read the letter Jarinder sent to me and that person posted it, not Jarinder.'

'If they did, then they'd have known where you were heading. You were lured there by the letter. But it was in Hindi—'

'Anyone could have scanned it into a computer translator, as I did.'

'Or they speak and write Hindi.' Marvik didn't need to spell out who that pointed to.

'Or the typewritten letter wasn't properly destroyed but thrown in the bin, or there was a carbon copy—'

'Which the killer found when he searched Daniel's flat. And Webb could have ransacked Jarinder's boat looking for a copy, or the original, which he might have secreted there.'

'And here's some more theories,' Strathen went on.

Marvik threw himself down on a chair, running his hand through his hair in exasperation.

'Let's say Daniel typed an account of what he'd been doing either for the paymaster or for Jarinder. Jarinder could have kept a copy in his safe, meaning Nishan is suppressing it because he doesn't want his family dragged into it.'

'But if it is to do with terrorism, whether that be the Real IRA or any other group, surely Nishan would have taken the report to the National Crime Agency. He or his firm of lawyers would have good contacts there. I just can't see him involved in terrorism. It doesn't fit.'

'Perhaps he believes it's safer to keep quiet. Nishan knows the attack on Tarina was used as a threat, and his father is dead. He doesn't want any more incidents and he certainly doesn't want to be knocked off himself.'

That made some sense.

'If Daniel had typed a report of what was going on, what would he have done with it?' posed Strathen.

'Given it to a lawyer for safe keeping, only to be released on his death or when Jarinder was able to expose the truth.' Marvik wiped a hand over his face. 'Maybe he gave it to Nishan's firm.'

'Or a lawyer in Woking.'

'Even if we phoned all the lawyers in Woking they wouldn't tell us if they had it, client confidentiality and all that.'

'They'd tell the police, if Crowder's officers asked. But as you said, Art, they're not going to . . . yet.'

Marvik knew he meant unless anything fatal happened to him or Shaun.

Strathen picked up Jarinder's logbook. 'There was no code in Hindi under the Falmouth entry. Why draw attention to the Sawes one?'

Marvik shrugged. 'Because he wanted Sawes exposed? But if so, then where does Lingfield fit in, save that Jarinder could have confided in him? But if he's honest he'd have gone to the police, which means he's too scared to or he's being paid not to. Why did he show up at the crematorium, the only one to do so aside from me and Webb? And then he's in London when Tarina is attacked, having a meal with Rohan and Ferrer to discuss funding, which according to Ferrer he badly needs or his company could go down the pan. I think it's time I had a little chat with Lingfield.' He rose and stretched. 'I'll call him tomorrow morning.'

CHAPTER TWENTY-THREE

Wednesday

After a restless night, Marvik learned that Lingfield was on his way to Plymouth for a meeting the following day, Thursday, and wouldn't be back in London until Monday. Marvik left his name and a message saying he needed to talk to him urgently about Jarinder Vaidya. He wondered if Lingfield would think it was in connection with a memorial. Maybe he'd ignore the message. He rang Rohan.

'What now?' Rohan answered wearily.

He could have ignored the call, thought Marvik, if he was that sick of him. But Rohan was clearly too curious to learn how far he'd got with his enquiries and if he'd discovered anything incriminating. 'I'd like Steven Lingfield's mobile number.'

'Why?'

Marvik heard the wariness in his voice.

'I'm thinking of investing in his company. George Ferrer said they're a good prospect.'

'Then you can talk to me,' he snapped. It was obvious from his tone that he didn't believe him. He was right, Marvik was kidding.

'If you don't want to give it to me then I'll ask Ferrer for it. Or maybe Nishan can give it to me. He'll have it on file, having been successful in prosecuting Lingfield's company.'

'If it's about my father, why can't you just let it go? It's nothing to do with you.'

'You're not going to give me his number?'

'No.'

'Then tell him I need to speak to him urgently. I think he can help fill in some of the remaining gaps.'

'There aren't any gaps.'

'There are.'

'You're bullshitting.'

'Am I?' Marvik rang off. 'That should stir things up,' he said to Strathen. 'I'm heading back to the West Country on my boat.'

'It could be a wasted journey. By the time you get there, he could have got the message and returned to London.'

'He won't. I've got a feeling Lingfield will ring me quite soon.'

Marvik refuelled his boat and took on board some extra fuel in his containers and some basic food supplies. According to the weather forecast a storm was blowing in later that day. He hoped to make good time before it blew in from the south-west.

Lingfield returned his call later than Marvik had expected. He had just cleared the Royal Island of Portland in Dorset.

'I hear you've been trying to get hold of me. My office called me.'

Not Rohan then. Or he had and Lingfield was lying.

'I need to talk to you about Jarinder. I believe I know what was troubling him before his death. It wasn't an accident.'

There was a short pause. 'You mean he was killed, deliberately.'

'Yes. I can't talk over the phone. A member of your staff said you had a meeting in Plymouth tomorrow and would stay down in the West Country until Sunday night. I'm heading for Plymouth on my boat — I could meet you there tomorrow.'

There was a moment's silence. Marvik wondered if Lingfield would say he'd return to London and meet him there, but he was banking on Lingfield wanting somewhere private with few people milling around. And he wouldn't want to risk being seen with him at his London apartment if he had something to hide.

'It's an all-day session and I'm dining out. Put in to Falmouth. I'll meet you on board tomorrow evening at eight.'

Marvik agreed. He gave Lingfield the name of his boat.

'Text me if you can't make it,' Lingfield added, before ringing off. That confirmed to Marvik that Lingfield knew something about this affair. Perhaps it was only to tell him that he and Jarinder had clashed over Nishan's handling of the negligence case, but he doubted it.

It was good to be back on his own boat even though the sea state was getting choppier and the wind was gathering speed. It was as well that he wasn't seeing Lingfield that night. He soon realized he wouldn't make Falmouth, let alone Plymouth. He only hoped he could tomorrow. The forecast was highly dubious.

Strathen called just as he was about to put in to Brixham Harbour. 'You're not going to like this, Art.' His voice was solemn.

Marvik's heart skipped several beats. 'Not Tarina? Not again?' he asked anxiously.

'No. A car's been found in a ditch on a narrow road just off the A379. A Skoda.'

Marvik let out a long sigh. 'Alive?' he asked, already knowing the answer.

'No.'

* * *

His heart was heavy. Despite their manipulative wickedness and complete indifference to the sufferings of Jarinder's family and his colleagues, he would never have wished Dawn Snell and Lee Barker serious harm or death. OK, so he had used strong-arm tactics on Lee and hurt him, but nothing that couldn't be mended. They hadn't asked to get involved in this murderous scheme but they hadn't refused either. And they'd paid the price.

He'd warned them. They had got out after that quickly enough, but that damp washing in the machine made him wonder if they'd had a visitor who had forced them to leave precipitately or had received a warning somehow, not by mobile or laptop, though, because he had taken them. Webb would never have shown himself in the neighbourhood, where he could possibly have been identified, not unless he was growing careless or didn't think it mattered anymore. Or had the warning come through the post or a note dropped into the letterbox? Or did they have another phone or device stashed away somewhere? Maybe it would be discovered on their bodies. Alternatively, and Marvik thought this more likely, Dawn had messaged Webb using a public computer. She'd had another way of getting in touch with him she hadn't revealed and it had cost her her life.

That left only him for Webb to dispose of, then he quickly amended that with alarm. There was Tarina and Amanda, if Webb or his paymaster thought he had confided in them. There was the chance he was walking into a trap laid by Lingfield, but he thought it an outside one because Lingfield would want to know how much he'd discovered first, and just how close to the truth he was. He needed to convince him that Tarina and Amanda knew nothing.

Again Marvik speculated if Lingfield was the main man behind this, but he couldn't see Lingfield being involved with terrorism. Strathen was of the same opinion. He'd been pre-occupied before Marvik had left. He'd said something was nagging at him and it was so obvious he couldn't think what it was. Marvik had smiled at the contradiction, but understood what he meant. There was something staring them in the face but they couldn't see it. Maybe that was because they were so focused on Sawes.

If Lingfield were involved, and his motive wasn't vengeance, then, as Strathen had said, it had to be money. He recalled their meetings — there had only been two, and yet from both Marvik had got the impression of a confident, controlled, clever man.

As the wind howled around the boat, rocking it even in the harbour, Marvik ran over what Strathen had told him about Lingfield. His company was making a loss, as Ferrer had said, but personally he didn't seem to be doing too badly. He owned an apartment in a select and expensive area of London, and the house in Falmouth, which was also in a desirable location. Strathen had found nothing relating to professional misconduct. It was either too long ago, buried deeply, or had been dropped. Nishan had discovered it though. That indicated to Marvik that Jarinder at some stage must have told his son about it. He had won a record amount of compensation in the medical negligence case against Lingfield's company. Jarinder must have been embarrassed on seeing Lingfield after the verdict, if he had. Marvik only had Lingfield's word for that and that they had been good friends. They could have hated each other, and not spoken for years. As Marvik had said to Strathen, he'd taken Lingfield's version of their friendship on trust, and that they had met up the weekend Jarinder sailed to Falmouth. The logbook made no mention of that.

He called Amanda.

'My God, Art, are you in the middle of a hurricane?'

'Feels like it.'

'Where are you? Florida?'

'No, Brixham. I'm on my way to Falmouth.'

'Why there?'

'I'm meeting someone who could help me, but it's best you don't know about it.'

'You think I'm in danger?'

'Dawn, aka Debbie, and her boyfriend Lee are dead. A car accident.'

'Shit! Like Jarinder?'

'Yes.'

'I told you before, Art, and I'll say it again, you should take all this to the police.'

'Not yet.'

'But you will. When?'

'When the final pieces of this horrendous puzzle are completed.'

'What did you say? This connection is appalling. I can hardly hear you. The situation on the explicit emails from Jarinder has gone quiet. There's nothing more on that. The autopsy on Sawes is tomorrow.'

'I don't think I need the results of that now, or any information on him. I can rule him out.' He didn't want her involved any further.

'How? OK, so it's best I don't know. Look, I'll go before the connection does. Call me when you can and let me know how your meeting goes. To hell with it, I want to know. Jarinder was my colleague and my mentor.'

The line went dead.

* * *

Marvik wasn't able to leave Brixham until late the next afternoon. And he couldn't get a connection to Strathen until the wind had subsided and he was almost approaching Falmouth.

'Jack Temperley is, as Tarina said, an investment director. He's with Hambleleigh Wealth Management. A qualified accountant, he used to work for a top accountancy firm on mergers and acquisitions before joining FXL, where he rapidly made a name for himself, according to his profile on the internet. He was poached by Hambleleigh to spearhead their expansion into the IT healthcare sector with a specialism in cybersecurity and artificial intelligence. He has an apartment in Chelsea and a yacht in Brighton Marina. He would certainly have the contacts to be involved in this, which could also have provided him with a dual identity — or come to that, multiple identities.'

'Wouldn't he earn enough money legitimately?'

'Depends on how much is enough. He might also gamble like Rohan. He might be diverting part of the funds raised from private investors into his own pocket instead of his clients.'

Be that as it may, Marvik didn't believe it was enough to have warranted Jarinder and Daniel's involvement and subsequent murders. Not unless . . . Not unless it was connected with a healthcare company, and one that both Jarinder and Daniel knew.

It was sunset by the time he moored up on the visitors' pontoon at Falmouth. He paid his dues and settled down to wait for Lingfield. Eight o'clock came and went. So too did nine, ten and eleven. Marvik called Strathen.

'Lingfield hasn't shown.'

'Done a runner or . . . ?'

'We got this wrong. Have you got his address?'

Strathen gave it to him. He didn't need to tell Marvik this could be the real trap. Marvik quickly looked up the directions. It would take him forty minutes to walk there, quicker if he jogged. He made it in thirty.

The house was set back off the road above Gyllyngvase Beach. It was in darkness and a BMW was parked on the driveway — not a bike, a car. With his senses on full alert, Marvik retrieved the larger of his two torches from his rucksack. He was glad the house had no automatic security lights and was shielded from the road and from the only neighbouring property on the right by thickly leaved trees. He ran his torch beam over the front door, then, taking the side entrance, crept round to the rear. There were no lights here either.

The rear door leading into a kitchen was ajar. Not a good sign. With his heart thumping, his body tensed for an attack — Webb could be waiting — stealthily he stepped inside, his ears straining for any sound and his nose for any scent of Webb's aftershave. There was nothing, but he didn't let down his guard. The same feeling he'd had in the cottage above Ballycotton returned with a vengeance. It was one he'd experienced many times before. All his instincts screamed that he was about to face death. Not his.

He found Lingfield on his stomach on the sitting room floor, the back of his skull a bloody mess and blood spatter all around. His left arm was crooked into his side, while the right arm was outstretched, fingers clenched. He had on a waterproof jacket, which indicated that he had been about to make their rendezvous when he was killed.

Marvik took a deep breath, still fully alert to the possibility that the killer might be lying in wait for him in the house. He stood stock-still for some time. Only the sound of wind rustling through the trees greeted him. He felt for a pulse in the neck, knowing he wouldn't find one. Then, straightening up, he swept the room with his torch before speedily searching the rest of the house, arranged over two floors, while listening for the sound of a car, which could be police, or a motorbike, which could be Webb. Nothing had been disturbed. There was no sign of a computer.

Returning to the body, he gently eased it over. Lingfield's face was contorted, his eyes closed. Marvik swiftly searched the pockets. His wallet and keys were there but no mobile phone. Webb had taken that, as well as any computer Lingfield might have owned. The man's death indicated that either he was involved in this or he knew something about it. He'd become a liability.

Marvik made to go, then turned back. He lifted the outstretched arm, noting that rigor hadn't reached that far although it was present in the neck. That put the time of death about two to four hours ago, between seven and nine. That, and the fact that Lingfield was dead, indicated that he had told someone about their rendezvous, or his phone had been hacked into. If the killer had picked up news of their prearranged meeting shortly after Lingfield had called

Marvik, that would have given him plenty of time to orchestrate this. He could have come from miles away, London even, very quickly on a powerful motorbike.

His torchlight swept the floor and with a quickening heart he picked out traces of blood away from the body, which lay close to a low coffee table. On the table were a newspaper, a book and a notepad, open, with a small piece torn off the bottom. The pen was under the table. Lingfield's body to the right. His heart raced. Lingfield had not died instantly. He'd crawled along the floor after Webb had left.

Marvik knelt down and prised open the fingers. In them was a small scrap of torn paper and one word scrawled on it that he couldn't make sense of. He pushed it in his pocket and stuffed the notepad in his rucksack. After taking one further quick look around the sitting room, he left the way he'd entered. He was surprised Webb hadn't waited to dispose of him, but two bodies in the house might not be part of the paymaster's plan, or Webb's if he was the boss.

He rapidly made his way to the boat, continually checking he wasn't being followed. On reaching it, he scanned it for any tracking or explosive device. He'd given Lingfield the name of his boat. There was nothing, and no one, lurking, or any sound of a motorbike.

He cast off, and in the blustery dark night made his way out of Falmouth Harbour. His head ached with thinking and with Lingfield's death. He felt badly about leaving him there but he had no choice. Three deaths and for what, he thought for the hundredth time that evening, as he turned into St Austell Bay. There he moored up for the night and, before ringing Strathen, examined the paper he'd got off Lingfield's body. There was only one word written on it. It was almost illegible, the scrawling of a dying, desperate man, but Marvik thought he could make out the word *Ultranon*. It rang a bell. He'd seen it somewhere before or heard it spoken, perhaps both.

He poured a large glass of water and swallowed it in one go. His head was thudding and his scar itched like mad. He reached for some painkillers and his hand froze. Pills. Now he remembered. It was at the recovery centre. Yes, he was certain of it, but in what context?

He swallowed some tablets and sat staring at the scrawled paper on the table in front of him. Mentally he ran through the first meeting with Elaine in the café. He was certain she hadn't mentioned the word. He'd then spoken to the receptionist, trying to identify the man Elaine had seen talking to Jarinder in the garden. He'd wondered if he'd been handing Jarinder some medical supplies. The receptionist had summoned the medicines management nurse, Roy Searle, who had checked the order. Marvik had looked over Searle's shoulder at the list of medicines on the laptop with delivery dates beside them, noted as received, checked and signed in by Searle. A couple had an annotation beside them of being out of stock.

Marvik sat up with a cry. He reached for his mission mobile and rang Strathen, who by now must have been on the verge of calling the cavalry. It was long after midnight.

'I ran into some trouble,' Marvik said.

'Webb?'

'No, he got there before me.'

Strathen quickly caught on. 'Lingfield's dead.'

'Yes. Either he told the paymaster he was meeting me or his phone is bugged — it's missing, by the way, and no computer in his house. Rohan and an employee of Lingfield's knew I was trying to get hold of him, but they didn't know what we'd arranged. Lingfield's obviously involved in this; whether Jarinder confided in him or not is another matter. Lingfield conveniently lived long enough, and was desperate enough, to leave us one lead, a word scrawled on a piece of paper I found in his hand. Ultranon. It's a medical supply, a drug or dressing — I saw it on the list of drugs at the recovery centre. It wasn't delivered because it was marked as unavailable.'

'Is it relevant?'

'I'd have thought so. A dying man doesn't go to that much trouble otherwise.'

'No.' Strathen sounded thoughtful. 'Perhaps Lingfield's company is connected with them.'

'I'm going back to the recovery centre tomorrow — correction, later this morning — to see what I can find out about it.'

'I'll do the same my end. Hold on. I've just searched the internet. It's a wound-healing drug manufactured by a company called Cortex based . . . guess where?'

'Cork.'

'Got it in one. I'll dig deeper. Are you going to update Crowder?'

'I think I'd better.'

This he did after he'd moored up once again at Mayflower Marina in Plymouth. Crowder listened silently and no doubt intently. Marvik could visualize his round, weatherworn face with its deep, solemn brown eyes. Marvik knew nothing about Crowder's background; neither did Strathen. They'd never delved into it. There was no need to. They knew they could trust Crowder, a man in his early fifties, fit, intelligent, determined, who could handle a boat and had an inner strength that showed in his calm, unperturbed manner.

'You're making progress,' he eventually said, almost as though Marvik was a pupil, he thought with a small smile. It was Crowder's way of paying a compliment, of saying 'Good work'. 'I'll be ready when you need me.'

Marvik rang off, wondering if he knew more about this than he was letting on.

CHAPTER TWENTY-FOUR

Friday

After sustaining himself with a cooked breakfast and drinking three mugs of coffee in an attempt to get rid of his muggy head, Marvik made for the recovery centre, where he was pleased to find Searle on duty. He didn't need to remind the medicines nurse who he was; his scars made him memorable. 'I'd like to know about Ultranon. I understand it's a wound-healing drug.'

'Yes, manufactured by Cortex. It's a potassium-based drug used for those who have amputations, not only service personnel injured in conflict and those in traffic incidents, but those with diabetic foot, which accounts for the majority of amputations. I worked in the hospital before here and the healing process of a surgical wound resulting from amputation in the diabetic foot is complex. Healing is mainly hindered by infection and vascular disease. Ultranon can speed up the healing process. That and the company's sprays and dressings are all highly thought of. Testing shows remarkable results and, while other companies supply them, Cortex's are the best, but we can never get hold of them.'

'How long have Ultranon and the other products been available?'

He tapped into his laptop. 'Five years.'

When Temperley left FXL Wealth Management, Rohan's company. 'Have you ever used their products?' he asked.

'Not personally. As I say, they're difficult to get hold of. They've been approved and are on the online pharmacy catalogue.'

'And they're a reputable pharmaceutical company?'

'Yes. They wouldn't have got through the tendering and contract award process if they weren't. Why do you ask?' he said, puzzled.

As casually as he could, Marvik said, 'The name Ultranon came up in conversation with someone when I was talking about Jarinder Vaidya, and I was curious.'

'He would certainly have prescribed it.'

'Is it complicated to get a licensed drug accepted?'

'This is the NHS we're talking about.'

Marvik returned his smile.

Searle continued. 'In brief, pharmaceutical companies submit their new drugs or dressings to the Commercial Medicines Unit in each regional health authority. Once it's approved by the CMU, the contract is handed over to the regional purchasing group to monitor its use, cost, effectiveness and compliance. The contracts with the drug companies are usually awarded for a set period of time, maybe two or five years, possibly more, but can obviously be renewed if they're still proving to be value for money and effective. New drugs, of course, come onto the market that prove better or more cost-effective. Research, as you know, is ongoing.' His bleeper went. 'Sorry, I have to go. I hope that's been of help, although I can't see how.'

'It's been great, thanks. Just one quick question: can anyone view the contract details?'

'Only authorized NHS pharmacy staff on the CMU web catalogue.'

Marvik left, deep in thought. Back on his boat, he called Strathen and told him what he'd discovered. 'My gut, and Lingfield's murder, tell me there's something wrong about Ultranon and Cortex's other products. They're listed but never seem to be supplied, according to Searle, and he's worked for the hospital as well as the recovery centre. Maybe he's wrong and it's just locally they can't get hold of the products.'

'You really believe that?'

'No. But if the company aren't supplying them, they can't be paid — unless it's fraud.' Marvik went up on deck and surveyed the marina in the bright, blustery day, hoping the wind would blow away his foggy head, which seemed determined not to shift. 'But how on earth could that be, and how could they have got through the tendering process, and all the checks and regular monitoring?'

'The days when you met the buyers face to face over several boozy dinners or lunches are gone, Art. You don't take them on an all-expenses paid so-called conference, which is really a luxury holiday on some Caribbean island, or slip them a brown envelope with a wodge of money and ask them to get you on the suppliers list.'

Marvik knew where this was going. 'Not much glamour to be got sitting in front of a computer in Barrow-in-Furness.'

'I've heard it's a very nice place. Not much chance of a suntan though.'

Marvik smiled. 'It's done by computer, remotely.'

'What isn't these days? And they call it progress. Yes, most of it is. And if the data says what you want it to say, then everything gets a nice fat tick by it and nobody asks questions because they're all too overworked, underpaid, short-staffed and running around looking for the cure to the healthcare crisis. But to be successful at this kind of fraud takes inside knowledge, someone who knows the purchasing system inside out. He or she might still work for the authority.'

'Lingfield would have known the process. His company are contracted by various health authorities.'

'Yes. And perhaps that's the reason for his involvement, and his murder and expensive properties. As you were getting close, or maybe because of Jarinder's death, he developed a conscience and was about to tell you of it. Aside from inside knowledge about the system, it also requires a highly capable IT professional, a hacker, to set it up and to keep it running without getting caught, and I don't think that was Lingfield.'

'It could be someone Temperley knows. He acts for clients in the cybersecurity sector as well as those in healthcare.'

'Yes, and it would also take a competent and curious IT professional to spot the fraud.'

'Daniel Carrol.'

'Sounds like it to me.'

'Could Cortex supply the London health trust?'

'They might. Or perhaps Jarinder got curious as to why Ultranon never seemed to be available and yet the company were still on that catalogue. Perhaps he discussed it with Daniel, who smelled a rat and got digging. Jarinder could also have mentioned it to Lingfield, who passed on that conversation to the people behind the fraud. Cortex, on the surface, look legit. Their registered address is on a business park not far from Cork Marina. But if we were to knock on their door, I doubt anyone would answer it.'

'Jarinder could have done.'

'I expect he did. Le Grewe too. Only he was discouraged from pursuing his curiosity.'

'Not because he could expose Hugh Sawes then? This has nothing to do with terrorism.'

'I think that was a blind to throw us off the scent. The three registered directors of Cortex all have addresses in Ireland. Those addresses also exist but, if I was to email or visit the General Register Office in Ireland, I suspect those three names would be those of deceased or fictitious people.'

'And Temperley with an accountancy background would certainly know how to set up a limited company and draw up fake accounts.' Marvik scratched his scar.

'If we were a specialist fraud squad, or the NHS Counter Fraud Authority, and dug deeper, I believe we'd unearth fraud on a major scale. I could do it but it would take time and resources that neither you nor I have. Crowder would need to take this over and work with the NHS fraud people.'

'And he will, but not before we fulfil our remit, and you know what that is, Shaun. To flush out a killer, because, although the motive might be fraud, we're still looking for a murderer. That's who Crowder wants. And the brains behind this, if they're not one and the same. I've got to start talking about Ultranon and Cortex. And Rohan's my best bet as a starting point.' Marvik counted off. 'One, he knew I was meeting Lingfield; two, he's involved in the healthcare sector; three, he knew of Le Grewe's cottage; four, he has expensive tastes, drives a fast, high-end car and lives in a luxury apartment. He also likes to gamble and womanize, which costs money. And we suspect he could be in hock to Temperley, who could be Webb. There's also the fact that Rohan arranged for Tarina to meet him for a drink when she was attacked. He also showed up on Jarinder's boat, possibly to look for the logbook or an account of Jarinder and Daniel's findings. I hate to think he was involved in killing his father but it's got to be considered. He might not be forthcoming unless I put pressure on him.'

'And there's someone else we need to consider who could be involved in this. You're not going to like this much, Art. I don't either.'

Marvik scrambled his brain to think.

'That thing that was bugging me finally dawned. It was when you said that you'd taken Lingfield's version of his friendship with Jarinder on trust, and that they'd met up the weekend Jarinder sailed to Falmouth. The logbook made no mention of that. It kept going round in my head. We've taken a great deal on trust, Art. Too much. I asked myself about those emails alleging an affair and when they were put on the system. If it was before Jarinder's death, then why didn't anyone find them? Why didn't Jarinder, who would have deleted them? I know they can still be retrieved, but why would the health authority dig that deep? They wouldn't have suspected Jarinder of inappropriate conduct. That leads me to two conclusions: either they were put on after Jarinder's death to sully his reputation in case anything emerged that could damage someone within the health service connected with this fraud, which is possible, or they were never there.'

That jolted Marvik. 'Someone made it up!'

'Someone *told you* they existed.'

Marvik groaned. 'No, it can't be. Not Amanda.'

'Yes, and you and I took her at her word.'

Marvik returned to the helm and sat down heavily. 'The DVD of those manipulated pictures was real enough, and Dawn told me she was paid to say she had an affair with Jarinder.' Then he cursed. 'God, you're right. I must have left my brain in France with those people smugglers.' He felt dejected. 'Of course Dawn was paid, but that doesn't mean to say the emails existed. She didn't know or care if they were there or not. And those pictures were Dawn and Lee's idea; they thought they'd do a bit of freelance blackmail. So whatever Webb was trying to give to Jarinder in the recovery centre garden, it wasn't a DVD with pornographic pictures on it. I can't believe Amanda would be out to discredit Jarinder, or be involved in his murder and Daniel's. And now Lingfield's. Heather, Jarinder's secretary, wouldn't lie about the emails . . .'

'You spoke to her?'

Marvik groaned. 'No, I left a message on her voicemail for Amanda to call me as she was secretary to them both. Amanda called me back quicker than I expected.'

'Too quickly perhaps.'

Marvik didn't want to believe this but knew he had to. 'I thought it was because she was close to Jarinder and worried over what had been discovered.'

'But she rushed to tell you about the emails.'

Marvik was doing some rapid thinking.

'She told you to find out what you could and to let her know. She knows you and I are close, so she wanted to know if you believed the story about my suicide. And she wanted to keep tabs on your progress.'

'What would she gain from this? She's a renowned surgeon, she earns good money,' Marvik said, anguished. 'She's intelligent, not easily fooled or influenced. She has a reputation. Shaun, I can't see her throwing all that away, or being conned by someone. She didn't seem at all uneasy or anxious. I was the one who asked her to find out about the autopsy on Sawes, she didn't pump me for information.'

'She didn't need to, she knew that was a dead end. I too hope she isn't involved,' Strathen said solemnly. 'I have a very high regard for her, and, like you, I'd be surprised if she's being used or manipulated by anyone. But if Lingfield wasn't our inside man, then Amanda could be. She knows the NHS inside out, she knows all about drugs, she's a strong-minded, clever woman. But although she'll know about the purchasing system, she won't know how to manipulate the data. We need to find that person.'

'And find Webb.' Marvik took a deep breath. 'I'll use her to see if I can flush him out before tackling Rohan. I'll update her on what I've got on Jarinder and Cortex and see where it leads.' He rang off, feeling wretched. He hoped to God Strathen was wrong.

CHAPTER TWENTY-FIVE

Amanda eagerly agreed to meet him that evening. He'd chosen his boat, saying it was more private and that he didn't want flapping ears overhearing what he had to tell her. He wondered how it would play out. He'd also updated Crowder, who had agreed his and Strathen's plan of action.

She made no apology for her tardiness. He hadn't expected her to. She looked a little more tired than previously but still vibrant enough to cause him to catch his breath. Again he hoped she wasn't mixed up in this. Her hair was damp, as were the shoulders of her jacket, which he took from her, and indicated for her to go down to the saloon. She had a way of moving that exuded confidence and sensuality. And her expensive, snugly fitting trousers and top accentuated the latter.

'You look tired,' she said.

'I was thinking the same of you.'

'That's not very gallant,' she answered with a smile. 'I had a long, difficult day in surgery. Any news of Shaun?'

'No.'

'Will you go over to Ireland for the inquest?'

'I'm still waiting for the Garda to come back to me on that. Would you like a drink?'

'Large red wine if you've got it.'

He reached into a cupboard and withdrew an unopened bottle and two glasses. She sat as he uncorked it.

'Nice boat.'

'Thanks. A present to myself when I left the Marines.'

'Can't give up the sea, eh?'

'No.' The cork popped and he poured her a full glass and a half for himself.

'So what have you found out?' she eagerly asked, after taking a large swallow of her drink.

'You first, the autopsy on Hugh Sawes.'

'I thought you weren't interested in that anymore.'

'That wouldn't have stopped you,' he answered with a smile that he hoped looked like the genuine article. 'Did you get anything?'

She returned his smile. 'Of course. There were lots of old wounds, evidence of extensive facial injuries, fractures in his right arm in two places and in his wrist, and interestingly enough not on his medical record.'

'That's because his real name is Peter Shoulter and his injuries were incurred in the Hong Kong riots of 1968.'

Her immaculately shaped eyebrows rose. 'How do you know this?'

'He was treated by Alexander Le Grewe in a Hong Kong hospital after being airlifted there by a Royal Navy helicopter. After which, he served fifteen years in prison for planting a bomb and returned to the UK on his release and became Hugh Sawes.'

'You amaze me.'

She genuinely looked it.

'I know of Le Grewe,' she said. 'He was a brilliant surgeon, retired far too early on account of his wife's invalidity. He's the surgeon who operated on Sawes after his injuries in a Birmingham explosion, according to his medical records.'

'I know.'

'But how?'

'Jarinder left a note in his logbook that he had visited Sawes shortly before his car crash and I paid Sawes a visit before he died.'

Her eyes widened. 'Why would Jarinder have gone to see him?'

'Because he inherited Le Grewe's estate and all his papers. Le Grewe had documented the fact that when he operated on Hugh Sawes he recognized him as Peter Shoulter. He was going to tell the authorities about Sawes' true identity and that he suspected Sawes had been planting that bomb and not innocently happening to walk past it.'

'You think Le Grewe was intimidated into keeping quiet on account of his wife's accident?'

'It's one theory.' He studied her closely. She merely looked intrigued. 'What was Sawes' cause of death?'

'Asphyxiation due to lack of oxygen. He wouldn't have lived much longer anyway. A matter of weeks. His lungs were in a pitiable state.'

'Anything suspicious, such as bruising or a bang on the head?'

'Some bruising on his arm where he fell from his wheelchair while trying to reach for a new oxygen supply, nothing untoward, and no blunt force trauma to the skull. He was discovered on the floor in front of his wheelchair with his oxygen tube pulled out from his nose, which could have got loosened as he struggled to breathe and reach the new supply.'

Marvik didn't think so. He was convinced Sawes had been helped on his way. But not by those involved in the fraud. 'Time of death?' he asked, sipping his wine.

'Between ten and midnight. If Jarinder inherited the details from Le Grewe, then Nishan and Rohan must know of it. Tarina too, I expect. Will they do anything about it?'

'I doubt it. Unless Sawes was killed, but there doesn't seem to be any evidence of that.'

'Jarinder could have been killed by the same people, if his car crash wasn't an accident.'

'No proof of that either.'

She sat thoughtfully. 'Shaun went to Ireland though. Could he have been following up on something Jarinder told him?'

'He was, but it wasn't anything to do with Ireland except for the fact that Le Grewe had lived there and owned a cottage above Ballycotton Harbour.' He thought he saw a flicker of something in her eyes. Maybe he was mistaken. 'Or I should have said it wasn't connected with terrorism but with a company called Cortex.'

She took a long, slow pull at her wine.

'You've heard of them?'

'Yes. They're a pharmaceutical company. They supply the NHS.'

'With a drug called Ultranon and some wound-healing dressings.'

'Yes, but what have they go to do with this?'

'They're phoney, as are their drugs.'

'But they can't be!' she cried.

'Have you ordered them?'

'Yes.'

'And used them?'

There was silence for a moment. She scowled. 'No. They're so good the supplies go out of stock. The company should manufacture more but—'

'They need more finance. Perhaps Rohan's company could help them. Or Jack Temperley's.'

She looked at him a little askance. Then took another sip of her wine. 'What are you implying?'

'I think you might be able to guess that.'

'Fraud? But I can't see how they could get through the system. I believe it's rigorous.'

'It can be rigged by a resourceful IT hacker and someone who knows how the NHS tendering and contract system works and how the pharmaceutical industry works.'

'Yes, but . . .'

'Steven Lingfield is dead.'

'Lingfield?' She looked baffled.

Marvik helped her. 'He ran a pathology diagnosis testing company called Horizons.'

225

'I know that,' she said somewhat irritably. 'I told you I'd met him. I just can't comprehend what you're telling me. You mean he's dead as in—'

'Murdered, yes. Last night. I had arranged to meet him. When I got to his house he'd been struck, violently.'

She sat back and ran a hand through her hair. 'This is serious stuff, Art, and dangerous. Did you go to the police?'

'No, because they'd probably suspect me. And how can I tell them that I suspected he was in on the fraud when I've got little evidence of it?'

'Little. Then you have some?'

'Yes, but it's nothing concrete. I believe Jarinder discovered what was going on and that's why he was killed, not because of Sawes or anything to do with terrorism. I thought that at first but Lingfield left me a note, or rather one word on a scrap of paper: Ultranon.'

'Then you don't know that Cortex are fraudulent.'

'No. But there's enough pointing that way. Who told you about the emails alleging an affair?'

She shifted. 'No one told me. I received an email from the clinical director, as had other senior consultants in the department, I assumed. It was marked strictly confidential, telling us that an investigation was currently underway into the alleged professional misconduct of the late Jarinder Vaidya regarding impropriety with a former patient. We were not to speak of it to anyone. I shouldn't even have told you, but I had to because of Shaun, and I didn't believe it of Jarinder. I still don't. I haven't spoken about it to anyone else. You said not to. I'm not a gossip and I won't fuel the disgusting rumours. But if it is being done to discredit him, then it seems pointless now he's dead.'

'I think they're as phoney as Cortex.'

Her eyes widened. 'You mean I was duped.'

Or you fabricated it. 'I said there was a hacker behind this.'

'This is incredible, Art. You must be mistaken.'

'We're talking fraud on a large scale. There's a lot at stake, enough for someone to kill for.'

'Pour me another wine. I need it.'

'I hope you're not driving,' he joked.

'No, I came on foot. I have a marina apartment.'

He poured her another glass.

'A guy called Paul Webb, not his real name, is behind all this.'

'Do you know who he is?'

'Not for certain.'

'But you have an idea.'

'Yes.'

'And you're not going to tell me.'

'It's too dangerous, Amanda. But I should have the answer soon. Maybe even tomorrow. That could depend on you.'

'Me? How?'

'You have access to the Commercial Medicines Unit catalogue database?'

'Yes.'

'See what you can get on Cortex's drugs and dressings. Find out when the contract was awarded, how long for, and how many health authorities they supply. Can you contact any of your counterparts in London and at the other health authorities, or would you have access to what they've ordered?'

'I can get access.'

'Don't say anything to anyone. I mean it, Amanda. I would hate for anything to happen to you.'

'I won't.'

'Also find out who else was told about Jarinder's alleged affair.'

'Right.' She tossed back her wine. 'What will you do?'

'I'd like to find out who Jarinder sent his evidence of the fraud to.'

'Did he?'

'Yes, but not electronically. He typed it.'

'It could be in his safe. If he had one.'

She didn't ask how he knew that Jarinder had typed it. He felt a stab of disappointment, which he didn't show. 'He did, which means if he put it there then Nishan knows all about it, and possibly Rohan. I don't think Tarina does, or she would have told me, and I haven't requested her help. I don't want to say anything about it to her until I'm certain I have the culprits and she's safe.'

'Will you talk to Nishan or Rohan?'

He hesitated. 'No. I might be wrong about that. I have some ideas of where the copy might be. It could be hidden on Jarinder's boat. I'll get on board tomorrow morning and take a look.'

'You should inform the NHS Counter Fraud Authority.'

'I will in due course. See what you can get first, Amanda. Can you do that right away?'

'Of course. I should have something soon, by tomorrow night, say. Here?'

'Yes. I'll wait until I hear from you. I can see you home.'

'No need.' She pushed her arms into her jacket.

'Text me when you get back. Don't let anyone know about the suspected fraud.'

She leaned over and kissed his cheek. 'I promise.'

He watched her walk down the pontoon. She turned and waved and then disappeared from view. He tipped his almost untouched wine down the sink and let out a breath. He didn't want her to be involved, but sadly he felt she was.

He made some coffee to help keep him awake, not that he needed it — his adrenaline would see to that. Then he settled down to wait.

CHAPTER TWENTY-SIX

Saturday

'No one came,' he said to Strathen the following morning.

All night there had been nothing but the sound of the howling wind, moaning and whistling through the masts, and the slapping of the halyards against them. A squally shower had swept across the marina in the early hours, thudding on the cover and decks. Now, an hour after dawn, the rain had ceased, but the sky was moody and the wind gusting.

He'd showered and shaved on board with an eye and ear open for an intruder. He'd eaten breakfast, and now with his second mug of coffee he stood on deck and gazed around the marina. There wasn't a soul in sight. Or was there? 'Hang on, Shaun, someone's just turned onto the pontoon where Jarinder's boat is moored. I can't see from here who it is but, yes, from the build it's either Rohan or Nishan.' He grabbed the binoculars. 'It's Rohan.'

'It had to be one or the other of them because there's another thing that I took on trust and shouldn't have done. I don't know about you leaving your brains in France, but I think I left mine in Ireland. The logbook entry written in Hindi under that Salcombe trip? I thought that had been written in code by Jarinder — it wasn't. I've compared it with what Jarinder wrote to me in his letter in Hindi. The logbook entry is a forgery. A good one too. It's written naturally and not as though copied by someone who doesn't write the language, so it has to be Rohan or Nishan.'

Marvik rapidly caught on. 'The logbook was left on the boat, which was deliberately ransacked, for me to find. To divert attention from any possibility that it could be linked to fraud. Jarinder probably never even went to see Sawes; he had other things on his mind and just went sailing there. But someone knew Sawes lived there from his Plymouth hospital records, which also showed that Le Grewe had been his consultant in Birmingham.'

'Amanda,' Strathen said dejectedly.

'Yes, and she and Rohan cooked up the Sawes trail. I'd told her about the DVD Dawn and Lee had fabricated, which appeared to have shocked her. Maybe that was an act, or perhaps she really didn't know about it, because I wouldn't mind betting Dawn put that on board after I'd left her. As she confessed to me, her plan was to call one of the brothers at their workplace on Monday to tell them where they could find evidence of their father's affair, which they might wish to suppress for a nice fat sum of money.'

'Then the package that Elaine says she saw Webb trying to give to Jarinder was . . . ?'

'Daniel's belongings — his passport, wallet, mobile phone — to prove to Jarinder that Daniel was dead. To use as a threat that the same thing would happen to him if he didn't keep quiet.'

'We've got so much wrong, Art.'

Yes, they had, and the word 'trust' had loomed large in Marvik's thoughts overnight.

Strathen said, 'Let's try and get the rest of this right.'

'Time I spoke to Rohan.'

'I won't have the cavalry at the ready. I'm joining you. I'm heading for Plymouth. Don't leave without me.'

Marvik remembered Amanda saying that. 'I'll try not to. Don't have any accidents.'

'I'll check the car over and take it steady. Should take me about four hours with no hold-ups. I've got one more thing to do before I leave. I think I know where that account of the fraud is. Good luck.'

Marvik alighted and made his way to Jarinder's boat, scanning the marina for any sign of Webb, or anyone acting suspiciously. Despite it being Saturday the marina was quiet, probably on account of the weather, which was blowing up into a storm.

Rohan must have heard, or sensed, him climb on board, but he gave no sign of it, or of alarm when he saw him. He was in the saloon, looking miserable and fatigued. He hadn't tidied the boat as he had said he would after their last encounter on board. In fact, nothing had been moved. 'Nishan rang me last night and told me that as I wanted the boat I had to come down today and make an inventory of what's on board.'

'Why the urgency?'

'Probate, I guess. I couldn't sleep anyway, so I drove down in the early hours of this morning. I tried to grab some sleep at the house but kept seeing that bloody coffin with Father lying in it. Now that I'm here I'm not so sure I want to keep it. I think I only said I wanted it to annoy Nishan. The memories on board aren't as happy as I thought.' He ran a hand through his hair. 'I told you before that Nishan and Father were always arguing. It was no different when we were kids on board. Nishan was a terrible sailor. Couldn't stand being on the sea for long. But then he hated anything Father liked. He only went to medical school because Father said he had to. Then after excelling there, he chucked it in to become a lawyer, specializing in a field that Father was uncomfortable with, medical negligence. Not that Father would cover up anything like that, but he and Nishan could never have a civil discussion without it resorting to an argument.'

'Like you and your brother.'

'Yes.' He stared around him. 'I don't know why anyone would mess up an old boat like this.'

'Did you find the logbook in the house?'

'No. Nishan said it wasn't in Father's safe or his study and Tarina hadn't found it, because if she had she'd have given it to Nishan. He said I must have missed it when I came down here previously. Maybe I did. I looked in the usual place, by the navigation table, but I didn't search anywhere else. I couldn't bring myself to do so and I can't now.'

'What do you know of a company called Cortex?' Marvik asked.

Rohan didn't even change his expression. It was as if Marvik's question had been the most natural in the world following on from their discussion. Surely if he was part of the fraud he would have looked guarded, whereas he just seemed anaesthetized.

'They're a small pharmaceutical business.'

'And they supply the NHS?' Marvik knew they did, but he wanted to see Rohan's reaction. Still that vague disinterest.

'Yes. They're very successful.'

Unless Rohan was putting on a good act, it hadn't been him who had written that code in Hindi. 'How do you know that? You've seen their accounts?'

'No. George was interested in possibly investing in them but he said they seemed to be thriving on their own without any outside funding.'

Oh, they were getting outside funding all right, for doing sod all. It was as Marvik had thought in the small hours of the morning. Trust had come into his reflections a great deal. Amanda's emails, the phoney logbook entry and Lingfield's continued friendship with Jarinder weren't all he had taken on trust.

'Have you had anything to do with Cortex, Rohan?'

'No. Why do you ask? What have they got to do with Father?' He seemed at last to be coming to life.

'I believe Jarinder discovered something was wrong with them.'

'There can't be. George wouldn't be taken in by anything dodgy. He's very thorough when he considers a business to invest in. He can burrow deep into accounts, systems and data. He's a geek at heart, although you'd never think it to look at him.'

No. Ferrer was fit and tanned. No pallid skin and paunch for him as a result of burying himself in front of a computer for days. Marvik had been blinded by his prejudices and shouldn't have been. Strathen too was a geek, and you couldn't get further from that stereotyped image than him.

'Everything George touches turns to gold.'

Or death, thought Marvik. Rohan wasn't speaking with admiration or resentment, simply in a matter-of-fact manner. Did Rohan know just how far Ferrer's obsession had gone, causing so many deaths, including his father's? But Marvik had no proof of that.

'How do you know that Ferrer was considering investing in Cortex?'

'He told me. I said I'd look into them on his behalf but he said he'd take care of it himself and let me know if he needed my help.'

'But you did more than that. You wanted in for a percentage, to pay off your gambling debts to Jack Temperley.'

'I admit I owe Jack money, but I don't know what you're talking about.'

No, Marvik didn't think he did, but he'd stick with it a bit longer. 'I'm talking about the Cortex fraud that you're involved in.'

'Me? Fraud? No.' He seemed genuinely baffled.

'Cortex and their supply of drugs and dressings don't exist.'

'Of course they exist.'

'How do you know?'

'The company accounts.'

'Faked.'

'The drugs then.'

'Always out of stock.'

'George's interest.'

'Oh yes, he has that all right. And you've colluded in it, resulting in murder.'

He shook his head. 'I've done some stupid things in my life but not that. Never that.'

The phone in Marvik's pocket vibrated. That meant someone had boarded his boat. He had locked it before setting out but there were still places on deck where an intruder could hide. He had the advantage though of knowing his boat inside out, and all the potential places where a man could secrete himself without being seen.

'I honestly don't know what you're talking about,' Rohan protested.

'Then think about it: a phoney medical company, drugs that don't exist, a surgeon, your father, killed in a car accident on his way to confide in a friend of mine. Your sister, attacked. Her boyfriend, a man who worked in a hospital IT department, also dead.' Marvik saw the horror cross Rohan's face. That was no act. 'And Steven Lingfield is dead too. I saw his body. A man with gambling debts can be bought and cajoled into doing anything, even murder if pushed hard enough.'

'I swear to you I know nothing about this. It can't be true.' He ruffled his hair. The colour drained from his face.

Marvik stared at him a moment longer before disembarking and hurrying to his boat.

CHAPTER TWENTY-SEVEN

Marvik climbed on board, his heart pounding, his body as taut as steel. He smelled Webb before he heard him, that strong leather scent Tarina had told him of. In an instant he ducked down, sprang round and punched Webb full in the stomach. Webb doubled up. The knife clattered from his hand onto the deck. Marvik kicked it away and with full force landed Webb another blow in the kidneys. He couldn't strike the back of his neck or his face because of the motorbike helmet. Webb cried out and fell forward on his knees. Marvik, using his leg, shoved him down flat on the deck, then, bending over, roughly pulled him round.

'Now, let's see you.' He knew who he would find. Rohan had told him as much and Marvik's overnight machinations had got him there himself. George Ferrer.

His tanned face was screwed up in pain. 'Don't like it much when someone gets the better of you?' Marvik sneered. 'Should have taken off your leathers. I'm not Daniel Carrol or Steven Lingfield, who you can creep up on and slaughter without them putting up much of a fight. And I'm not in a car that you can force off the road.' He raised his fist. 'This is for Jarinder.' But it froze in mid-air as a voice hailed him from the pontoon.

'I wouldn't do that.'

Marvik turned round but didn't lower his fist. 'Why not, Nishan?'

'Because this gun is loaded.' He climbed on board. 'And I have no hesitation in using it.'

'Don't you think that will alert the other berth holders?'

'There aren't any on this pontoon or close by. But I'd thought of that. While you were doing your gymnastics I loosened the for'ard line. George, cast off aft. Do it! Hurry.' Ferrer pulled himself up with a groan. 'Marvik, go to the helm and start her up. We'll go somewhere nice and quiet. No one to bother us. Move one inch out of line and I'll pull the trigger. Don't even think of trying your commando stuff on me because the gun will go off before you do.'

Marvik did as he was told. Looking over his shoulder, he saw Ferrer climb back on board with a grunt. Behind him, Marvik also saw another figure walking along the pontoon with a puzzled and shocked air. He gently reversed and stalled the engine, restarted it, and swung away from the berth.

'Take it steady and slow,' Nishan urged. That suited Marvik fine. Ferrer, still nursing his stomach, moved to the right of Nishan. His face was contorted with pain, but fury blazed in his eyes and it didn't take a *Brain of Britain* champion to work out that he was building up to get his revenge. He could try, but unless Marvik was tethered he was confident he'd get the better of the man. Both of these men could only threaten and kill with a weapon in their hands and now both had one, Ferrer having retrieved the knife from the deck.

Marvik, raising his voice above the gentle purr of the engine, mocked, 'I didn't hurt you, did I, Ferrer? Maybe you need to spend more time in the gym. You should have stuck to hacking into computers, much safer for you and others. I guess it started some years ago when you were working in that chemist as a sixteen-year-old. You found a way of automating their ordering and prescription delivery systems, as you told me. But instead of them telling you that you were talking rot, they said go ahead, and you did. You also set up fake patient details, phoney prescriptions and deliveries, and soon built up a store of drugs to sell on the dark web. Of course, I don't know all this for a fact, but going on your current record I'd say I've guessed right.'

Ferrer was still grimacing in pain but the hand that held the knife was steady and the eyes full of hate. 'You have. Not that it will get you anywhere,' he growled.

'From there, with glowing false references, because no one suspected you, you moved into the pharmaceutical industry as a rep, as you told me. And yes, I believe you were highly successful. You looked good, you were smooth and fluent. You knew your stuff and rapidly got promotions and made a lot of money, but it still wasn't enough. You told me you could spot the investment opportunities, how to invest in yourself. You could hone your criminal intentions and the rewards would be high.'

'Do we have to listen to this drivel?' Nishan sniped.

Marvik answered. 'Can't you humour me? After all, it's your intention that I won't be around much longer.' Marvik turned to Ferrer. 'Planting false information on the drug manufacturers' systems, sending deliveries to places that you directed them to, selling the drugs again on the dark web, under an anonymous identity or false name. Then you met Nishan in Cork, six years ago, when he was prosecuting a company over a faulty medical implant. It was the company you were working for. It takes one corrupt, greedy person to spot another. Together you hatched the plan to create the fictitious company and defraud the NHS on a massive scale.' Marvik knew it needed a third party for the idea to have developed. Or perhaps the idea had come from that person — Amanda — but he wasn't going to say. He suspected that Ferrer had met Amanda at a seminar hosted by the pharmaceutical company.

Nishan said, 'Stop talking and head out to sea.'

Marvik did so, as slowly as he could because if he sped up and got up on the plane the uneven roll of waves would be gone. The higher and deeper the trough of waves, and the more erratically the boat rocked from side to side, the better. The wind was whipping up further. The sea was growing ever more swollen. Good. 'Have you always been corrupt, Nishan?'

'Just steer the boat.'

'And you, Ferrer. Why, when you obviously have a brilliant business brain and a talent for developing and turning around companies, go in for fraud? You can obviously make good money legitimately, although probably not enough to have been able to buy the Battersea apartment and the one at Clink Wharf. How many others are there? Possibly abroad? And in different names. Got to spend your ill-gotten gains somehow. And you, Nishan, have you other properties hidden away from your wife and family?'

'Shut up.'

'But it's not just about money. You both want to cheat the system and you get a thrill from it. You need that hint of danger to turn you on. Should have joined the Marines — ah, but they wouldn't have either of you.'

Ferrer was recovering. He stepped forward with the knife, a malicious smile on his face.

'Is that how you get your kicks, Ferrer?' Marvik continued casually, though he was far from relaxed. 'Watching someone die, having the power to take a life?'

Ferrer's hand thrust out, but Nishan stalled him. 'We're not out far enough yet.'

Marvik continued. 'It's a pity for Daniel Carrol that he was honest and just as clever as you, Ferrer. How did he stumble onto Cortex? Or was that Jarinder?' The slight flicker in Nishan's eyes told him that it was. 'Jarinder casually voiced to Daniel one day — he was in London on a seminar and staying at Rohan's — that it was strange that no matter how many times he ordered Ultranon it was never available. Daniel, curious, did some investigating over time and didn't like what he found. He told Jarinder. And Jarinder asked your advice, Nishan. He probably asked you what evidence he'd need to successfully prosecute, instead of going to the NHS Fraud Authority as he should have done. Was that because he suspected Rohan was involved? A suspicion that you and Ferrer then played on further. Ferrer, or you, Nishan, made sure that Jarinder knew how heavily in debt Rohan was to Temperley and others because of his gambling addiction.' Marvik swung his gaze to Ferrer as the boat rose and dipped like a manic rollercoaster. 'Did you try and recruit Daniel Carrol?'

'He would never be up to my level, although he would have been useful.'

'But he couldn't be bought. So you tried to take him out when he was cycling to the shops in Woking. He survived. He and Jarinder knew then that they faced real danger. Daniel typed a full account of what he'd discovered, on a typewriter in his flat, and Jarinder typed a letter to send to my friend, Strathen, should he never make a meeting with him, which he didn't. He also wrote it in Hindi. That was a smart idea, Nishan — you making up the code under the Sawes entry in your father's logbook in Hindi, laying the false trail to Sawes and his past terrorist activity, which you'd learned about through Le Grewe's papers. Was it your own idea?'

Nishan was looking a little paler than when they had started. He was frowning but the hand that held the gun was still steady. Marvik didn't know how much longer he'd be allowed to continue with the deadly tale. There was more he had to say yet, but he knew time was running out.

'Or yours, Ferrer?' Marvik sadly knew it was neither. Raising his voice above the wind and the rain that now swept over the sea, he continued, again addressing Nishan. 'Jarinder took Daniel Carrol to Le Grewe's cottage, hoping to keep him safe until he could expose the fraud. But our knife-happy friend here went to despatch Daniel to the other world. Don't you care anything for your religion?' Marvik shouted above the soft sound coming from the cockpit. Neither Nishan nor Ferrer seemed to notice. Marvik didn't have much time. 'Rohan told me you were a strict Hindu

239

because it's what everyone believes. Outwardly, you are. You chastise him for having white girlfriends, for drinking and gambling. But he's not half as bad as you. Your life, and your righteousness, is an act designed to fool people, or to be used as it suits you. Inside, you're corrupt. How many Hindu sins have you committed?'

'I'll leave you to count them up, seeing as you're so keen on them.'

'There's greed for starters. But then it's not about money, it's about ego, another Hindu sin. You need to feed that enormous ego of yours.'

Nishan swayed a little. Ferrer looked at him with irritation.

Marvik hastily continued. 'Then there's lust and adultery. I shouldn't think Amanda is the first woman you've shagged while married.'

'No, but she's the finest and the best. I would have married her if my wife hadn't come with such a vast sum of money and property. But thankfully she's stupid and faithful like a dog.'

Marvik resisted the temptation to smash his fist into the handsome, smooth face because Ferrer would be on him in an instant. And, despite the fact that Nishan was growing paler and beginning to sway even more, and not with the movement of the boat, he would still be able to shoot that gun. Ferrer was beginning to look agitated at the delay. Marvik had to hold his interest for just a moment longer. The knife was steady in his hand but his eyes were on Nishan.

'Then there's seething resentment and anger, leading you to a terrible hatred and jealousy that had to be assuaged at all costs. You were jealous of your father's success and heroism. He was fearless and upright, two qualities you lack. Hatred and bitter resentment drove you to become so corrupt that you thought nothing of him being murdered.'

Marvik raised his voice against the wind and the gentle throb of the engine. The boat bucked and rolled. 'Oh yes, you've committed every sin in the Hindu book. But as you say, that means nothing to you. And now you think you're safe. You think you'll be allowed to live? Ferrer has got his breath back. He'll dispose of you once you've got rid of me. He'll set the boat adrift after dumping our bodies overboard and then he and Amanda can carry on as before. They might not even need to fold the fictitious company with everyone gone. She and Ferrer will have bank accounts in other names. Easy enough for them to disappear, if they need to, which has probably always been their plan.'

Nishan was having difficulty focusing. His eyes were all over the place. Marvik didn't think that was caused by fear of what he was saying. *Nishan was a terrible sailor.* Timing was everything. 'You really think you can go back and everything will continue as before?'

'I . . . I'm going to throw up.' Nishan spun round to race to the cockpit. As he did, Ferrer glanced after him. It was the moment Marvik had been waiting for. In a trice, he struck a carotid slap just below the jaw on the side of Ferrer's neck. He collapsed on the deck. Stepping over him, Marvik raced to where Nishan was now leaning over the side, being violently sick. Behind him with the gun in his hand was a soaking wet, shaking Rohan.

'Give me the gun,' Marvik shouted above the roaring wind.

'He killed Father. I will kill him.'

'And become as bad as him? No, Rohan. That way he wins. He'll be punished. Let the courts decide. Give me the gun.'

Rohan hesitated. He looked from his brother to Marvik and then back to Nishan. Marvik could see the thoughts chasing over his streaming face — fury, confusion, despair, and finally mental exhaustion. His body slumped. Meekly, he handed Marvik the weapon. After quickly making sure it was safe, Marvik tucked it into the waistband of his trousers. Then, taking hold of Rohan, he said, 'Leave him. He's not going anywhere. Come inside.'

Rohan was too numb to protest as the ramifications of what he had heard while hiding on the deck dawned on him. He sank heavily onto one of the seats close to the helm. Marvik checked Ferrer was alive. The blow he delivered could kill, although he'd made sure not to render the full force. He was breathing but, whether Marvik had done any damage to his brain by suddenly depriving it of oxygen, he didn't know. He didn't think there was any need to tie up Ferrer. He wasn't going anywhere for some time, and Nishan was still retching over the side. He swung the boat round, put the throttle at top speed and returned to the marina, calling Crowder as he travelled. There was still one more player in this dirty game to face. He steeled himself for the bitter, unpleasant task ahead.

CHAPTER TWENTY-EIGHT

Three hours later, Marvik found Strathen in the consultants' break room just off the operating theatres. They had the place to themselves. Only the theatre Amanda was operating in was in action. He crossed to the coffee machine. 'Need a top-up?'

Strathen handed over his mug. He looked as weary as Marvik felt. Although both had a supply of amphetamines, neither liked to take them unless really necessary. And this fatigue wasn't solely physical.

Marvik had handed over Nishan and Ferrer to the police, who had met his boat at the marina on Crowder's instructions. They'd been brought to this hospital by ambulance with a police guard. Nishan would soon recover but Ferrer would be kept in longer to make sure there was no long-term damage caused by Marvik's strike. Ferrer would be charged with murder and Nishan as an accessory. There would also be the fraud charges when it was unravelled. Rohan had been taken to the station, where he'd been given dry clothes before making his statement. Marvik would give his later to Crowder, which had been accepted because of Crowder's rank and position. Marvik had thought of Tarina. His heart was weighed down with sadness at the torment she'd suffer over the news of a triple tragedy — the murder of her father and boyfriend and the terrible deceit of her brother.

He'd showered and changed. Crowder had told him that Amanda had been called to an emergency, and that was why she hadn't seen Nishan leave her apartment and Rohan climb on board when Marvik had reversed and stalled the engine. He hadn't known how long Rohan would remain in hiding on hearing the truth from his brother and Ferrer. He had hoped it would be long enough for him to get clear of the marina and out to sea, recalling how Rohan said Nishan hated sailing. Maybe Rohan had been waiting for Nishan to get sick too so that he could seize his chance. When he had, thankfully he hadn't taken it by shooting his brother.

Crowder had cleared it with the clinical director that they could use the room and wouldn't be interrupted. He'd also confirmed that no one had found emails on Jarinder's computer regarding professional misconduct with a patient.

Marvik said, 'Amanda would have seen Rohan arrive and me go to Jarinder's boat before being called away. Rohan said Nishan was away for the weekend. He must have been staying with her. He was in her flat last night when she came to meet me on board and they planned what to do.' He put together some of the remaining threads. 'Nishan called Rohan and told him to come down to take the inventory. He knew I'd be watching Jarinder's boat but he couldn't know I'd be looking out all the time. I just happened to be on deck calling you.'

'They'd have thought of another way of getting you off your boat for the time it took for Ferrer to slip on board. Amanda could have called you and said she'd seen someone go on Jarinder's boat.'

'They didn't have to involve Rohan though. Ferrer could have waited until I went to the marina showers or took a walk. He hoped to kill me, take the boat out, dump me at sea and then set the boat adrift after climbing in the tender to get off. He was good but not good enough.

'And Tarina didn't recognize him as her attacker because of the visor.'

'Even if she had fleetingly thought there was something familiar about him, her shocked mental state would have dismissed the idea of it being anyone she knew. Ferrer was hiding in that passage when Tarina walked past. He grabbed her, dragged her in and pushed her to the ground. As she lay traumatized, he whipped off the helmet and jacket, stuffed them in a dark alcove by one of the fire exit doors and cried out after an imaginary figure. I trusted him when he said he scared off the attacker, when he *was* the attacker. He then leaned over her as George, planting in her mind that he'd seen the attacker run off. As you said, Shaun, we took a lot on trust, and your words made me think of that attack. And the more I considered it, the more convinced I grew that it had been staged,' he added sadly. 'Did Amanda know Nishan would turn up with a gun? Or was that his own idea?'

'We'll ask her,' Strathen said sorrowfully.

'Do you know how long she'll be in theatre?'

'The sister says she doesn't know. Amanda is trying to save the man's leg. Maybe both of them. I don't know how badly they were crushed. Could be a few more hours yet.'

Marvik nodded. He needed more caffeine. The adrenaline rush was subsiding, making him weary. Strathen also looked drained. But there was a way to go yet. 'I find it so hard to believe she would want to kill me, or anyone, come to that. It just doesn't stack up.' He crossed to the filter machine and topped up his mug.

'It appears to be the truth though.'

'Crowder said you had found the proof of the fraud?'

'Daniel was a Catholic. You found a rosary in a drawer in his bedroom and I took the crucifix from his body.' Strathen stretched into his jacket pocket and retrieved the small gold crucifix with a stone in the centre. 'I thought that he wouldn't wish to burden a priest by telling them what he knew. Besides, a priest wouldn't remember the complexity of the fraud, only that Daniel had uncovered one, and we know he and Jarinder conspired to type up a full account of it. So I thought leaving that account with a priest would be possible, and, as Daniel worked at St Thomas' Hospital, the Roman Catholic priest there might be the man to whom he had entrusted it. I was right. I didn't have time to pay him a visit but he confirmed it — I can see you're going to ask why he should tell me off the cuff, so to speak. We arranged a video call.' Strathen held out his mug, and Marvik topped it up. 'Daniel had given a full description of me, courtesy of Jarinder, to the priest, including the fact that I was an amputee. Father Munroe could see that. I also showed him my ID. He said he had the document and that he had instructions to hand it over only to me. If I hadn't survived, and if we hadn't teamed up, then the fraud could have continued.'

'Did you find anything more on Cortex?'

'No, I'll leave that to the fraud authority. Our job is done, or nearly done. I can hear movement.'

So too could Marvik. They waited in silence.

The door opened and Amanda waltzed in. Even in her scrubs she looked vibrant and attractive, and although there were dark smudges under her eyes they still sparkled with life. She drew up with a start and looked at each in turn, registering their expressions.

'I see you're still very much alive, Shaun.' She crossed to the coffee machine. 'I never believed for a moment you would take your own life. George slipped up there. Not that I wanted you dead — or you, Art. I admire you both, but if you got in the way then I would have had no choice. Where is George, by the way, Art? Did you kill him?'

He felt a deep sense of sorrow and loss. He was looking at a talented surgeon, yet an intoxicating, dangerous woman. 'He's in police custody, as is Nishan.'

'He's a fool,' she said dismissively, swallowing some coffee. 'Don't tell me he turned up on your boat?'

'With a gun. Was it yours?'

'Of course not. Nishan belongs to a gun club. He fancies himself something of a sharpshooter.'

'That he might be but he's no sailor. He got seasick. Why, Amanda? Why did you do this?'

'The fraud? It's only money and what's another million pounds in this vast black bottomless hole of the NHS? Fraud goes on all the time, most of it legitimately perpetuated by the drug companies, peddling medicines that most of the population don't need anyway. They — the food manufacturers, fast-food chains and private medical companies — rub their hands with glee at the rise in obesity, diabetes, stress, heart disease. It's good for business.'

'But murder! Jarinder, Daniel Corral, Steven Lingfield — all dead. And you were willing to kill me and Shaun.'

'People die.' She shrugged and swallowed her coffee. Her expression impassive.

Did she really not care? Had she become so desensitized to death? 'But murder,' Marvik insisted. Strathen looked downcast.

'I murder people all the time — well, not all, but it happens. We live. We die. I fight to keep some of them alive but they die despite that. And some that live would have been better off dying.'

'You don't really believe that?'

'I do. That's it, another patient dead, another statistic.'

Marvik felt cold inside. Strathen's face was a picture of sorrow. 'Don't you have any conscience?' he asked.

Her eyes bored into Strathen's. 'I did where you were concerned. I hoped you'd get away. And I hoped Art would give up trying to find you and prodding and interfering. I didn't ask for you to die. Ferrer is not a man I can control.'

But Marvik disagreed. 'You're wrong. He'd do anything for you. So too would Nishan.'

She tossed back her coffee. 'I take it the police are coming for me, or are you taking me to them?'

'They're waiting outside the hospital,' Marvik answered.

'Then I'd better change. But I tell you this.' She turned at the door. 'A court of law will never convict me.'

Ferrer would take the full blame, of that Marvik was certain.

Marvik felt disconsolate. Strathen looked to be holding himself together with difficulty. They didn't need to speak. They waited in silence, listening to the movement beyond the room, a clatter of instruments, voices, footsteps. Then came a loud cry and a buzzer. Marvik jumped up and threw a startled and worried expression at Strathen. They rushed through the door into the operating theatre, where Amanda lay on the floor. Beside her were two nurses and a doctor still in scrubs, fighting to keep her alive. No one took any notice of them. Then finally the doctor straightened up, his face a picture of horror, disbelief and shock. On the floor some distance from her hand was a syringe.

Strathen said, 'Is she dead?'

'Yes.'

There was a smile on her face and those sightless eyes still looked lively to Marvik. He felt overwhelming grief.

'How?' asked Strathen. 'What was in the syringe?'

'Nothing. An air embolism. Death was instantaneous. Such a bloody waste. My God, such a waste.'

Marvik took Shaun's arm and gently led him away. There was nothing he could say. Nothing to say. The medic had said it all.

* * *

It was almost midnight when Marvik and Strathen returned to the boat. Crowder had been informed and their statements taken. Ferrer was still in hospital but would recover, and Nishan, on hearing the news of Amanda's death, broke down.

Nishan had told them that Ferrer had killed Sawes by removing his oxygen tube and putting the oxygen cylinder out of his reach, the sole purpose of his murder to make Marvik think terrorism was the cause of Jarinder's death.

Lingfield had been killed because Ferrer had realized he was a risk. Jarinder had mentioned his concerns about Cortex to Lingfield when he had sailed to Falmouth and met up with him. That had been the truth. Jarinder hadn't known Lingfield had got involved after Jarinder had confided in him.

Marvik said, 'It wasn't until my meeting with Lingfield at the crematorium and saying I didn't believe it was an accident that he knew Jarinder had been right. He, like Jarinder, had made the mistake of confiding in Nishan — after all, he was the one with the legal brain. Nishan told Ferrer, who came up with the idea that he would tell Rohan he was interested in providing funding for Lingfield's company. That had diverted attention from Nishan and enabled Ferrer to keep an eye on Lingfield, in case he had more information than he was letting on. He didn't. But after speaking to me on the phone, Lingfield again made an error, a fatal one for him. He told Nishan he'd arranged to meet me. If Lingfield hadn't left that scrawled name on the piece of paper, we might never have discovered the fraud.'

'We said it was about money, if we ruled out terrorism, and we even said it was fraud but we didn't know how, what or the scale of it. We might have got there eventually, but Lingfield helped us speed things up.'

'And died as a result.'

Strathen nodded solemnly. 'Amanda didn't believe I was dead, so they had to keep you alive until they were certain or you led them to me. If I was still loose there was always the chance that I'd blow the whistle. Amanda knew I was an intelligence specialist and I'd get there in the end.'

'And when you broke cover to come to Plymouth they knew you were alive. How?'

'They didn't. You did that.'

'By telling Amanda what I knew when she was with me on my boat.'

'Yes.'

'And Nishan was already in her apartment at the marina. He got Rohan down to Jarinder's boat, not only to get me off my boat so that Ferrer could get on it but to keep up the charade that Rohan was involved in the fraud, not his brother.

I suspect Ferrer was with Amanda when I met her in the marina restaurant that time and not in Frankfurt as she said.'

'If he was in Germany then she told him about it, keeping him and Nishan informed. Well, that's it, Art. It's over for us, sadly not for others.'

No. He thought of Tarina. He stared at the small box that Strathen had placed on the table. Inside it was a gold chain crucifix with a tiny diamond in the centre. Daniel's. Tarina didn't know he was dead or how he had died. Then there was Steven Lingfield, an innocent victim of greed and corruption like Jarinder and Daniel Carrol. It left a sour taste in his mouth. And what of Tarina and Rohan? Their lives were blighted by their brother's treachery. Perhaps Rohan would learn a lesson and change his ways. Perhaps he wouldn't. Tarina would throw herself into her work to try to blot out Nishan's evilness, and the tragic loss of her boyfriend and father.

He conjured up those beautiful, soulful dark eyes, her gentle, kind manner. Her earnestness and her plea to him to keep her informed. How could he look at her knowing he had been instrumental in Nishan's arrest? But this wasn't about him and how he felt — it was about her and her sorrow. So what if she gazed at him with anguished, accusing eyes? There would be so many questions she would want answers to. He might not be able to provide them. She might not want them now, but he had to leave the door open for her to ask at any time, however long that might be. He had to give her that. He owed her the truth.

He picked up the tiny box and placed it carefully in his pocket. Then, with a determined smile, he said, 'I'm coming back to London with you, Shaun. Let's go now. There's something I need to do and someone I need to see.'

THE END

THE JOFFE BOOKS STORY

We began in 2014 when Jasper agreed to publish his mum's much-rejected romance novel and it became a bestseller.

Since then we've grown into the largest independent publisher in the UK. We're extremely proud to publish some of the very best writers in the world, including Joy Ellis, Faith Martin, Caro Ramsay, Helen Forrester, Simon Brett and Robert Goddard. Everyone at Joffe Books loves reading and we never forget that it all begins with the magic of an author telling a story.

We are proud to publish talented first-time authors, as well as established writers whose books we love introducing to a new generation of readers.

We won Trade Publisher of the Year at the Independent Publishing Awards in 2023 and Best Publisher Award in 2024 at the People's Book Prize. We have been shortlisted for Independent Publisher of the Year at the British Book Awards for the last five years, and were shortlisted for the Diversity and Inclusivity Award at the 2022 Independent Publishing Awards. In 2023 we were shortlisted for Publisher of the Year at the RNA Industry Awards, and in 2024 we were shortlisted at the CWA Daggers for the Best Crime and Mystery Publisher.

We built this company with your help, and we love to hear from you, so please email us about absolutely anything bookish at feedback@joffebooks.com.

If you want to receive free books every Friday and hear about all our new releases, join our mailing list here: www.joffebooks.com/freebooks.

And when you tell your friends about us, just remember: it's pronounced Joffe as in coffee or toffee!